EXPERIMENT

Marina Simcoe

To My Captain

1

Experiment

Marina Simcoe

Marina.Simcoe@Yahoo.com

Facebook/Marina Simcoe Author

This is a work of fiction. Names, characters, places and incidents are a product of the author's imagination. Locales and public names are used for atmospheric purposes. Any resemblance to actual people, living or dead, or to businesses, companies, events, institutions or locales is completely coincidental.

Cover Design by Naomi Lucas and Cameron Kamenicky

First Edition

Spelling: English (Canada)

Editing by Two Horses Swift

Proofreading by Nikki Groom, The Indie Hub

Experiment is a Science-Fiction romance. It contains graphic descriptions of intimacy and discussion on topics that may be triggers for some. Intended for mature readers.

Chapter 1

"ISABELLA BRUNO." THE man in a dark suit wasn't asking. Staring at me from the other side of the front entrance as I held the door open, he stated my name confidently, as if he already knew it was me.

"How can I help you?" I asked cautiously, glancing at the two others behind him. The large, black vehicles parked at the curb in front of our house did not put my mind at ease either.

"Michael Trevin." He offered me his hand. "May we come in?"

"Trevin?" I stared at him in shock, ignoring his hand. "*The* Michael Trevin?" I asked, dumbfounded, even as I had already recognized the face of one of the three North American representatives in the coalition of Earth Governments. "You're here? In Deer Rock?"

The fact that someone so high up in the government personally visited our small town—far up North on the territory that used to be Canada before the three countries of the continent had been merged into one—should be a huge event.

Had his visit been made public? How had I missed the news? And why was he at my house?

"Can we come in?" he asked more persistently, moving forward, which forced me to step back.

"Um, sure," I mumbled, as if my permission meant anything at that point—all three had entered our small hallway.

I smoothed my hair quickly and brushed my palms down my t-shirt, feeling painfully underdressed in my pajama pants. It was midmorning on a weekday, but I had an evening shift at the store today and hadn't changed yet. Luckily, I had at least put a bra on.

"Who is it, Bella?" Mom came out of the kitchen, bouncing Lily, one of my sister's twins, on her hip. "Mister Trevin . . ." She stared at the representative, her eyes opened wide, her mouth agape. "In my house?"

"Mrs Bruno." He shook her hand energetically. "Where would be the best place for us to have a quick talk?" Without waiting for an answer, he shoved past her and into our kitchen. His escort followed.

"Um . . . About what?" Mom hurried after them. "Would you like anything? Tea? Water?"

"We don't have much time." Trevin pulled a chair from the table and sat down. "Secretary Carter. Agent Miller." He gestured at the two men accompanying him as they took seats at the table too.

"What is it all about?" Mom moved her gaze from one man to another. Both her and I remained standing.

"We are here to collect Isabella Bruno," Miller blurted out, earning a stern glare from Trevin.

"Me?" I stepped into the kitchen from the entrance where I had been standing.

Surely this was some kind of misunderstanding.

"What did she do?" Mom sent me a questioning stare.

"Before I explain," Trevin raised a hand in a calming gesture, "allow me to remind you that although our coalition is the main human governing body on the planet, it has been under the jurisdiction of the planet Keala for the past nine years. The extraterrestrials have left us to administer our population, but the Kealan laws take precedence over ours."

The aliens had come to Earth suddenly one day. Several giant flying saucers had hovered over a few major cities, and it didn't take long for them to make it clear they did not come in peace.

All military attempts by the coalition to attack the spaceships resulted in the immediate annihilation of our aircraft and missiles.

Then *they* attacked *us*. Entire populations of several towns and small cities around the world were eradicated within minutes when bright rays of light had descended from the ships. All structures, machines, and animals were left intact. However, the people in those places were turned to dust in seconds—white ash all that remained.

Human capitulation came right after the aliens threatened to annihilate the entire population of Earth in the same fashion if we didn't surrender.

As Trevin pointed out, the Kealans left the coalition in charge of Earth's administration, not getting involved much in our politics or our way of life. They built two facilities, one on each of Earth's poles, and implemented mandatory annual medical evaluations for all humans aged eighteen to sixty.

Other than that, it was easy to forget with time that Earth had been conquered at all.

"Please take a seat, Isabella." Trevin's stare carried a power I found myself unable to disobey. I sat at the table across from him, folding my hands over the large red strawberries printed on the plastic tablecloth. "About a week ago, the coalition received a request from the Kealans. They demanded you be handed over to them."

"Me?" I repeated, stunned, a fog of confusion and denial settled over my brain. "There must be some mistake . . ."

"No mistake. They want you," Miller bit off.

Trevin leaned in, resting his hands on the table. "We were able to negotiate some time to discuss the situation last week. However, this morning, their request was made urgent—" A sudden thought appeared to flash through his mind. "When was your last medical examination?"

"Yesterday," I replied, clutching my hands tight. "What do they want with me?"

The exams were done by the local doctor, for free and with no known health consequences observed. Alien robot-drones delivered the test kits and collected the data obtained. After nine years, the global medical exams had become the norm. By now, hardly anyone questioned it, begrudgingly accepting having to go see the doctor once a year as something that had to be done—kind of like renewing one's driver's licence, or filing taxes.

"You had one done yesterday?" Trevin exchanged a knowing look with the other men at the table. "That may explain the urgency."

"How?" Even more perplexed, I moved my gaze from one face to another. "What do they want?" I asked again, since no one had answered me the first time.

"Well." Trevin leaned against the back of his chair, stretching his neck and obviously stalling his answer.

"Your current physical state may be of some importance to them," Carter joined in.

"What do you mean? When will I be able to come home?"

Carter glanced at Trevin. Something in the expressions of the two sent a chill of trepidation down my spine.

"I *will* come back, won't I?" I insisted, louder.

"The extraterrestrials offered you Kealan citizenship. Through marriage." Trevin shifted in his chair, making it squeak. "To that extent, they also agreed to honour our traditions and have a proper wedding ceremony—"

"What wedding?" both Mom and I said at once.

Rolling his eyes to the ceiling, Miller leaned back in his chair and crossed his arms over his chest. "Yours," he explained, with a dramatic sigh of exasperation. "The aliens want one of them to marry you."

"Which is a good thing when you think about it," Carter rushed in. "It could be presented as a gesture of good will—"

"Presented to whom?" I jumped from my seat. All of it stopped making any sense whatsoever. "What are you all talking about? I'm not going anywhere. I'm perfectly fine where I am. Why would the aliens want me anyway? I've never met them and don't want to."

I'd watched the news broadcast of the few official visits of the Kealans with the coalition. The images of their tall figures, draped in black cloaks, hoods drawn low over their faces, left an unpleasant impression on me, bringing the Grim Reaper to mind.

"And . . . a wedding? Really?" I wrung my hands, pacing in front of the table, as if moving could help me wrap my mind around all of this.

"Miss Bruno . . ." Carter jumped out of his seat, too.

"This is just stupid!" Skipping down the stairs, my sister, Mary, barged into the room, her son Luca under her arm. "His diaper is changed." She handed Luca to my mom, who put him on her other hip, opposite to his twin. "Honestly, guys." Hands propped on the tabletop, Mary stared down Trevin and his escort. Less than two years younger than me, she had always been the more assertive and outspoken one. "Just listen to you! An alien wedding? What the hell are you talking about? Is this some kind of a joke for reality TV or something?"

"It *will* be televised," Carter announced, brightly. "The preparations for the event have been in full swing since the initial demand was received."

"Even before I was notified?" I muttered, wishing I could just wake up and stop this nightmare.

"And who are you?" Mary threw at Carter sarcastically, one corner of her mouth lifting up. "The wedding planner?"

"Ma'am." Miller rose from the table and moved on my sister. "It's imperative we deliver Isabella Bruno—"

"What do you mean by *deliver*?" Mary scoffed. "Bella is a free woman, she has rights—"

"Exactly," Mom stepped in, balancing the twins on each hip. "You can't just come in here and take her—"

"You're forgetting that *none* of us are free, miss." Trevin got up, shoving the chair back with a screeching noise, his jaw muscles flexed. "Not since the capitulation to the Kealans nine years ago."

"We have orders to take your sister." Miller crossed his arms over his chest. "Your permission is not required."

"I don't want to go." Dread slithered up my spine, cold and sticky. "My home is here. My job. I have a life . . . I—"

"Isabella." Trevin took a step my way.

"No." I glared at him.

"She is not going anywhere," Mary insisted stubbornly.

"This is all definitely way too fast." Moving her gaze across the room, Mom appeared completely lost. "Why all this rush? Who is this man . . . um, this *alien*, who wants to marry her? Why? Does he like her? They've never met . . ."

"*Like*?" Miller grimaced. "What does that have to do with anything?"

The front door opened with a knock.

"Bell? Are you home?" I heard the familiar voice of Johnny, my boyfriend of four years.

Mom bounced on her heels to calm the twins who started fussing. "What I'm saying is that this is not a proper way to ask someone to marry you," she argued with Miller.

Trevin pinched the bridge of his nose. "You're missing the point, ma'am. *We* are not the ones who make demands here."

"Who is getting married?" Johnny walked in, tossing back his shoulder-length blond hair, some of which perpetually hung over his face.

"The freaking aliens are planning a wedding with Bella!" Mary blurted out, gesturing at Miller and Trevin, as if they were the aliens in question.

"Mary . . ." I exhaled, feeling like my knees were about to give out, a pounding headache threatened to set in.

Johnny moved a confused glance from her to Miller then finally to me. "Is that true?"

"We don't have much time." Trevin ignored him. "The flight to Capital City will take at least two hours. With the ceremony scheduled for tonight, the team will have to start getting you ready soon."

Ready . . .

Ready for what? The wedding?

Tonight?

My heart skipped at the realization that all of this was real after all. Fear settled heavily in my chest, threatening to turn into panic.

"How will you ever get anyone ready to marry some alien dude?" Mary yelled at the three. "No matter how much time you have. Who the hell is *he* anyway?"

"We have not been given the groom's identity," Trevin replied coolly.

"Mary is right, though." Mom shook her head. "This is insane."

"Your family will be well compensated, of course," Carter started.

"This is not about money!" Mary snapped.

"Her dad is in the hospital," my mom muttered softly, shifting her pleading gaze from one of the men to another. "At the very least, you need to let her say goodbye . . . Why this rush?" she groaned.

"Johnny . . ." I grabbed my boyfriend by the arm and shoved him into the hallway, desperate to get away from it all, to shut the noise out, to get some time to do something . . . Anything.

"Is it true what they're saying, Bell?" Johnny asked as I dragged him around the corner and out of everyone's sight. "Are those SUV's outside theirs? And is that Michael Trevin, for real?"

"Miss Bruno!" Miller's voice thundered behind me.

"A minute, please. Give me one freaking minute!" I yelled back. "Johnny." I whispered quickly, panic vibrating through me. "This can't be happening . . ."

"Do they really want you to marry an alien?"

"Apparently, it's the aliens who want this. Johnny." Gripping his shoulders, I gave him a shake. "Please, help me. Let's run."

There was no way I was going to return to that kitchen where they all waited for me.

Until this morning, I'd been a regular small-town girl, working in a convenience store since I graduated high school eight years ago. With my oldest brother in and out of jail for the past several years and my father in and out of hospitals with his ailing heart and lungs, I had been helping my mom with my four younger brothers who were still in grade school and more recently, with Mary's ten-month-old twins.

My plans for the future had mostly included marrying Johnny—whenever he saved up enough money to buy me a ring and asked me to be his wife—and eventually starting a family.

It was not a glorious life, but it was *my* life, and I was content, living right here in Deer Rock, where I knew everybody and everyone knew me from the day I was born.

This whole thing now felt surreal and terrifying.

"Get me out of here, please," I whispered, not sure myself *how* that could be accomplished or *where* I could run to. I just needed to be far away from here. "I'm not going with them. I need to hide."

"Bell." His hesitant expression broke my heart. "You know their drones can find you by your DNA?"

I knew—that was how the Kealans traced those who tried to evade the medical testing—but I couldn't think rationally at that point.

"We'll hide in a cave, somewhere, where the drones can't fly?" My voice dropped, however, as did the hope in my heart. "I can't do this, Johnny . . ."

"Maybe just for a little while?" he suggested.

"What?" I stared at him in disbelief. "You actually want me to go with them?"

"Tony should be out next month," he spoke quickly. "I'm sure your brother will think of something."

Tony—my oldest brother and Johnny's idol since we were little—always came up with something. I wished he were here. Unfortunately, Tony's ingenuity had been wasted on raiding gas stations and convenience stores, which had put him in jail for the second time in his twenty-nine years.

"Together, we will find a way to get you out later," Johnny promised.

"It means I'll have to go with them *now*," I whispered, every fibre of my being refusing to accept the idea of that.

"Listen," he said soothingly, stroking my arms, but his gaze flickered to the wall behind me as he refused to meet my eyes. "If they want you . . ."

"Then you don't?" I snapped.

"No, it's not that. Just, you know, they always get their way . . ."

"Johnny. Are you afraid of them, too?" I stepped back, not wanting to believe the obvious, but feeling completely alone already. "Are you breaking up with me?"

"There is going to be a wedding, Bell," he sounded apologetic. "I don't want you to end up feeling guilty over what may come afterwards."

"Are you kidding me?" My throat tightened painfully, and I brought my hand to it.

"I just want to make it easier for you," he continued in a rush. "No matter what, I won't see it as cheating on your part. Okay?"

"I can't believe it!" With a sob, I shrunk further away from him, feeling both ashamed and disgusted.

He reached for me. "You know we don't have a choice—"

"Isabella, it's time." Trevin walked out of the kitchen, his voice firm.

Breathing hard, I backed away from both of them, moving to the front door.

"Miss Bruno . . ." Miller came from around Trevin, but I was no longer listening to whatever either of them had to say.

Twisting around, I dashed for the exit.

"You go, sis!" Mary cheered from the kitchen just as one of the twins started crying.

Shoving at the front door with my shoulder, I ran outside, without having any idea where I was going. Panic overtook me, propelling me to sprint as far away from this place as possible, away from the men in suits.

"Miss Bruno!" The doors of one of the black vehicles in front of our house flew open, and two men in black uniforms leaped out. They cut me off and tackled me to the ground on our front yard.

"Quickly, in the van with her," Miller bit out the command, catching up with us.

"Let me go!" I screamed, fighting against the hands lifting me off the ground. "I don't want this! I'm not going!"

The last I saw before they shoved me in and shut the doors were the pale faces of my family standing in the doorway of the house where I grew up.

My sister, comforting Lily in her arms. My mom, her hand over her mouth, Luca crawling at her feet. The thought of Tony and my dad flashed through my brain. The images of my little brothers who would come home from school that afternoon and find me gone.

I never got a chance to say a proper goodbye to any of them.

Chapter 2

"THE PLANE IS READY, sir." Carter shoved the phone back in his pocket.

"Good." Trevin glanced at his wrist device. "We're making good time."

Handcuffed in the back of the van, I glared at them from behind the few curls that had fallen over my face from my messy bun.

"As long as there are no more unforeseen delays." Trevin threw a meaningful glance my way.

"Fuck you," I hissed through my teeth. Panic shook me, breeding hot, seething anger.

With a long-suffering look Trevin heaved an exasperated sigh, as if dealing with a petulant child.

"Isabella . . ." He moved over to my side, and I slid away from him along the metal bench, as far as the handcuffs locked to the bar on the wall would allow. "I'm not enjoying doing this."

"Are you expecting sympathy?" I snapped.

"Unfortunately, our instructions were not to give you any al-cohol or pharmaceuticals," he cast me a semi-sympathetic look. "I would like to be able to give you something, to help you calm down."

"Right," I huffed, sarcasm thick as mud in my voice. "Because be-ing intoxicated is exactly the same as being calm."

Actually, the way my heart pounded against my ribs and every muscle and bone in my body trembled, I would have liked a shot of something. Anything to forget for a brief moment, the horror of my situation.

"I am, however, allowed to use any restraining device." His voice sounded firm now, with a clear note of threat. "As long as it doesn't leave permanent damage. I also have full authority to use force as necessary to get you to your destination."

"Really?" I tilted my head, hoping my expression was more mocking than terrified. "So the freaking alien doesn't mind his bride sporting a shiner at the altar?"

"You'll be wearing a veil," Trevin deadpanned.

"French lace," Carter enthusiastically jumped into the conversation. "Italian silk dress. Real pearls. I've heard they even have a pair of diamond-encrusted shoes for you. All this info is hitting the media as we speak. Millions have been spent on the outfit and the ceremony in the historical cathedral in Capital City. Lots of work, and all last minute."

"Why bother?" I scrunched my face in disgust and confusion that overshadowed my fear for a moment. "What is there to celebrate?"

"It's a goodwill gesture from both sides," Carter replied, seemingly unfazed by my expression. "A step forward in bringing the two races closer. The romantic aspect of a wedding doesn't hurt public opinion either."

"What is this? The eighteenth century?" I glared at him. "For you to try to unite two races through marriage? Do you honestly believe that any normal human being would buy the farce you're planning?"

"*The farce* is a distraction, Isabella—a way to pacify the masses, if you will." Trevin's voice remained even, although, I noted his eye twitch. "As of this moment, the world is soaking up the information we are feeding them. People are gawking at the pictures of your dress and church decorations, going through the celebrity guest list, and reading the fake love story between a human and a Kealan that someone at the coalition penned last week." He leaned back, muttering cynically, "I bet it will be made into a movie one day."

I smirked sarcastically. "Too bad any idea of a fairytale romance will be blown to pieces as you drag me down that aisle kicking and screaming."

To my surprise and disappointment, my threat didn't seem to affect Trevin much. The expression on his face was now more tired and worn than angry or concerned.

"And what good would that do anyone, Isabella? The Kealans are getting you tonight, one way or another."

"What if I fight this, like a rabid raccoon, every step of the way?"

"To what purpose? I was there when the coalition forces tried to fight their invasion nine years ago. The Kealan weapons turned people into dust. Our best fighter pilots were gone in seconds." He rubbed a hand over his face. "They got what they wanted—the Earth—within hours. What can *you* do to stop them from getting you now?"

I sat there for a moment, subdued by his words and the new wave of terror they brought.

"What will they do to me? Do you think they'll kill me?" I asked, knowing that no one in this vehicle could give me any guarantee that it wouldn't happen.

"They asked for you to be handed in alive," Carter ventured carefully, as Trevin fell frighteningly silent. "They are going ahead with this wedding, which appears to be a sign of good intentions."

None of it sounded convincing at the least.

Trevin leaned forward, elbows on his knees. "Fuck them all," he gritted through his teeth.

DURING THE DRIVE AND then a flight in a private jet, my anger simmered down under the overwhelming fear of the unknown. Dread and anxiety wracked me. When the plane landed in Capital City and they furtively transported me in a limo to a luxury hotel, I felt as if a tight ball of nerves bounced inside me, with no escape.

Rushed through the lobby between two rows of guards in black uniforms, I had a hard time getting a grip on reality all over again, going through the motions as if in a haze.

High in the penthouse of the hotel that apparently was entirely reserved by the coalition for today, I impassively let the team of beauty professionals do whatever they were trained to do to my body—a bath, a massage, a manicure and pedicure—while my mind kept beating against the bars of the cage the events of this morning had put it in.

"We will have to do some waxing," the woman who seemed to be orchestrating this whole beauty routine informed me while I lay on the massage table.

"Whatever." I shrugged. All their manipulations didn't exactly relax me but made thick numbness settle over me. I felt tired of worrying and worn by fear.

She nodded, and another woman, wearing a white coat, quickly and efficiently waxed the hair off my legs and underarms then lifted one of my legs up. The warm sensation between my thighs followed by a sharp pain ruthlessly snapped me back to reality.

"What the . . ." I lifted my head, to see what was going on in my neither regions. "What are you doing?"

The woman in the coat continued with her work, without paying me any attention. The one at my side nervously consulted her tablet.

"I'm afraid there was a specific request to remove all hair from, um . . . your private area. Leanne is a celebrity beautician." She pointed at the woman who kept working on my 'private area'. "She specializes in bikini waxing, including the Brazilian."

"Where did the request come from?" I asked Leanne, who proceeded to ignore me.

"The staff have strict instructions not to talk to you about anything related to the wedding," the woman with the tablet pointed out. "And I am here to make sure they follow all instructions."

Air left my lungs and my body jerked again as Leanne yanked the fabric strip off my body over and over, ripping the hair out by the roots.

"Those are the wishes of your groom, of course."

Turning my head to the side, I bit my lip, bracing for more. It was easy to pretend that the tears rolling down my face had everything to do with the physical pain, and nothing with the fact that my body was being custom groomed to be used by someone I had never met. Someone who was planning to see me naked tonight—hairless from the neck down.

Defiance bubbled hot inside me, pushing pain and fear aside. More hair was ripped off by the skillful Leanne, but I hardly paid any attention to what she was doing now. Trevin might be right that I couldn't fight this, but I refused to be silenced.

"My groom?" I croaked. "That's what they told you, didn't they? We're madly in love, right?" I barely winced from another rip of the cloth.

"Isabella." The voice of the woman with the tablet held a warning, but I was not going to stop.

"What if I told you I've never met any of them? I have no idea what is going to happen to me tonight. I may be raped . . . or eaten, for all I know—"

A shudder of uncontrollable terror ran through my body.

"Leanne, leave the room, please," the woman with the tablet ordered quickly as Leanne wiped the freshly waxed area with some oil, her hands shaking.

"All done," she muttered and rushed out of the room.

The woman with the tablet urgently called, "Madam Representative," into her wrist device.

"You know I haven't agreed to any of this . . ." I started again.

"Isabella." She draped a fluffy bathrobe over me. "The instructions of not talking were meant to apply to all parties. I thought it would be understood without further explanation."

"So, you're in on it, too?" I drew in a shuddered breath.

"Miss Pen works for the coalition," came the reply, said in a strong female voice from the entrance to the room.

"Madam Representative." Miss Pen inclined her head.

"Barbara Adan?" I gasped, hurriedly stuffing my arms in the sleeves of the bathrobe and closing it over my chest.

The second representative of the coalition I met today, Barbara Adan was the only woman of the three officials representing North America.

"Give us a moment, would you?" she asked Miss Pen, who obeyed with another bow of her head.

"I'd say nice to meet you, Isabella, but I really wish it was under better circumstances." Barbara leaned against the back of one of the two armchairs by the fireplace, gesturing me to take a seat in the other. "Do you mind if I smoke?

"Me?" Struck by her sudden appearance here as well as by her odd request, I needed a second to collect my bearings. "No, I don't, but I don't think it's allowed in here . . ."

"No, it's not." She marched to the climate control panel on the wall and punched in a few numbers. The soft hum of a fan filled the room. "But with the smoke and carbon monoxide detectors off now, no one will know if you don't tell them. Right?"

She took a pack of real cigarettes out of her pocket then lit one and took a long inhale. "We all have our vices," she said, blowing the smoke out. "What's yours?"

I watched, in fascination at the puff of smoke coming out of her mouth. Hardly anyone smoked nowadays—cigarettes were prohibitively expensive. I'd never seen anyone do it in person.

"Um." I remembered her question. "I have a sweet tooth."

"Hardly a vice." Barbara gave me a smile. The way her gaze lingered on my face, felt unsettling, as if she was taking a last look at a person about to die—or be sacrificed. "I can only imagine the morning you had." A kind note slipped into her voice, giving me hope.

"I don't want to go through with this." I was glad my own voice came out firm and clear, because I didn't want any doubts in anyone's mind about my objection to what was being done to me.

"Unfortunately, none of us has any choice about this." She took another drag of her cigarette.

The hope from the sympathy I had glimpsed in her was not that easily crushed, it slithered under whatever armour of composure I'd been trying to build in her presence, prickling my eyes with tears that threatened to spill any minute. "I just want to go home," I said, and this time my voice was much softer, trembling in my throat.

"I know, honey, and I wish I could simply let you go." She sat on the armrest facing me, the skirt of her grey tailored suit stretched over her thighs. "I don't think it would make you feel any better, but there were those of us who opposed the Kealan request to hand you over. The aliens left us no choice, though. They made it clear they wouldn't stop eradicating the population of the entire planet if we opposed. Billions of lives in exchange for you."

"Why me?" I protested. "There is nothing special about me."

"There must be *something* for them. Are you certain you've never met any of them face to face?"

"No. Never." I shook my head vehemently. "Only ever saw them on the news on TV."

"Well, since the request to hand you over tonight came right after your medical testing, I can only assume you've met the criteria of whatever they've been looking for all these years."

"This wasn't my first medical, though. Why now?"

"Honestly, I don't know. They never shared the reasoning either behind the testing or your selection."

I clasped my hands together, but it did nothing to stop them from shaking as my whole body trembled with fear. The words 'medical criteria' did not carry any reassurance.

"Here is what I've been thinking . . ." Barbara crushed her cigarette into the slate coaster on the coffee table then leaned in towards me. "They wanted you to have Kealan citizenship and honoured our laws and traditions by asking us for a better way to go about it. I find it encouraging. It tells me they aren't indifferent to your wellbeing and shows their intention of making the transition easier for you."

I huffed a nervous laugh.

"Giving me considerably more information and at least some time to get used to this idea would be a much better first step."

"There is definitely a time constraint on their part—they made that very clear. What I'm saying, Isabella, is that there is hope they don't necessarily want to harm you. They are willing to exterminate the population of a whole planet for you. You're obviously special to them in some way."

I dropped my gaze to my lap, there was too much uncertainty in her words to make me feel any better about my future, but they made me think about the race of beings who were taking me tonight.

"Do any of them speak English?" I asked. "Will I be able to talk to anyone there?"

"They sent a personal translator for you." Barbara perked up. "Another good sign. They want you to be able to communicate with them."

"They say the Kealans look like the Roswell Greys. You've met them. Is that true?"

There was no official information on their appearance. The few rumours out there compared them to the Greys, which was unappealing and terrifying, adding to my fear and anxiety.

"I haven't seen them without their cloaks." Barbara shook her head. "No one has. The rumour that they are the Greys stems from the fact that the towns they eradicated nine years ago were all small places in North America, the British Isles, and the Siberian region of Eurasia where UFO sightings have been reported during the past century, including Roswell. Also, the little glimpses that some of us have caught of their appearance seem to confirm some similarities—pale skin, large black eyes—"

She cut herself short, obviously catching the fact that her words were only putting me more on edge.

"Listen." She shifted on the armrest. "No matter their appearance, the Kealans are intelligent, sentient beings. You will be in their environment, closer than any one of us has had the chance to be. Communicate with them. There must be a way to reason with them."

"Is that what you would do in my situation?"

She straightened, perched on the armrest. "Yes. I'd definitely hope for a peaceful, diplomatic resolution."

BARBARA ADAN HANDED Miss Pen a small silver box, containing a bio-electronic translator for me.

"I believe communication is the key. With this, you'll be able to understand them," she said before wishing me good luck and leaving me in the care of Miss Pen and her team of beauty experts once again.

"Do not try to take it out by yourself." Miss Pen inserted the translator that looked like a blob of black rubber with prongs into my ear. "It will be rather painful if you do."

Afterwards, I was placed in a white armchair in front of a large mirror. Someone handed me a flute of champagne, obviously unaware about the aliens' instructions of no alcohol. I emptied it immediately before they discovered their mistake.

The bubbly effervescence warmed my insides, somewhat easing the anxiety vibrating through every cell of my body, enough for me to get through whatever they were doing to me, without passing out.

My long, curly mane, inherited from the Italian side of my dad's family, was straightened and tamed into a sleek up-do.

Then they put me in some lacy lingerie and stockings and carefully slid over my head the puffy cloud of my dress—a voluminous, creamy-white contraption, covered in lace and beads, with satin ribbons laced on the back.

"You're going to love these shoes," one of the women crowding me cooed.

The light flashed off the row of the diamonds encrusting the straps of the silver sandals she put on my freshly pedicured feet. Each of the stones was much bigger than I'd ever seen in my life, bigger than the ones Johnny showed me in a magazine when he told me he wanted to be able to afford one for me some day. Although he knew I would have married him yesterday, with a ring from a piece of electric wire, had he proposed.

A sharp pain pierced my heart again at the thought of Johnny's betrayal. Ours was the only wedding I had ever fantasized about. In my dreams there were no diamonds, no silk or fancy hotels. Just our families getting together, lots of yummy food made by my mom and aunts, and our happily-ever-after that would never happen now.

"Give it a twirl!" The woman at my feet glanced up at me. "Take these gorgeous heels for a test drive." She giggled excitedly.

And I twirled, mechanically following her command and sending the skirts of my dress flying in a swirl of lace and silk around my legs.

Swaying on the four-inch heels at the end of the full turn, I braced myself on the rolling cart holding the tray of gleaming manicure tools. My gaze felt on a long, sharp nail file, and I swiped it quickly while no one was looking.

A minute later, I pretended to adjust my skirt. Turning away from everyone, I stabbed the nail file through one of the gauzy underskirts, hiding it in the folds of my dress.

Despite what Barbara Adan said about searching for a diplomatic resolution to my situation, it made me feel better having a sharp object in my possession.

Champagne obviously still muted my terror, but for that moment I felt I might make it through the day without losing consciousness or my mind, even as the uncertainty of what was to come afterwards still weighed heavily on me.

Chapter 3

DRAPED IN SILK AND lace, my hair weighted down by beaded pins and several layers of hairspray, and with a thick veil over my face, I finally emerged from the hotel room shortly after the sunset.

The two rows of Coalition Security Squad marking my way to the limo and then from it to the entrance of a grand church didn't deter mobs of reporters with cameras and microphones pointed my way.

"Will you tell us your name?"

"Is it true that privacy concerns are the sole reason for keeping your identity secret?"

"Do you work for the coalition?"

"Did you really fall in love with the Kealan during one of his official visits?"

"Do you find the Greys sexy?"

"Do you think it's morally acceptable to sleep with the enemy?"

The questions hurled at me sharpened the reality of my impending doom, with some hitting me like rocks of judgment from the crowd.

Trevin and Barbara flanked me at the entrance to the church.

"Breathe," Barbara whispered, taking one of my elbows as Trevin took the hold of the other.

With smiles practiced to perfection, they walked down the aisle, tugging me along.

Anxiety was rapidly growing into all-consuming panic once again, urging me to scream, run, fight someone, everyone . . .

'Fuck them all.' Trevin's words came to mind, along with the tone of defeat and helplessness they had been said with.

I swept the church with my gaze. Row upon row of high-profile guests, none of whom I had ever met in person. The Coalition Forces in full uniform lined the perimeter, laser guns in their hands. They were clearly ensuring the safety of the proceedings, but they were also my guards, making sure I'd be handed over to the Kealans one way or another.

With the cathedral packed to capacity, I would never make it more than two steps in any direction before being stopped, tackled to the floor, and packed into the alien ship, which must be waiting for me outside by now.

There was no way to run.

Trapped, I felt acutely what everyone had been telling me all day—I had no choice.

Through the white haze of the veil over my face, I spotted a person dressed in the formal uniform of the coalition at the altar, the one who must have been chosen to conduct the ceremony. Reluctantly, I slid my gaze to the large, dark figure towering to the right of him.

My groom.

My heart seemed to skid to a complete stop, and my steps halted as my knees went weak.

"Deep breath, Isabella," Barbara urged me as she and Trevin nudged me to move ahead, towards the figure draped in black.

He stood with his back to me. His cloak was made of some sort of material that seemed to have absorbed all light completely, making him look like a black hole against the lustrous interior of the church.

Up close, he appeared even bigger than I expected. Taller. The black cloak clung to his wide shoulders.

Further to the right, I noticed four more of them standing silently, side by side, hoods obscuring their faces, leaving but slivers of pale chins visible.

A shiver ran down my spine when Trevin and Barbara positioned me next to the figure in black and then left my side. I was literally being *given away* to him now.

The official started the ceremony. Barely listening to the words he said, I still noticed that the speech had been shortened. He didn't invite anyone to voice their objections to the union. The most essential part of the whole ceremony, where the couple say their '*I do's,*' had also been cut.

Like me, the Kealan remained silent through the whole ceremony, letting the official read his part.

At the words '*with this ring*', the motionless black figure at my side stirred, the folds of his cloak shifted and a hand emerged from their depths, holding a slim wedding band of gold.

I stared at his hand. In the bright light of the church, it appeared absolutely white, like that of a marble statue.

With his other hand he found mine. I'd expected the contact to be cold, but his skin felt warm, his hold firm.

Watching him slide the ring on my finger almost choked me with the finality of it all.

"I don't want this," I whispered, repeating the same phrase I had said to everyone that day, without anyone listening.

"The choice is neither yours nor mine," came from the inside of the hood.

I snapped my gaze up. All I could see in the shadows of the hood, though, was the strong chin, unnaturally pale, just like the hand.

"I now pronounce you husband and wife," the official announced brightly.

The Kealan turned to the exit, my hand still in his. The other four joined us on our way out.

Organ music started to play. It was replaced by some symphony from a classical quintet when we stepped outside.

People threw white rose petals over us.

I believed I spotted a flock of white doves being released, too.

Someone with a microphone rushed up to us, but the cloaked figures shielded us from both sides. The guards from the Coalition Forces shoved the reporters away quickly.

My head swam. My vision blurred by the veil over my face.

The only thing that felt real was the warm, firm contact of *his* hand holding mine. And I followed its guidance down the wide, seemingly endless stairs out of the church.

Then my attention was fully absorbed by the dark disk-shaped craft descending from the sky to the plaza in front of us. It hovered about a metre or two over the ground as a side of it literally seemed to melt. The solid material of the hull liquefied and dripped down, creating an opening and forming stairs that extended to the cobblestones at our feet.

One of the dark figures at my side ascended the stairs then someone nudged me from behind, prompting me to follow. Only then I realized that no one was holding my hand anymore, and I had no way of telling which one of the cloaked shapes around me I had just married.

Without sparing so much as a glance at the people outside—there was no one I knew or would miss, anyway—I gathered my skirts and focused my attention on navigating the smooth metal steps without tripping in my heels.

Chapter 4

"WELCOME," ONE OF THE aliens greeted as we all took our seats that lined the walls of the circular interior of their craft. As soon as I sat down, a flexible strap extended from the side of the seat and stretched across my lap, keeping me in place, as if I wasn't trapped already.

Somehow, I understood what he said, although I was certain the words were not spoken in English or Italian, the two languages I knew.

I realized that the only sentence my now-husband had said to me at the altar was also spoken in the same language. Although, I couldn't immediately confirm if this was him talking to me now.

"I am Professor Iar Ricread," the alien across from me introduced himself.

Raising a pale hand, he slid his hood back, exposing his face.

I hurriedly swept the annoying veil off my head, ripping the whole thing out of my hair-do—the comb, tiara, and all.

With the tulle gone, I could see clearly again.

I didn't even make an attempt not to stare, taking in every sharp feature of his pale face. In the soft yellow lighting inside the aircraft, his skin had a warm glow, making it appear less gleaming white and more alive.

His eyes were the most striking. Huge, the shape of wide almonds, they took up almost one third of his face. Completely black, they had no visible pupils or irises, no eyelids either. Every time he moved his head, though, I noticed a hexagonal web of iridescent lights glimmer through their black surface.

"I am glad to have you with us," he said, not hiding from my scrutiny.

I sensed a slight movement of the craft and assumed we were now airborne.

"Where are you taking me?" I asked, my voice husky. With the tension crushing me all day, my patience stretched thin, I had no time for pleasantries.

"To your new home," Professor Ricread replied evenly and added, "We skipped the wedding feast. You must be hungry."

The floor in the middle of the cabin rose between us, forming a circular table with a round container sliding up in front of me and a smaller one that seemed to have water inside it.

My throat parched, I opened the water container quickly and drank most of its contents greedily, trying not to spill most of it as my hands shook uncontrollably.

The alien at my right, still completely out of sight behind his hood, opened the lid of the other container revealing a green salad, and silently handed me a narrow, dark-grey utensil.

"Eat, please." Ricread gestured at the food in front of me. "There will be no time for dinner when we arrive."

"Why?" I took the fork-like utensil but couldn't even attempt to eat. With my throat tight as it was, I doubted I could swallow any food, and with the way my hands shook, I didn't think I could even spear a leaf. "What do you want with me?"

"Only what all humans traditionally do after a wedding. I would like you to consummate your marriage tonight."

His words seized me with shock. The fork fell out of my weakened fingers and hit the table with a loud clank. I should have guessed their intentions—the wedding, the waxing, the 'biological criteria' I must have met during my last medical exam . . .

"Are you . . . my husband?" I blinked, swallowing hard.

"No. I represent the interests of all the Kealan race in this matter. Your marriage and its outcome hold importance for all of us."

The other aliens present had made no attempt to either talk to me or even lift the hoods off their faces, remaining silent and motionless like statues.

"How?"

He leaned back a little, the hood framing his angular face not allowing me to see whether or not he had any hair. Unlike the thin, narrow chins and sunken cheeks of the grey aliens in popular culture, though, Ricread had a well-defined, strong jawline and high cheekbones, making the shape of his face closer in appearance to that of humans.

"We have some time before we arrive at our station at Antarctica. I may as well share some of our background with you since you are a citizen of Keala, now."

Drawing in a lungful of air, I nodded silently.

"We are a strong, intelligent, and beautiful race," he said with pride that bordered on arrogance. "For the past many decades, however, our numbers have decreased, due to a drastic drop in the fertility rates."

"You're going to *breed* me?" The idea sounded as appalling as it was terrifying.

"Right now, I am sharing the tragic situation of my people with you." The indignant rebuke in his voice failed to offend or embarrass me—concern about my fate had taken over all my other emotions. "Our birth rate has been at zero for years," he continued. "With the last live birth registered a decade ago, we have not achieved a successful pregnancy between two Kealans since. I've dedicated myself to searching for a way to reverse the situation and prevent the extinction threatening us. By now, Kealan females have a considerably smaller egg reserve compared to humans. The quality of the remaining ones has also been compromised—"

"So, you want to use *my* eggs instead?" I interrupted him, fighting a new surge of panic at the thought of the many ways that could be accomplished—from bloody and gory to painful and cruel.

"It is definitely a part of it."

"Through . . . surgery?" My hand went to my stomach.

"I'm afraid surgical methods wouldn't help us. What humans call 'in-vitro fertilization' is no longer a possibility for us. The sperm of Kealan males has weakened to the point that it is unable to survive outside of their bodies, no matter how hard we try to replicate the environment for it by matching the temperature and other physical parameters."

"Hence the need for the *consummation* . . ." I exhaled as a chilly feeling of dread tightened around me.

"Exactly." I couldn't read his facial expression, his eyes remained completely unchanged—unblinking, but the trace of satisfaction in his voice was unmistakable. "I'm glad you understand."

"Not entirely. Why me? There are billions of people on Earth."

"We had identified you as one of the potential subjects about a year ago, however, we narrowed it down last week. You are the only one."

"Well," I huffed nervously, sarcasm slipping in my voice. "Maybe you shouldn't have exterminated a whole bunch of people nine years ago? What if there were other matches among those you killed in places all over the Earth when you first invaded us?"

"There were none." His tone remained even, unremorseful about the destruction they had caused. "Our Group tested the population of those areas excessively during the preliminary studies conducted on Earth long ago. I reviewed the results before our coming here. None of the humans tested then or after turned out to be a good match to the male subject of this experiment."

"Who is he?" I glanced around the circle of black cloaks. None of the aliens inside them had rushed to claim the honour.

"He is the last known Kealan male capable of producing viable sperm with proven results."

"How romantic," I deadpanned.

"We can't afford romance, Isabella," he retorted coolly. "Our race is facing extinction."

"Professor . . . Ricread," I struggled to accurately reproduce the sounds of his name. "We are entirely different species. Everyone knows that it is impossible to breed dogs with horses."

"But it is very possible to breed horses with donkeys, isn't it?" He tilted his head in a rather human way, gazing at me with those huge, unblinking eyes that made my skin crawl with unease. "*Mules*, I believe, you call their offspring."

"Mules aren't capable of reproducing." I remembered seeing some information on that in one of the many books I had read during those late-night quiet shifts at the store. "Also, breeding horses and donkeys works because they share the same ancestor, I believe."

Ricread nodded with what seemed like approval. "We have determined that humans and Kealans have just enough genome similarity for us to make the interbreeding between you and our male subject possible—with some intervention on our part, of course. The reason for the similarity does stem from the fact that humans and Kealans share a common ancestor."

"How is that possible?"

"We are not indigenous to Keala. Evidence has been found that our ancestors were abducted from Earth, with the first abductions possibly happening hundreds of thousands of years ago."

"By whom?"

"Another alien race who had mastered interstellar travel way before Earthlings even discovered fire. We believe we were a part of their own experiment when they brought early humans to Keala and gave them just enough to survive, choosing to observe our development from a distance. Just the way the early humans on Earth had been watched by them, too."

"Where are they now? Still watching?" All of this felt surreal, and I half-expected to wake up any moment.

"We have reason to believe their entire civilization disappeared as a result of some global tragedy that took place fairly recently, possibly less than two to three thousand years ago. We have firm evidence of their presence on Earth during the time of the ancient Egyptians."

"You do? What evidence is that? The pyramids?"

"It doesn't matter at this point, Isabella, does it? What's important is that Kealans share a large portion of DNA with humans. The physical differences between our species are attributed to evolution in different environments and to the small traces of the DNA of that extinct alien race spliced into ours during the early stages of our development."

"So, you are aliens who came *from* Earth?"

"Yes, technically, we are. And I have determined that interbreeding between our species will be possible. We only have one male subject and, so far, only identified you as his possible match. I was hoping for a few more when we came here, but I'll work with what I have."

"I don't think two people are enough to continue the species," I argued, in desperation. "I don't know any specific research on this, but isn't there inbreeding to be concerned about?"

The detached way with which Ricread spoke about all of this made the whole thing sound hypothetical and abstract. It was hard to believe he meant for me to be a part of it.

"I have developed a technique of eliminating the results of inbreeding on a chromosomal level. Besides, as I've mentioned, the main objective of the research is to continue *our* race, not to create a new one. I will breed human DNA out of the offspring by adding more Kealan DNA with each generation, until the ratio matches the one we currently have."

"How?"

"Using the protocols and technology I have created and perfected over the course of my life. But you don't need to concern yourself with any of this at the moment."

"I think I do. You're talking about the offspring . . . the babies." I said, trying hard not to think that those would be *my* babies.

"At this stage of the experiment, there is a very slim chance of an actual pregnancy," Ricread revealed with a sigh. "During this phase, we will be focusing mostly on your body's reaction to the male subject's reproductive material."

Trepidation chilled me from the inside, but I needed to get any information I could from him, since he continued answering my questions.

"How many stages are there? How long are you planning to keep me?"

Clasping his hands in front of him, he leaned across the table towards me.

"For as long as it will be necessary." His tone was firm and unyielding.

"Do you have any plans to ever set me free?" I asked, my voice hollow, just like the dreadful emptiness spreading inside in anticipation of his answer.

"You are a citizen of Keala now," he reminded, snuffing out any hope I might still have. "The Earth gave you to us. To *me*. Indefinitely."

"I don't want to be part of this," I whispered, unable to move under the horror descending on me.

"I'm afraid you don't have a choice."

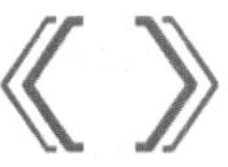

STUNNED BY RICREAD'S revelations, I lost any sense of time. There were no windows in the Kealan craft that allowed me to see outside. At some point, I felt that the whole aircraft tilted slightly.

Ricread yanked his hood down to cover most of his face again. "We are here."

The table disappeared back into the floor, taking my untouched salad with it. The wall shimmered as if dissolving into the air. The solid structure melted down, forming the stairs.

The same warm, yellow light greeted me when I stepped outside. Focusing on making it downstairs without tripping over my useless skirts, I wasn't able to take a look around until I was fully on the ground.

We had landed inside a building. The high, dome-like roof must have been opened to let us in. It was now closing—the round opening shrinking, obstructing the night sky outside and shutting me in.

The huge indoor space was lit by curved strips of light that ran along the circumference of the ceiling. I saw grey walls far in the distance. The floor under my sandals felt a bit springy as if made of hard rubber.

"I will personally show you to your room." Ricread appeared at my side. By the tone of his voice, I understood, it was a great honour to be escorted by him.

I followed him across the spaceship hangar, with two other cloaked figures joining us. The rest of our traveling companions seemed to have disappeared somewhere while I had been surveying our surroundings.

We entered a wide corridor. Empty just like the hangar.

"Where is everyone?" I asked, just to break the silence in which dreadful thoughts roamed through my mind.

"Around," Ricread replied briefly. "We have several hundred personnel at the station, not including the security team. However, it is a large facility and it is late in the night. Most are asleep."

"Would you have preferred a large greeting party?" Another male voice asked unexpectedly, coming from one of the two Kealans accompanying us. "That is customary in human culture, isn't it? To organize a ceremony to welcome a newcomer?"

"That's enough, Valran," Ricread stopped him sharply. "No more of that human tradition nonsense," he added grumpily. "In fact, you're dismissed for today."

With a brief nod, the other man fell behind, leaving just Ricread and me, along with one more male at Ricread's side.

With each turn of the grey-walled corridors, the fear and anxiety kept rising in me at the thoughts of the actual purpose of my being here.

'They are intelligent, sentient beings. Reason with them.' Barbara Adan's words came to mind.

I swallowed hard, trying to calm my nerves. From our previous conversation, I got a feeling Ricread was not exactly someone who listened to anyone's reason but his own.

"I am very tired," I attempted. It wasn't even a lie. Throughout the day, the tension never left me, as panic spiked and ebbed. Combined with the fact that the last meal I ate was the breakfast at home, it was a miracle I still remained upright at all.

"I believe you," Ricread agreed calmly. "Things ended up being rather rushed."

"Can I rest tonight?" All I wanted was a few hours of sleep. My brain was shutting down already, and I could pass out the moment the adrenaline receded—if only there was a chance for it to do so.

Tomorrow was another day, and I'd be able to think better in the morning, I hoped.

"Absolutely." Ricread stopped again, turning to face me fully. The hexagonal mesh of light inside his eyes glistened, bringing an insect to mind. "You can have as much rest as you want *after* the consummation has occurred. My plan is to attempt insemination for the next three consecutive nights."

"Insemination?" My heart fell.

"Yes. By intercourse," he clarified. "Our tests have confirmed you will be ovulating within hours. We have performed a number of procedures on the male subject already, to ensure the optimal performance of his genetic material. If we miss this cycle, all our preliminary work will be wasted." The clinical note in his voice made it sound even colder than before.

"Please, this is all too much and too fast. I—I just need some time."

"Time is exactly what we don't have. We have made some allowances for your customs and traditions, to make the transition less jarring for you. I cannot allow for any further delays at this point."

My back to the wall, I moved my gaze quickly between Ricread and his companion, who had slid his hood back, too, revealing the same large, black, unblinking eyes.

"I don't want to do this," I said firmly, wanting it to go on record somewhere—even if just in my own mind—that I had made my wishes clear to everyone.

"Like I said, you don't have a choice." Ricread moved my way. "The only thing I can allow you to choose right now would be whether to consummate your marriage in the privacy of your bedroom—one on one with the male subject—or under the supervision of the medical team on duty."

I stared wildly at him for a few moments as the realization that this was it, he truly meant what he said, hit me fully.

"I don't want any of this," I kept repeating, although any hope that anyone would listen had gone.

He moved closer, hovering over me exactly like the Grim Reaper in his black cloak, with bottomless, emotionless eyes.

"Privacy or supervision?" he asked, his voice sharp and hard like a knife.

"Privacy," I whispered, struggling to breathe.

"Well then." He stepped back immediately, hitting something on the wall over my shoulder.

The support at my back disappeared suddenly, and I nearly fell backwards, staggering in my heels.

"Sikril," Ricread threw over his shoulder to the Kealan who had came with us, then back to me, "We'll see you in the morning, Isabella."

Then, the two grabbed me under my arms and shoved me into the void behind me.

Chapter 5

"WAIT." I DOVE BACK, but the wall quickly solidified again in front of me, cutting me off from the corridor and the two figures draped in black. "You can't do this!" I slammed both fists into the matte grey surface, hard and unyielding as it was.

"Yes, they can," a quiet voice came from behind me, startling me.

I spun around, as quickly as my skirts would allow.

Bathed in soft, yellow light, the room was quite spacious. Although, the only piece of furniture was a wide bed in the middle, covered with a thin, black blanket.

A tall figure stood by the wall on the other side of the bed. His back to me, he had the same black cloak on as the rest of them.

"Who are you?" I squeezed past a thick lump in my sore throat, already having guessed the answer. His sombre tone sounded identical to the voice of my 'groom' in the church.

Without answering me, he took his hood off, revealing a mass of thin braids. Glossy and snowy-white, they were clipped together with black and silver rings in an intricate weave at the back of his head. The ends of the long pleats streamed free down his back and shoulders.

Running his fingers over the wall, he made a shelf slide out then shrugged his cloak off, making me the first human who had ever laid an eye on the Kealan without their ever-present black shrouds.

As he unhurriedly placed the cloak on the shelf, I quickly slid my gaze down his torso.

He was dressed in a grey body suit so tight, it seemed to be painted on him. The top was sleeveless, leaving his muscular arms exposed, white skin glaring in contrast to the black material of a wide armlet circling his left forearm.

As if sensing my stare, he glanced at me over his shoulder. The reflective light sketched the hexagonal pattern in his large eyes the moment before he lifted his hand and . . . peeled them off.

With shock spearing me like lightning, I made a strangled noise and pressed my back into the wall behind me, watching as he placed 'the eyes' onto the shelf calmly, as if removing body parts was an every-day occurrence to him.

Breathless from fear, I took a tentative glance at his face, expecting to find gaping eye sockets. Instead, a pair of human-sized eyes met my gaze.

"Those things weren't your eyes?" My hand at my throat, I let out a long breath, still shocked but relieved that no body dismemberment had taken place in front of me.

He cast a curious glance at the shelf, as if figuring out what could have caused this reaction in me, but still didn't say anything.

Silently, I continued to watch him for a moment, as he slid a finger around his middle, separating the top part of his bodysuit from the bottom, then along the front, opening it up.

Only when he peeled the vest-like piece off his torso and laid it neatly on the shelf did the meaning of what he was doing filter through to my exhausted brain—he was stripping.

The next moment, he brushed his hands along the side of his pants, and they fell off to the floor, revealing two gleamingly white legs, like columns of marble, and . . . a hard alien backside.

The shock of seeing him literally butt-naked jolted my ability to speak again.

"I don't want to do this," I repeated for what felt like the millionth time. And just like every other time, my words seemed to fall on deaf ears.

"As I have previously stated . . ." He turned around. Kicking his boots must have opened them somehow, because he stepped right out of them and stalked my way—completely nude. "The choice is neither yours nor mine."

Back pressed into the wall, I shrank away as he approached and closed my eyes, wishing I could just melt into the hard surface behind me.

Hands propped on the wall over my head, he hovered over me but made no move to touch me.

"It has to be done," he said unexpectedly softly. "One way or another."

The words were harsh. However, the tone of his voice gave me the courage to open my eyes to face him.

"Not right now," I begged, staring straight at him. "Not like this."

The shape and size of his eyes were human, however, their colour was nothing like I'd ever seen. Despite the dimmed lighting in the room, the dark pupils in the centre were small, not dilated at all. The irises were just as white as the rest of his eyes, except for the vividly iridescent, violet rims marking the outer edge. Thin rays of shifting colours of lavender, magenta, and violet stretched from the rim to the pupil. They seemed to shimmer and change with every move he made and every breath he took, making staring into his eyes truly mesmerizing.

"There will be tests to confirm it has happened," he said evenly, staring at me with those out-of-this-world eyes. "And consequences if it does *not* happen."

The fact that he hadn't lunged for me, gave me a reason to hope. I shot a furtive glance down his body to his crotch. There, his penis hung placidly, without so much as a twitch of an erection.

His brain led his actions, I figured, not lust from hor-mones—and a brain could be reasoned with, I hoped.

"When?" I drew in a lungful of air, bracing for an argument. "When are the tests going to be done?"

"Six in the morning. Local time."

"What time is it now?"

"Well past midnight." He glanced at the wide armlet covering most of his forearm. "Almost one, actually."

"We still have time," I said, frantically grasping at straws. "At least a few hours before anything needs to happen."

Everyone had been telling me that I had no choice whatsoever. And here I was, still desperately trying to influence something. Any-thing.

The fact that he didn't seem to be that into the immediate *insem-ination* either strengthened my hope, though.

"You will need to get some sleep, too," he said calmly, as if we were debating a business transaction.

"At least an hour then?" I pleaded, not giving up. "Give me an hour, please."

"What for?" He shrugged a wide shoulder. "The sooner it starts, the sooner it ends."

God, did this really come down to this? Was I reduced to begging not to be raped on my wedding night?

He didn't strike me as a rapist, though. More like someone who had a reason and determination to go through with this, but lacked the kind of violent aggression I assumed would be required to force himself on me.

"What difference would an hour make?" he asked. "What would you do with that time?"

"Um . . . talk." I tried to give my voice as much force as I could muster, as if I was negotiating, not begging. A negotiation, though, would require me being able to offer something in exchange for concessions from the other party, and I had nothing to give. All I could do was beg and hope he had a shred of kindness in his heart. "Could we just talk for one hour, please?"

"Why?" He leaned back, away from me, dropping his arms to his sides.

He hadn't agreed to anything yet, but he seemed to consider my request. After a day full of rejections, this alone felt like a win, and I was able to let out a breath.

"Maybe getting to know each other, at least a little, would make this night somewhat more . . . acceptable for me," I explained, really hoping he cared at all about my feelings on this matter.

He appeared to think about my words for a moment then gave me a brief nod.

Relief flooded me, as if I had just narrowly escaped a death sentence. In my mind I understood perfectly well I had *escaped* nothing, just postponed it, but an hour felt like an eternity at the moment, and I could breathe freely once again.

"What do you want to talk about?" he asked, sauntering to the bed, seemingly completely undisturbed by his nudity.

Finally, I was able to peel my back from that wall. Carefully, trying not to trip over the skirts of my ridiculous dress, I took a few steps his way. "What's your name?"

He glanced at me, fixing me with those unearthly eyes.

"Commander—" He winced and shook his head. "Just Tairan. Tairan Saryal."

"I'm Isabella Bruno." I walked over and sat on the bed about a metre away from him. With the adrenaline finally wearing off, my bones seemed to be turning to mush weighted down by extreme tiredness. "How old are you?"

"Thirty two."

"In human years or Kealan?"

"It's very much the same. Our planets are of similar size and their orbits are nearly identical."

"Really? I didn't know that." Not that I knew anything about Keala at all. "The gravity is the same too, then?"

He nodded.

"How about plants and animals?"

His less than enthusiastic responses had me worried that our conversation would fizzle to nothing way too soon. Would sitting in silence for an hour make *the consummation* any more tolerable to me? I doubted it would.

"Are your forests also green and the oceans blue?" I prompted, to chase away the silence that threatened to settle over us.

"No. There are no forests or oceans on our planet."

"What happened to them?"

"They have never been there. Our star is brighter than your Sun and much hotter. Through the day, the surface of Keala is burnt, and the ground melts into a black ocean of lava. At night the temperatures drop hundreds of degrees below freezing, solidifying the lava into hard crust. No life can exist in that environment."

"Is that why you came to Earth, because the surface of your planet is no longer habitable?" I asked, shaken by his description.

"I didn't say it has ever been habitable," he replied a bit abruptly.

"Well, how do you *inhabit* it then?" I asked somewhat tersely, too.

It was not my intention to turn this conversation into an argument, especially over something silly like that, but I'd had a gruesome day. I was tired and stressed, my patience worn too thin to remain perfectly diplomatic.

Tilting his head, he stared at me for one silent moment.

"Listen," I inhaled, shifting uncomfortably under his gaze. "I don't know about you, but all this . . . today has really tested my limits. I'm not trying to give you an attitude. I just want to have a conversation."

It wasn't exactly an apology, but I made an effort at sounding friendlier this time. He dropped his head down, seemingly relaxing, too.

"We live underground on Keala," he continued, calmly. "Your planet is of no interest to us. Your Sun hurts our eyes and burns our skin. Earth's crust is too thin and volatile, and the mantel is too soft and hot to accommodate our cities. Just like Ricread said, we came here for you. Well, the research team, sent by The Science Group, came here to find a solution for our race by the potential of using human procreation with Kealans. As you pointed out on the way here, breeding two different species is a challenge. But Ricread has high hopes for progress with this idea of his."

"Has he had many other ideas?"

"Quite a few. You are the first human who had been identified as a match. But there were numerous other attempts to perpetuate our race—DNA splicing, cloning, artificial insemination. All have failed."

"So, this here is truly their, I mean, *your* last hope?"

He shrugged. His expression of indifference in contrast to Ricread's passionate conviction on the subject spiked my curiosity.

"What do *you* personally think about all of this?"

He turned to face me fully, giving me another opportunity to study his features while he considered my question.

Despite his otherworldly appearance, I didn't find looking at him unpleasant.

Tairan's face was proportional and symmetrical, his strong features giving him a powerful expression even when relaxed. His whole body exuded power and strength. My gaze strayed to his thick, corded neck and wide shoulders, then to his biceps, which bulged as he leaned forward to prop his elbows on his thighs.

I didn't venture to examine him lower than that, raising my gaze back to this face instead.

"My opinion doesn't matter," he said.

"It matters to me," I protested. "I want to know what you think about having to marry me."

He shook his head. "The marriage is simply a façade. I hope you understand that."

"I do."

"Good."

He went silent again, making me realize he was not going to share his personal thoughts about the situation we both found ourselves in.

"Tell me more about Keala then," I said, giving up. "Do you live in underground caves?"

"Our cities are built inside the large tunnels created by one of the indigenous life forms, *ure* worms," he replied, somewhat mechanically.

"Must be some big-ass worms, to fit a whole city in the tunnels dug by them." I smiled, for the first time today.

"Huge," he agreed, not quite returning my smile, but his expression had definitely lightened a bit. "They have to be, in order to grind through the hard mantle of Keala. No matter how far our technology has advanced, we are still unable to produce tools similar in power and efficiency to the jaws of *ure* worms."

"It's nice of them to help you out then." I kept my tone light, encouraged by him growing more talkative now.

"There is nothing *nice* about *ure* worms." He huffed a small laugh. "They dig, searching for food, and love coming back to eat whatever life form takes over their tunnels in their absence."

"So, the ancient aliens that stole your ancestors from Earth just dumped you in that uninhabitable environment and left you there to battle the giant worms for survival?"

"Not exactly." He shifted on the bed, his features growing more animated, and I congratulated myself for stumbling on a topic of some interest to him. "Nothing can survive on the surface of Keala. However, life has existed in some form in the mantle of the planet for a very long time. The ancient race had terraformed the rock of the planet, to make the underground space more habitable for the early humans. They also provided the air-filtration equipment that regulates the oxygen content in the atmosphere inside the tunnels. After that, yes, they pretty much left us on our own."

"Why?"

"We must have been some form of an experiment for them, too. There is evidence of their interference in our biological make-up—the alien DNA spliced with that of the early humans', like Ricread mentioned. But no one really knows the ultimate purpose of starting our race. With them gone, we probably will never know."

I stared at him again, wondering which visual differences between us could have resulted from the alien DNA in their blood and which from the evolution in different environments.

"With the advance of technology and the discoveries that made interstellar travel possible for us, we ventured to rise to the surface of our planet," Tairan continued. "We have several spacecraft launch platforms that are raised from underground during the two hours in the day when the surface temperature is actually bearable—one in the evening, a little after sunset, and one in the morning, at sunrise."

I tried to envision what life on Keala would be like.

"Tell me about your cities? How many do you have?"

"Just one now. *Atar*. But we used to have six, back when there was enough population to sustain them all. Our cities are much larger than yours, though. Much more densely populated, too. Simply because we don't have the luxury of space as you have here, living on the surface. All six cities were also located close to each other, occupying a relatively small portion of the planet, for practical reasons and for security."

"Security? Do you have many enemies there?"

"Some, the main ones being those *big-ass* worms." I noticed the corner of his mouth twitch a little when he quoted me, as if he were fighting a smile. "They are one of the indigenous life forms that have adapted to the modified environment. And they are nearly inde-structible."

"*Ure* worms?" I recalled their name.

"Right." He nodded. "Every now and then they travel through the tunnels to feed, including the ones we have occupied. We found it is easier to organize and execute the defence against them if the cities are in a cluster, rather than being separated and on their own."

"How do you fight the worms?"

"The old-fashioned way, by hand. The City Defence Forces was the largest and the most influential organization until The Science Group grew in size and importance. We have several legions respon-sible for the city. When *ure* proximity is reported, the legions are sent to attack and divert the worm before it hits the populated areas."

I watched him grow more animated as he spoke, the subject of city defence obviously being one of interest to him. And I found my-self drawn into the life he described.

"What do you mean by saying you're fighting worms that must be the size of a subway train *by hand*?"

"A train?" He lifted a snowy eyebrow. "From what I've read about your underground transportation system, an *ure* worm is fifty to a hundred times wider in diameter than a subway train, and at least ten times as long."

I gaped at him. "Really? I have a hard time imagining something like that."

"Don't even try. It's ugly." He smiled, using mostly just one half of his mouth, so it came out rather lop-sided. Still, it was a smile. "We always need to be extremely careful when using explosives or any heat-generating weapons underground—the overheating can cause fire in the oxygen-rich air in the tunnels, with devastating results. That leaves us with small close-range, cold-laser blades and metal spears. Knowing exactly where on the worm's body to strike the blow to inflict the most damage is important."

"Have you ever killed one?" That was a pure guess, but the way he talked about that part of Kealan life made me believe he might have been personally involved in the city defense.

"Yes. Many," he confirmed my assumption.

"Was that your job back home? Did you work for the City Defence Forces?"

Tairan took a few seconds to reply this time.

"What did *you* do back home, Isabella?" he asked instead of answering my question.

"Oh, I worked in Shen's Variety Store."

He stared at me, as if expecting me to continue. I wasn't sure what to say next, though, because really there wasn't much more than that to my story.

Tairan remained silent, so I went on, "It's really more like a convenience store with an extended grocery aisle because it's the only place to get groceries in town, except for the farm store, of course, but they mostly carry seasonal produce . . ." I stopped myself, realizing that he may not be familiar with much of what I was saying. "Sorry, does any of it make any sense to you?"

"About fifty percent," he deadpanned.

"Right." I rubbed my forehead. "Basically, I help run the store in our town. Since graduating from high school, I've gone from working part-time to being an Assistant Manager. My boss, Mister Shen, is nice, we get along well. And I get to read in peace during the late-night shifts—"

I caught myself talking in present tense about my job, which made me stop abruptly. All of that was in the past now.

"*Got.*" I sighed. "I meant to say 'I *got* to read in peace.'"

"Have you ever been married? Had a partner?"

His question was unexpected, yanking me out of the gloom threatening to move in.

"I had a boyfriend," I nodded, with a spike of hurt and anger at Johnny's betrayal spearing through me anew. I understood he wouldn't have been able to stop them from taking me, but the way he gave me up, without even voicing an objection, still burnt inside. "We broke up. This morning."

It was hard to believe all of that happened just hours ago. Right now, Deer Rock and my parents' house seemed to be in another life and another dimension.

"I'm sorry to hear that." Tairan sounded sincere, and his expression turned sombre once again.

Did he have to part from someone, too? I wondered.

A sudden buzzing sound startled me.

"The hour is up." Tairan ran his fingers over the armlet on his forearm, and the sound stopped.

"Is it?" I exhaled heavily. The anxiety that had settled somewhat during our conversation rose again.

Having this hour had definitely helped. Tairan no longer seemed like a complete stranger to me. I had not expected to like having a conversation with him as much as I did.

Except that there was still a long way from liking talking to someone to having sex with him.

The fact that Tairan didn't seem to be that excited about going through with it didn't actually help. His cool, business-like demeanour towards the impending *insemination* made it worse, I realized. It felt like getting intimate with me was a chore for him, necessary to accomplish.

'The sooner it starts, the sooner it ends.' His earlier words came to mind, and I wondered once again what he really thought about all of this. About me.

"Tairan?" I whispered as he leaned over, placing his hands on my bare shoulders. "Do you find anything strange—ugly maybe—about human appearance?"

"Yes," he confessed simply.

"Like what?" I braced inside for a list of things about me that repulsed him, then stopped him the moment he drew some air in to reply, "Wait. Don't answer that. Can you tell me about what you find pleasant, instead? Is there anything you *like* about me?"

I'd never been intimate with someone I hadn't loved before. There simply was no time to see if that fragile connection I might have established with Tairan had a chance to grow into anything yet. What was about to happen had nothing to do with love, but I longed for some kind of emotion, a positive feeling—even if it mostly had to do with physical attraction—between us that would help me go through with it.

Tairan paused for a moment, leaning back slightly then looking me over slowly, as if seeing me for the first time just now.

"I . . . I like your shape." His gaze lingered on my breasts, pushed up by the beaded bodice of the wedding dress, which made them seem ready to burst out at any moment.

Men. I rolled my eyes inwardly. Human or alien, they definitely had things in common. The thought made me smile, easing my mood.

His hands still on my shoulders, he stroked the sides of my neck with his thumbs. "The *feel* of your skin." His voice deepened as he moved closer, hovering his mouth over the spot he had just caressed with his thumb.

"How about you?" His whisper hit my neck, fanning it with warmth, which spread with a flock of pleasant tingles through my chest.

"Me?" I found myself tilting my head to the side, as if inviting his mouth closer.

"Is there anything you find attractive about me?" he asked softly.

Was it possible that he shared my insecurities, worrying what I might be thinking about him, too?

Lifting my hands, I carefully placed them on his shoulders then slid my palms down. "I like your shape, too," I admitted, admiring the bulging cords of muscles in his arms.

His lips brushed against my neck as he drew me closer. The light contact sent another rush of ripples down my body.

The physical attraction to him seemed to be there for me.

Wishing for more, I leaned into him. My nose skimmed the few long, thin braids draped over his shoulder, his hair feeling smooth and silky.

With a series of light kisses and nibbles, he moved his mouth along my shoulder then down to the swell of my breast rising over the edge of the low neckline.

I slid my hands to his back, along the hard planes of muscles under his warm skin, and inhaled a lungful of air mixed with the exotic spice of his scent—warm and masculine, yet of no flavour I could compare it to.

"I like the way you smell," I murmured.

He drew in some air sharply, roaming with his hands up and down my back then over to the front, pausing at my breasts.

"How do I take this off?" he muttered with clear frustration, tugging at the beaded neckline.

"Oh." I exhaled a brief laugh. "The ribbon lacing on the back . . ." I twisted out of his arms, getting up and turning my back to him. "See? You'll have to untie it, down here . . ." I tried to blindly find the bow at my waist with my fingers, feeling for the end of the ribbon. "This one. I think."

I felt him firmly tug at the ribbon as he unlaced me with more fervour than skill.

"It took a team of professionals to pack me into this." I laughed, still feeling a little apprehensive, but no longer scared or wracked by anxiety.

My laughing stopped abruptly, as he shoved the bodice—along with the strapless push-up bra I had on—down to my waist. Still at my back, he circled me with his arms, cupping my breasts from behind.

"I like the sound of your laughter," he murmured, placing another kiss on my shoulder and massaging my breasts gently.

Swaying in my heels, I leaned back against his tall frame for support and covered his hands with mine, the warmth of his palms invigorating against my chilled skin.

"Now what?" he asked, between kisses around my neck. "How do I get rid of all this?" He kicked at the hem of my skirt, which puffed in a cloud all around us on the floor.

"Just like this," I replied, somewhat breathlessly, and shoved the whole dress down, forcing the bodice past my hips.

The voluminous contraption heaved in layers of underskirts, as if some life form had trapped my legs. Hands on my waist, Tairan twisted me to face him, then lifted me up, and I kicked my feet free from the beaded silk.

He didn't set me back on the floor but pressed me to his chest, hands under my butt, and I wrapped my legs around him.

"Ready?" He nuzzled my ear in a strangely intimate way that made my skin prickle with pleasure and my chest fill with warmth.

For the first time today, someone actually asked me if I was ready for whatever was about to happen. The sudden realization of this made my eyes burn with tears. Leaning my cheek against his shoulder, his braids tickling my nose, I nodded, not trusting myself to speak.

And strangely enough, also for the first time today, I truly felt ready to go through with what the rest of them had planned for me. I wanted more of his hands on my body and of his kisses on my skin.

Without letting me go, Tairan climbed on top of the bed then laid me down. Lowering his head to me, he touched my lips with his—light and gentle, not quite a kiss, yet so tantalizingly exciting in its promise of more. His braids fell over his shoulder, caressing my skin, as he trailed his lips down my neck to one of my breasts then sucked the tip into his mouth.

I felt his hand travel down my stomach, then his fingers running along the straps of the garter belt and the edge of the stockings.

Apparently having decided against asking any more questions, Tairan simply yanked at my lace panties, ripping the thin strap on the side apart, then slipped a finger between my folds.

Startled for a moment, I halted my breath, but the apprehension never took hold of me again, melting away as wonderful sensations spread through my body from the smooth glide of his finger between my legs combined with the light swirls of his tongue over my nipple.

Panting, I trailed my fingers along the braids fanning over the wide expanse of his back, then gripped his shoulders hard as he increased the speed of his hand, rubbing harder.

Suddenly, I realized what he was trying to do—make me come—although it would surely be a wasted effort on his part. After everything I'd gone through today, orgasm couldn't possibly happen for me tonight.

'*There is no way,*' I thought, even as my body responded to whatever he did to me.

Stress and tension melted away as lightness floated through me, relaxing every muscle under the heat that came from wherever our bodies touched.

The hard, cold spring that seemed to have been winding tighter and tighter inside me with every passing minute throughout the day, finally began to relax under the warmth of his attention and tenderness of his touch.

I let my mind drift with the flow, too, forgetting where I was, whom I was with, and most importantly, why I was there.

All that mattered at that moment was his mouth at my breast, the silky, warm sensation of his tongue on my nipple, the slight grazing of his teeth.

The slick glide of his fingers in and out of me.

The tantalizing pressure of his thumb when he rubbed it against my most sensitive spot.

A slight tendril of pleasure fluttered through me, curling warm, low in my belly. Tairan circled his thumb, pressing it harder, making the pleasure grow and ebb in waves with every move.

My hips jerked, my thighs trembled, and I moaned, writhing under him, fisting my hands in his braids.

He removed his hand at that moment, and I felt something significantly thicker than a finger press against my opening.

There was definitely nothing flaccid about his penis this time. Hard and strong, Tairan slid inside me in several deliciously slow, shallow thrusts, replacing with sweet pleasure the achy pressure that had been building in me.

With a long exhale, I circled my legs around him, linking my feet together behind his back. He eased his hand between us again, pressing his thumb to where I wanted it most, then slowly began to move.

His thrusts remained unhurried, deep and powerful at the same time. Slowly, gradually, the waves of heat that flowed through me grew until they began to crest, taking me higher and higher.

The swells collided, crashing inside me. My legs tensed, locking him with me, as I rode the shudders of my orgasm.

Removing his hand from between us, he propped himself against the bed with both arms. In just a few determined thrusts, he pumped his release into me.

My eyes closed, I stretched under him, crossing my arms above my head, the post-orgasmic glow settling over me with a languid flow of warmth rolling through my veins.

I opened my eyes, unable to keep a smile off my face.

Tairan remained completely still over me, his arms straight, his eyes met mine.

I couldn't read his expression. His eyebrows furrowed, but he didn't seem to be angry, just pensive. Unsure what to do, I kept staring back at him, the smile stubbornly refusing to leave my face.

Although the silence was beginning to grow uncomfortably long, I wasn't sure what to say to break it.

What was the appropriate thing to say after something like that?

It was nice? Nicer than I had expected? Thank you for making me come, after all?

What he just did to me wasn't simply sex for science. It felt like lovemaking, although neither of us was anywhere near being in love.

'I'm glad it turned out to be you,' rushed through my mind—the only thing I actually wanted to tell him, but the moment was lost. Breaking our eye contact, he slipped out of me and moved to the side.

Sliding his hand down my leg, he circled my ankle with his fingers and lifted it up, making me bend my knee.

"You have to stay like this for a little while now," he said unexpectedly, lifting my other leg, knee to my chest, too.

"What? Why?" I kept smiling, sure he was joking, despite his serious expression.

"Ricread's instructions," he replied gloomily. "He believes this position may increase the chance of conception."

"He said nothing is expected to happen during this phase," I reminded. "Besides, I got a feeling you weren't into this . . . um, *experiment* that much. Definitely not at the level Ricread was."

His jaw flexed.

"No one could ever match Ricread's zeal."

"Well, then. Who cares about his instructions?" I made a move to straighten my legs, but Tairan held his hand over both of my ankles, keeping them in place.

Before I could ask him any more questions, he slid his hand to one of my shoes. Turning it side to side, slightly, he found the buckle and figured out how to open it.

"These must be painful to walk in," he muttered under his breath, closely examining the strappy stiletto after he took it off.

"They are."

"Why wear them then?" He tossed the sandal to the floor and removed the other one, massaging my feet afterwards.

"Vanity?" I shrugged. "They add some height." There was no need to remind him that I had no say in choosing my attire today. Besides, being on the shorter side of average, I often wore high heels by choice, too.

Carefully sliding his hands under my back, he tugged my garter belt down and over my hips, taking the ruined underwear with it. Without unclipping the stockings, he rolled them off my legs, making sure I pressed my knees back to my chest right after again.

"What is the purpose of this contraption?" he asked with a genuine confusion on his face.

"Garter belt and stockings? There is no real purpose to either nowadays, just aesthetics. The look of it, I guess. Most men find them sexy."

Holding up the bunched-up nylon tangled with straps and ribbons, Tairan regarded it for a few more seconds then tossed it on the floor next to the diamond-encrusted shoes.

"Is there a shower here?" I asked, feeling uncomfortable, lying on my back like this, hugging my legs to my chest.

"You can't have a shower yet," he said firmly, shaking his head. "It's in the instructions."

"What instructions?" I snapped, extreme tiredness making me sleepy and irritable at the same time. "Why do you care about them? What are *you* getting for participating in this?"

There were so many more questions I could ask, had he given me any sign right now that he would actually answer.

Something warm flickered through Tairan's expression, struggling to break through, but then the serious frown returned, settling firmly over his face.

"What am I getting out of it?" He rose from the bed. "The pleasure of your company, of course." Said in a cool, detached voice, it was hardly a compliment.

"The shower is right here." He touched the wall to the right, which dissolved into an arched opening to another lit room. "You are allowed to take one after the tests tomorrow morning."

He entered the bathroom.

"Wait a minute!" Taken aback by his suddenly chilly behaviour, I jumped off the bed the moment the wall solidified behind him—Ricread's instructions be damned—and slammed my fist into the closed-off opening.

The wall remained solid.

"Fuck it," I muttered under my breath, no longer sure who or what I was angry with, Tairan, Ricread, the wall, or this whole situation I found myself in.

Rummaging through the skirts of my discarded dress, I found the nail file I'd hidden there earlier and tucked it into the narrow gap between the bed and the floor. Despite still feeling irritated, I was extremely glad I didn't end up needing to use it as a weapon to defend myself tonight, but who knew what tomorrow would bring.

Right now, only one thing was certain—I was deadly tired. Shuffling back to the bed, I lifted the thin, black blanket. There didn't seem to be any other bedding than that, just a plush mattress with a raised headrest instead of pillows.

Yawning, I climbed under the blanket, which turned out to be warmer than could have been expected, and curled into a ball.

As I made myself comfortable, my forearm brushed by my nipple, still warm and sensitive, reminding me of the sensation of Tairan's mouth on my breast.

My mind then went back to my walking down the aisle in the church just a few hours earlier, when I was shaking to the core with horror and trepidation.

Tonight could have gone so, so much worse.

Chapter 6

LIGHT FILTERED THROUGH my closed eyelids. The noise of someone bustling about startled me awake. It took me a few moments to remember where I was—no longer in my bed, under my grandma's quilt, but at the Kealan lab, on the South Pole of all places.

I rubbed the remnants of sleep out of my eyes and made an attempt to open them. Blinking, I sat up in bed, pressing the cover to my naked chest. Pearls and crystals rained from my messy hair to the mattress. My scalp itched from the crusted hairspray.

A group of Kealans had invaded the bedroom. None of them wore goggles or cloaks, and I identified some as females by the shape of their bodies. Most of the group were dressed in tight, grey bodysuits, identical to that worn by Tairan. Although, the uniforms of four of the men were black.

"Who are you all?" I mumbled, scratching my head, which still felt foggy inside from sleep. "What is going on?"

"The tests," the reply came from Tairan in the bed next to me. I had fallen asleep before he came out of the shower, but he must have stayed with me for the rest of the night.

I noticed iridescent swirls of make-up mixed with the black streaks of mascara on the heels of my hands, which I had rubbed my eyes with.

Great, I must be looking like a raccoon.

I groaned inside.

"I really, really need a shower," I told the female attendant who approached me.

"After the tests are done." She gently pushed me back to the mattress. "Lie down, please."

Several automated equipment racks rolled in, and the Kealans arranged them in positions around the bed.

A tall, narrow, white box was placed at the foot of the bed, then a chrome arm extended from it, spreading a grey, plastic divider between Tairan and me.

"Will this hurt?" I asked with apprehension, sweeping the faces of the Kealans crowding me with my gaze.

"Not if you co-operate," a man at the entrance replied, and I recognized Ricread's voice, snapping my attention to him.

While the technicians readied the equipment, I studied him. Ricread wore no cloak or goggles this time. He appeared older than the other Kealans, his braids duller than Tairan's glossy white, as if time had rubbed the shine out of his hair, giving it a greyish tinge. He took a few steps closer, and I spotted a web of fine lines crisscrossing his face.

The woman at my side tugged at the blanket I clutched to my chest.

"No." I tightened my grip.

"If you fight, it will take longer," Ricread observed calmly. "With a higher chance of it being painful."

"Painful?" I gasped, clinging to the blanket like a life raft.

"Just relax," the female assistant cooed, patting my shoulder. "My name is Zavis, and I promise to be very careful." She tugged at the blanket again.

'The sooner it starts, the sooner it ends.' I recalled Tairan's words. But Ricread was hovering over me, his stare making my skin crawl. A number of his assistants, male and female, gathered around, staring, too.

What was I to do? Say *I don't want this?* Again? It hadn't helped me avoid things before. No one would listen now either, I was sure of it.

A muffled groan reached me from behind the grey partition.

"Tairan?" I turned my head to the sound but couldn't see a thing through the plastic-like material. "What's happening?" I demanded from Ricread.

Without replying, he gestured to the men in black uniforms, and two of them moved on me.

Another groan came from behind the divider, a little louder this time, and definitely filled with pain, which tugged at my compassion, even making me forget about my own situation for a moment.

"What on earth are you doing to him?" I raised my voice. Zavis stood aside, as the two men pressed on my shoulders, prying the blanket out of my hands.

"No!" I screamed as they forced my hands up, over my head and pressed them into the headrest.

I frantically kicked my feet just before someone got hold of my ankles, pushing my heels into the mattress.

"Hold still," came Ricread's cool voice. "Or I'll have no choice but to strap you in restraints next time."

"It'll be fine." Zavis climbed on the bed between my spread legs, and I felt her warm palm on my belly. "This won't be any worse than the routine exam in your doctor's office," she assured me, patting my leg. The men who held my ankles, shoved them up the bed, bending my knees. "Just hold still now."

This was nothing like my doctor's exam—no one had ever held me down in the medical office. Neither were there this many people, staring at my naked body.

Unable to deal with the crowd around me, I closed my eyes, shutting them all out. Panting heavily, I struggled to get air in and out of my lungs, the weight of several men holding me down seemed to compress my insides and even my awareness.

My mind floated on the fringes of consciousness, leaving me only half-aware of something sticky being glued to my skin in several places and something cool and hard probing between my legs.

"Her heart rate is elevated," I heard Zavis' concerned voice, as the probing continued.

No kidding!

I felt like screaming. One didn't need to be a scientist or use a bunch of sophisticated equipment to figure out that their treatment of me would stress me the hell out.

"Keep going," was Ricread's cool reply. "I need a complete set of data for today."

The tests continued for what felt like forever, until finally they let go of my arms and legs.

I opened my eyes, watching with relief as the rest of the team move away from me. Zavis stood at my bed. A milky-white screen extended from the black armlet on her left forearm, and she poked at it with the fingers of her right hand.

Feeling hollow, as if drained from the inside, I didn't even care about covering myself with the blanket right away, focusing on getting my breathing back under control first.

The grey partition rolled back into the tall, box-shaped robot at the foot of the bed, revealing a gurney-like board hovering on Tairan's side. He was no longer in bed with me but strapped to the gurney now. Avoiding my eyes, he rolled his head away, but I caught the expressions of suffering and utter exhaustion on his face.

"What did you do to him?" I rose on my elbows, glaring at the Kealan standing by the gurney.

Ignoring my question, he silently punched in something into a panel on the side of the frame, sending the gurney into motion.

"Where are you taking him?"

The Kealan finally met my eyes. "You'll see him tonight."

His voice sounded familiar, although I couldn't place it right away.

"We're done, Valran," Ricread called firmly on his way to the exit. "Let's go."

The man broke eye contact and followed the gurney, which was taking Tairan out of the room. The rest of them exited too, leaving me completely alone.

"Good morning," the voice came from next to the bed unexpectedly, making me jump.

"What the hell?" My nerves were still on edge from the events of this morning.

"Sorry if I startled you," the same voice said soothingly, and I realized it was coming from the grey cylinder by the bed. About thirty centimetres wide by a metre tall, it could have been easily mistaken for a nightstand or a side table.

"What are you?" I stared at it, getting hold of the blanket again.

"GRAN-1421-B. A special edition of robotized personal assistant." The top panel of the cylinder tilted up, displaying two pale-white lights in the upper part of the circle. A line of small blue lights flickered and curved in sync with the words the thing spoke, giving it the appearance of a smiley face, with white eyes and blue mouth—a little goofy in its simplicity.

"G, R, A, N, one . . . what?"

"GRAN-1421-B," the robot supplied helpfully in its soothing, androgynous voice. "I have been assigned to help you navigate your new environment."

"Can you help me make sense of what just happened?"

"Certainly. If you are referring to the tests being performed this morning, they were to confirm that copulation between you and the male subject had occurred, as well as to collect data to monitor the response of your organism to his genetic material and to identify the areas where intervention may be required."

"What kind of *intervention*?"

"This will be determined by the professor and the medical team. I have no access to the details."

I placed my hand on my belly as my stomach churned. For what it was worth, there was no soreness from the tests, just the lingering memory of their invasive touching.

"What did they do to Tairan then?"

"I do not have the information on the procedures performed on the male subject."

"Can you *get* that information?"

"Sorry." The blue smile shone brighter. "You do not have the necessary clearance for this request."

"I believe Tairan has been hurt. He also happens to be the only person who's shown me any understanding in this place. You see, I don't want him to suffer."

"I see." The robot's 'expression' didn't change and its voice remained cheerful.

"Do you now?"

"Absolutely. The level of sensitivity of my optical sensors is twice as high as that of humans."

"I was talking about a different kind of *sensitivity* here, Gran." I waved him off, getting out of bed. "One that obviously couldn't be programmed into a robot." I sighed. "Never mind, we're not speaking the same language."

"I have the basic database to speak any known language on Earth and advanced artificial intelligence software with expanded vocabulary for Kealan and English," the robot hummed, whizzing softly after me as I headed to the wall, behind which Tairan had mentioned the shower was located.

"Can you tell me then, how to open doors here?" I patted the wall where I thought Tairan had, but without any result.

"Certainly. To open an entrance in a wall, you need to approach it within the distance of approximately twenty to forty centimetres, position yourself under the marker indicating the entrance then place the pads of your right-hand fingers on the section approximately at your eye level."

"A marker?"

"The break in the light on the ceiling indicates a passage had been programmed into the wall."

I glanced up to the ceiling, spotting the line of white light running along where it met the wall. The line broke with a gap of a few centimetres about two steps to the left of me.

"This sounds tricky," I muttered under my breath, remembering how smoothly the doors opened for others.

I shifted to move under the gap and pressed at the wall at my eye level.

The dark surface seemed to waver and thin, then melted away as if absorbed into the sides, forming an arched doorway.

"Hmm, it worked," I said, stepping into the lit room on the other side.

"Or you could give a voice command," chirped the robot, rolling in behind me.

"What do you mean?"

"The equipment in your living quarters has been programed to obey your voice commands, in English.

"Really?" I faced the wall that had already solidified behind me. "Open," I ordered and watched the hard material instantly shimmer and dissolve. "Wow." I stepped back into the bedroom. "Wouldn't it be easier to start with that?"

"I am required to provide you with all available options. The doors outside your rooms will not respond to commands in English."

"Will they respond to this?"

I hurried to the wall that I remembered led to the corridor, too eager to get out of the room to worry about possibly being seen by someone on the other side, naked as I was.

Glancing up, I aligned myself a little better with the marker and stepped a bit closer, putting my fingers on the wall.

Nothing happened.

"Open," I ordered.

Again, the wall remained unchanged.

"That entrance is not on the list of approved equipment," the robot behind me announced.

"Of course it's not." I sighed, turning away. "Shower it is then."

Chapter 7

THE BATHROOM HAD NO visible fixtures. The toilet and sink slid out from the floor and the wall, following my voice commands, and disappeared again when I told them to.

To take a shower, I followed the instructions given to me by the robot and ordered the jets of warm water with shampoo to stream from the ceiling to wash my hair, followed by the ones with liquid soap from the wall to wash my body. The voice command to rinse activated clean water to run from both.

Kind of like a car wash, I thought. The illusion grew even stronger when warm air blasted from the jets at the end, drying most of the water off my skin and hair. Freed from any trace of hairspray, my hair immediately sprang up into thick curls.

"I'm hungry, Gran," I said, upon returning back to the bedroom where the robot was waiting for me. "And, do you know where I could get some clothes?"

I glanced around the room. The bed had been made, my wedding dress was gone, and a couple of flat, white cylinders whizzed along the floor, reminding me of the robot vacuums back home.

"Breakfast is served in your living area." The robot rolled ahead of me to the wall opposite from the bathroom. "The closet can also be accessed from there."

"My living area?" Only now did I spot another break in the line of light under the ceiling. Coming closer, I ordered the wall to open.

The new entrance led me to a room at least four times as large as the bedroom. One of the walls was smooth and completely bare. The other three had shelves with green potted plants and held some unknown-to-me wall-mounted devices and cabinets.

Opposite to the smooth wall stood a white couch, curved in the shape of a crescent, with a few stands arranged around it. Several bright throw cushions on the couch, along with the green of the plants, were the only splash of colour in this grey-and-white room. Still, it appeared someone had actually made an effort to decorate this place.

"How many 'areas' do I have here?"

"Two. One for sleeping and one for taking meals and socializing."

"With whom?"

"With company. Whenever you're allowed to have a visitor. This is the food compartment," the robot informed me, rolling across the room to a medium-size cabinet on the wall. "Your breakfast will be here shortly." It proceeded to roll to the bare wall. "This is your window. You can select any degree of opacity from the inside. However, it will always remain completely non-transparent to anyone outside."

"Did you say 'outside?'" I rushed to him, anxious to see beyond the grey, depressing walls. "How do I make it clear?"

"Slide your finger in a vertical line anywhere on the surface. Up will increase the opacity, down will make it more transparent."

Following the instructions, I slid the tip of my finger down. The grey seemed to dissipate from the wall, leaving it as clear as a pane of glass.

"Wow!" I stepped back, taking in the dark, snowy landscape outside the room. Illuminated only by the yellowish light that seemed to come from the wall, the snowdrifts did not come all the way to the window, as if kept a short distance away by something invisible.

Beyond that the Antarctic winter reigned. The night sky was clear, with the stars twinkling high above the snow that had been blown into shapes, similar to ocean waves. The white crests glistened under the pale light from the sliver of the moon.

"It's beautiful." I inhaled, wishing I could feel the crisp outside air. Although, from what I remembered reading about winter in Antarctica, a deep inhale would have most likely burned my lungs with frost. Earth's southern pole was considerably colder than the northern one.

"This must look gorgeous in sunlight," I wondered out loud. "How long is it until sunrise here?"

"You will not stay at this facility in summer," the robot assured me. "The entire staff will relocate to the North Pole before full sunrise, to minimize the exposure to sunlight."

"Are Kealans that afraid of the sun? How bad is it for them?"

"Skin damage can be extensive and extremely painful, especially in cases of prolonged exposure. Even indirect sunlight can cause unpleasant reactions if no protective clothing is worn. Without the specially developed goggles, permanent blindness can result."

"No wonder they don't come out much." I remembered the hurried way the Kealans had departed the church, even as the wedding ceremony had taken place fairly late in the evening.

"Your closet is in this wall," the robot chirped, continuing his tour through the room. "It is accessible either from here or from the bedroom."

"Do I also give it voice commands?" I stood in front of the rectangular panel, which seemed to be made from dark, tinted glass.

"You could. Or you could simply open it yourself, using your hands."

"My hands, huh?" I touched the glass panel. It shimmered and lit up, like a computer screen coming to life.

"This is the display of what is inside," Gran explained. "Slide the images aside, until you find what you like."

I went through the slide show of mostly loose white dresses, all of a very similar cut. "Not much variety here," I observed, choosing one at random.

"This style of clothing was deemed to be the most suitable for you."

"Deemed by whom?" I asked when the panel slid to the side, revealing the folded dress pressed between two clear pieces of plastic. One of the pieces opened like an oven door, the dress falling out on it for me to take. "And how is it *most suitable*?"

I shook the garment out, eyeing its loose-fitting shape, with a plunging neckline and a wide belt made from the same soft material.

"It's unrestrictive to movement and blood flow, and adjustable in size," the robot explained as I slid the dress over my head.

The skirt fell down to my ankles. There were no sleeves, and the front seemed to be just two wide strips of material sewn together below my chest bone, wide enough to house a breast size a few cups larger than mine.

"That's not what I've seen Kealan females wear," I noted, thinking about their skin-tight bodysuits that seemed comfortable, despite fitting like a glove.

"The uniforms of the personnel have been found too restrictive in terms of access, with the danger of accidental overheating if the temperature control is not operated properly."

The word 'access' jolted me with unease, highlighting to me once again the purpose of my being here. Even fully dressed, my body needed to be 'accessible.'

"Do I get any underwear to go with it?" I asked quietly. Swiping through more pictures on the panel, I found a pair of underpants—wide, soft, and stretchy—but no bra.

"Some undergarments can severely impact your blood flow."

"Why is there such a concern about my blood flow?" I asked, sharply.

"It is necessary to support a successful pregnancy."

"I've been told a pregnancy is unlikely to happen." I remained by the screen, but my attention was no longer on the images.

"At *this* stage," Gran agreed evenly.

"How many stages are there? Where can I get any details on their plans for me?"

"You do not have a clearance to receive this information."

"Why am I not surprised?" I mumbled, walking to the couch, my legs suddenly weak.

"Because you have been made aware of your clearance level before?" Gran supplied helpfully.

Ignoring him, I propped my elbows on my knees and rested my head in my hands, spearing my fingers through my hair. Obviously my Kealan citizenship came with no rights, and every moment spent in this place reinforced that to me.

Locked in these rooms, like a prisoner with no crime committed, I'd lost not only my freedom, but control over my body no longer seemed to belong to me either. The privacy I currently had was not guaranteed. And I had hardly any information on what was to come.

The little I had managed to find out painted a bleak future of a life closely resembling that of a lab animal—confinement, controlled environment, tests . . .

I forced my mind out of the gloomy thoughts that threatened to plunge me into misery.

This couldn't possibly be all there was for me.

My head swam, reminding me I hadn't eaten anything for nearly twenty-four hours, now. "I need some coffee."

"Breakfast." Gran's voice picked up as the robot rolled to the wall with the food compartment and took out a tray with dishes, using two thin chrome arms that extended from the sides of its cylinder-body.

Gran placed the tray on one of the stands in front of the couch. "Or would you prefer to eat at the table?" At his words, a large panel descended from the ceiling near the window, forming a table suspended by thin silver chains.

"It doesn't matter." I shook my head.

The table slid back up and into the ceiling as I grabbed the cup, taking a big swig of the warm liquid inside.

"This is not coffee." I stared at Gran. "It's tea. Chamomile, I think. Weak and unsweetened."

"Caffeine and sugar can be harmful during pregnancy—"

"What pregnancy?" I snapped, cutting the robotic voice off. "I'm *not* pregnant."

"Many substances may interfere with the process of conception. Your diet will be strictly regulated to improve the chances for success at every step of the process, from conception, through implantation, pregnancy, and hopefully, consequent labour and delivery. Taking good care of your body will help the medical team preserve your reproductive functions for longer."

Despite being mostly empty at this point, my stomach roiled. I set the teacup down on the tray, my appetite deserting me.

"How long am I to be kept here like breeding stock, Gran?" I asked, not expecting an answer but needing to voice the dread and anxiety that threatened to suffocate me from the inside. "Will I be slaughtered at the end, when I get too old to be useful? Will whatever *offspring* I manage to produce face the same fate?"

A shudder ran through my body. I'd always wanted children of my own, a family, but this was like a cruel and twisted parody of my dreams.

"There are no plans for termination of your life," the robot informed me brightly.

"Well, that's a relief," I said blankly, rubbing my face with both hands.

Sitting on the couch, I absentmindedly turned the wedding band on my finger. My thoughts went to the man who put it there.

'The choice is neither yours nor mine.'

Tairan's words implied he was not a willing participant here either, although I couldn't tell exactly to what degree, because of his contradictory behaviour. He seemed to be following instructions, even if unenthusiastically.

I recalled him telling me about life on Keala. There was definitely more excitement in his words and expression then. The slip of his tongue when he introduced himself as *Commander* came to my mind, too.

Back home, Tairan seemed to have had a rank, a job, a purpose. What made him give it all up? Wouldn't a man who held a position of power be resentful when lowered to the level of breeding stock? Was that the reason behind the gruffness in his attitude?

"Gran." I turned to face the robot that silently waited nearby. "What can you tell me about Tairan . . ." I strained my memory for the full name he'd given me. "Commander Tairan Saryal?"

"Your instructions are to eat all daily rations of food," the robot replied impassively.

"Will you answer my question?"

"Not until you finish your breakfast." He wouldn't give up.

"Are you blackmailing me?" I narrowed my eyes at him, feeling annoyed at the piece of machinery that acted way too human for its own good.

"Negotiating." The smiley face stared at me, innocently.

"Is that how you choose to use your artificial intelligence? To argue with me?"

The blue smile grew wider, as if he was turning up the charm.

"Just follow the instructions, Miss Isabella, and we will remain friends."

"That sounds like a threat." I released a frustrated breath, reaching for the whole-grain toast on the tray.

"I would never threaten you."

"Liar." I listlessly chewed on the bread.

"On the contrary, one of my main tasks is to look after your health and safety."

"Fine. You win." I took another bite off the dry toast and moved the plate with two poached eggs and a salad closer. "I'll eat."

There was no dressing on the salad and no seasoning on the eggs, not even salt. Still, as I started eating, I realized how hungry I actually was. Finishing the breakfast turned out to be an easy enough task.

"So." I leaned back in the couch, pushing the tray with empty dishes aside. "Tell me about Tairan now."

"Tairan Saryal is a former Commander of the City Defence Forces of Atal, the capital of Keala."

"What exactly does 'commander' mean?"

"It's the highest rank possible to achieve in the Forces."

"Tairan is only thirty-two," I pointed out.

"He started the Academy at the age of fourteen, two years younger than the average age of admission."

"Why?"

"Tairan Saryal demonstrated exceptional aptitude and character during the entry exams, and was granted permission for an early admission."

Gran's round 'face' grew brighter, swallowing 'the eyes' and 'the mouth,' before turning into a screen. The picture of a young Kealan appeared on it, and I immediately recognized the violet-rimmed eyes as Tairan's.

Upon a closer look, the boy's stern expression also seemed familiar. His braids were considerably shorter back then, and they hung freely, the only rings were the ones on the ends.

"He graduated the Academy at the age of eighteen, as first in his class." The picture changed to that of a portrait of a young man now, with Tairan's eyes and a look of hard confidence on his face. "He became Keala's youngest Commander of City Defence Forces at the age of twenty-six."

The picture changed again, the screen showing Tairan as a grown man. He wore a black uniform, with both shoulders and one of the sleeves decorated with all sorts of insignia. "What are these for?' I asked pointing at his sleeve on the screen.

"These are given every time someone distinguishes themselves during an *ure* attack. Some are also to mark advancement within the Forces. Each mark is accompanied by the honour ring that Kealans in the Forces display in their hair."

"The braid rings?"

"Yes. Each is engraved with the date and the symbol of the event or accomplishment."

The screen dulled. Tairan's portrait disappeared, replaced by the unblinking smiley face again.

"Anything else?" I urged. Drawing my feet under me, I shifted closer to the robot. "This can't be it."

"This is the only information available for your level of clearance."

"Really? That's it?" I jumped out of my seat, my patience wearing thin from yet another denial for information. "What's so harmful about me getting to know more about him? I married this guy!" I shoved the hand with my wedding band into the smiley face. "I had sex with him, for crying out loud. And I'm not allowed to know anything about his life?"

"None of this information is necessary for a successful copulation," Gran stated brightly.

"I bet it was Ricread who fed you *that* line," I muttered under my breath, pacing the room, with the robot pivoting back and forth to follow my movements.

After a while of pacing the perimeter, like an animal in a cage, I finally calmed down enough to get back on the couch.

"Fine." I gestured Gran to roll closer. "Tell me about Keala then."

I figured if I couldn't learn more about the man, I could at least find out everything there was about the planet he came from and the people who now had full control over my future.

THE PICTURES OF KEALA taken from space showed a pitch-black planet, the light of its large star reflecting off the glossy, melted rock covering its surface.

Pictures of life underground, however, were much more vivid.

I still had a hard time imagining the giant monsters that dug the wide tunnels housing Kealan cities. In the pictures that Gran showed me, the tunnels looked like wide streets with arched ceilings over them.

Apparently, the vehicles in Keala moved along rails mounted in the ceiling, leaving the floor solely for pedestrian use. The two-story buildings, constructed along the tunnel walls, were just one room deep, as Gran explained to me, but could stretch a hundred metres or even longer.

I scrolled through the pictures on Gran's screen, fascinated by the alien way of life, flowing in front of my eyes—Kealans walking along the streets of their towns, holding hands, carrying groceries. Sure, the design and architecture of the cities was foreign and unusual to me, but the atmosphere of the pictures was very similar to that of any other city on Earth—people simply living their lives.

One striking difference was a complete lack of children.

The Kealans pictured might be of different ages, but they were all clearly adults, with some possibly in their teens.

"What happened there, Gran? How did the birth rate drop so drastically?"

"The cause was the significant drop in fertility, both male and female, which has been linked to the use of the Xaute chemical in the cities. When sucked into the filtration system, Xaute did not get fully absorbed by the filters or cleaned from the air supply bio-chemically, which resulted in its re-release into the breathable atmosphere of the tunnels. After several years of continued exposure to it, the people of Keala started experiencing severe infertility issues. Male sperm has weakened to the point that it is unable to survive in any artificial environment outside of the body. Women have much fewer viable eggs, too. The last Kealan born is ten years old now. Unless the experiment is successful, he will be the last of his race."

"How did that chemical get into the cities in the first place?"

"Xaute was invented after decades of extensive and expensive research as the only chemical weapon capable of effectively immobilizing *ure* worms."

"What?" I blinked in astonishment. "Are you saying that Kealans *created* the cause of their demise?"

"Yes."

"So, they basically chemically . . . castrated themselves?"

"Little was known about the full extent of the harmful, long-term effects of the chemical when it was approved for use in the tunnels."

"Well, if it paralyzes a giant worm . . ."

"As non-indigenous species to the planet, Kealans were believed to have vastly different biology to that of *ure* worms, with a completely different reaction to drugs or chemicals."

"Didn't prove to be the case, though, did it?"

"All preliminary tests appeared harmless to Kealans, and Xaute was approved for use against *ure*."

"And here we are now . . ." I flipped the picture to another peaceful scene of city life. It was hard to imagine that the silent tragedy of extinction was now hanging over the entire population of this planet.

"The last Kealan was born ten years ago. Before him, there was a period of five years of complete infertility on Keala, and there have been no live births since."

Chapter 8

AS MUCH AS I TRIED to stay awake that afternoon, my body did not want to obey. I had but a few hours of sleep last night and, really, should have had a nap earlier. But I remembered Valran's words about seeing Tairan again tonight. Since I wasn't sure when 'tonight' would start, I struggled to stay awake, expecting him to enter any minute.

I had mixed feelings when I thought about Tairan. Although something warm and sweet flickered inside me at the memories of our night together, his abrupt distancing from me afterwards was confusing and upsetting.

Whatever little I'd learned about him only bred more questions. He had clearly evaded revealing his true motives for participating in Ricread's studies. Still, I hoped he might have some information for me. As a Kealan and someone who had held a position of authority at some point, surely Tairan would have a higher level of the damn *clearance* here. I hoped if I spent more time with him, I might be able to persuade him to give me some answers—he was a man after all, not a robot.

His groans of pain during the testing and the way the medical team promptly whisked him away that morning had me puzzled and concerned too.

To distract myself from all the thoughts roaming in my head, breeding worry and apprehension, I explored my suite a little. Pressing buttons and sliding panels aside, I found a pair of shoes for myself—flat, white sandals with wide, soft straps. Gran promptly informed me that was the only type of footwear I was allowed to wear from now on—breathable with no heels.

After a dinner of yet another plateful of bland food and insipid tea, I could no longer keep my eyes open and figured I would just lie down on the couch for a minute.

I must have fallen asleep then.

Slight tickling on my forehead woke me up. Swatting at a lock of hair that had fallen over my eyes, I glanced up to find Tairan staring at me with those mesmerizing eyes of his.

"Hi." I blinked, sitting up, as he crouched in front of me.

"How did you do this to your hair?" he asked, with undisguised curiosity, then pulled the curl hanging in front of my face down, only to release it and watch it bounce up into a wide spiral again.

"What do you mean?" I smiled, confused but glad to see him. "I just washed it, nothing more."

"It was straight yesterday, wasn't it?"

"Oh, yeah." I rubbed my eyes. "They straightened it, sprayed it a lot to hold the whole thing in place . . ." I waved my hand over my head. "You know, for the wedding."

"Why? This feels so much better." He brushed the strand off my face then leaned in with an audible inhale of the air near my neck. "Smells lovely, too. Definitely better than last night."

"You didn't like the smell of the hairspray, did you?" I wondered if that was one of the repulsive things about humans on his list I hadn't let him recite to me.

"No," he confessed. "I did not. It was too strong. Pungent." He circled my waist with his arms, drawing me closer. "I like *your* smell," he said softly, burying his face in my hair.

I blinked in bewilderment, unsure how to take his sudden display of affection. It definitely felt enjoyable to be held by him, though.

"How have you been?" I asked, tentatively lifting my hands to his shoulders.

"Fine." He nuzzled my ear in an intimate way.

"Did they hurt you during those tests this morning?" I felt his arms stiffen around me. "You seemed to be in pain, and it made me worried—"

"Don't." He leaned back abruptly, finding my gaze with his. "You can't worry about anyone here but yourself, Isabella."

"Compassion is a natural human emotion," I argued, ignoring his stern tone. "It's not like one can switch it off."

"Nothing good would come out of it," he insisted. His voice remained firm, but his eyes flickered between mine anxiously. "Caring about anyone or anything would be giving *them* another tool to control you."

I stared at him, trying to read the true meaning behind his words.

"Tell me what you know about the research team and what they do here."

He shook his head, an expression of regret clearly visible on his face.

"I have no information that would be helpful or useful to you in any way. The findings aren't shared with me—I hold no official position."

Drawing him closer between my legs, I cupped his face.

"Tairan, are you no more than a subject of their experiments, too? Just like me?" Oddly, having confirmed this left me feeling less alone, even giving me a sense of camaraderie with him.

He stroked my hair with the tips of his fingers, pausing for a long moment.

"Last night, being with you felt like a reprieve from it all," he finally said, his expression contemplative but warm. "I did not expect that. Will you help me forget again? Just for a little while?" He lifted me into his arms, getting up. "Will you let me have you right now, Isabella?"

He was asking my permission for what I had no control over and what was already his to take.

Still, he asked.

I wrapped my legs around his hips, tucking my face into his shoulder.

"I liked being with you, too," I whispered as he easily carried me into the bedroom. "I like your company," I added, having my own list of things I was beginning to enjoy about him. "And your strength."

I gazed up at him as he kicked his boots off and climbed on the bed with me in his arms.

"I like your hair." He put me down on my back then raked his fingers through my curls. A smile ghosted his lips. "And your shade." He stroked the side of my face.

"My *shade*?" I lifted an eyebrow in question, and he traced it with the tip of his finger.

"Your skin is darker," he explained. "And your features are vivid."

I tried to look at myself through his eyes, to imagine how he saw me.

Having been surrounded by his people all his life, Tairan must find my dark hair, olive skin, and brown eyes unusual. The contrast of my almost black eyelashes and eyebrows against my skin must be stark for him.

Different.

Vivid.

"It must be weird for you to see any colour whatsoever in a person." I thought back to my initial reaction to him. Anyone on Earth, regardless of their race, had more pigment in their skin and hair than the snow-white Kealans who lacked even the hint of pink that Albino humans had.

"I don't know what 'colour' means," Tairan said, playing with my hair. His tugging at the strands was like a soothing scalp massage, pleasant and calming. "There is no word for it in Kealan."

"What do you mean?" I frowned in concentration, recalling the monochrome interior of the facility and the clothes worn by everyone here. The pictures of the underground cities had some colours, but when I thought about it now, the use of them might have been unintentional, simply the natural hues of the materials used. "You can't *see* colours?"

"No. Just shades, tints, and the intensity of light. I know, though, that colour is important for humans. I heard this word many times when I watched your life videos, just could never fully grasp the meaning of it."

"What videos did you see? Television?"

"I believe that's what you call that wave stream." He nodded. "I wanted to learn more about your world when they told me you had been identified."

"Why?"

"I . . ." He paused before continuing. "I knew what I'd have to do. They gave me lessons on human biology, which is not that much different from ours, by the way. But I wanted to learn more about human interactions and customs, to make sure I didn't end up inadvertently harming you more than you already would be—physically or emotionally—after having been *acquired* by Ricread and his team."

He didn't want to care about me, but he did care enough to try not to damage me further.

Simply having him here now warmed me from the inside, melting away the feeling of loneliness, and I wanted him closer.

"You must have watched the right shows." I smiled, sliding my hand up his chest. The hexagonal pattern lit up on the material of his suit under my fingers. "I enjoyed what you did to me last night." I traced a line in the middle of his chest, mimicking the gesture he had made to open his suit yesterday, but it wouldn't open for me. "How does it work?"

"It's programed for my finger prints." He lifted his hand, but I intercepted it before he touched his chest.

"Let me." I took his finger between mine and pressed its pad to the beginning of the invisible line at the hollow between his collarbones. Sliding his finger down between his pectorals then along the hard ridges of his abs, I watched the hexagonal mesh light up again, parting the material this time.

Sitting up, I kissed the pale skin revealed by the opening. His chest rose with a sharp inhale as he cupped the back of my head, tangling his fingers in the thick, curly mass of my hair.

I slid my hands under his clothing. His muscles rippled under my palms as he shrugged the top part of his suit off, then unclicked his belt, dropping both to the floor beside the bed.

Carefully, he lowered me down, his dark pupils dilated wide now, almost reaching the iridescent violet rims of his irises.

"I like this dress on you." He glided his hands down my front, cupping my breasts. My nipples pebbled under his caress, pushing against the soft, thin material. "It's much easier to unwrap you from it than that thing you wore yesterday," he murmured, sliding a hand under the neckline to fondle my naked breast underneath.

Easy access. I remembered what Gran said about my wardrobe but quickly chased the bitterness brought on by the thought away, focusing on the wonderful sensation of Tairan's warm skin against mine, instead.

Apparently, feelings weren't necessary to go ahead with 'copulation.' So, my having any sympathy or attraction for Tairan couldn't be in the plans of the research team. This closeness and true intimacy I felt towards him right now was for him and me only.

Despite being forced into each other's arms, Tairan and I had managed to carve out something for ourselves in this situation. I loved his hands on me, and he obviously was enjoying touching me.

Kneading my breast, Tairan leaned in and brushed his lips along my cheekbone, down the side of my neck, then over to my mouth. The light caresses heated me from inside, making me crave more.

Arching my back, I lifted my face to his, urging him to deepen the kiss, but he only responded with another light brush of his lips on mine.

I cupped his neck, keeping him close. "Kiss me," I murmured against his mouth, his warm breath fanning across my lips like a caress.

"Show me how to do it."

"Kealans don't kiss?" I asked surprised, not having considered this possibility.

"We do. Like this." His mouth closed, Tairan lightly touched his lips to mine, the side of his nose brushed by mine again in something between kissing and nuzzling, sweet and tender, but not enough for me at that moment. "I've seen humans do it differently on the videos I watched." He nibbled at my bottom lip, grazing it lightly with his teeth. "Is this right?"

"There is no wrong way," I assured him.

There didn't appear to be one with him—Tairan seemed to put care in his every move, making anything he did to me feel extremely sensual.

"More?" I begged, lifting my head to him.

He took my bottom lip between his again, and I kissed him back, tantalizingly slow.

With a soft groan, he yanked the dress off my shoulder, finding my breast with his hand again. A light pinch on my nipple shot a hot charge down my belly, making my hips buck. A moan vibrated deep in my throat.

"You like that," he whispered, breaking our kiss for an instance.

Swept into the moment with him, I slid my hands down his back, my fingers trailing the edge of his pants. The smooth material fit tight, with hardly any give for my hand to slide under.

As if sensing my intention, Tairan brushed along both sides of his hips, parting the fabric of his pants.

"That's better," I panted, shoving them off his hard backside with my hands then kicking them further down with the heel of my foot, freeing his straining hard-on.

My stomach flipped with anticipation as I wrapped my fingers around the hard length. Surprised, I felt a number of unusual raised ridges along it.

"It's . . . bumpy," I mumbled, confused. "Ribbed?"

"Is it bad?" He paused trailing kisses down to my breast.

"Bad?" I smiled. "No, definitely not."

"Good." He sucked the tip of my breast in then nibbled at my nipple.

Writhing under the onslaught of pleasure brought by his hands and his mouth, I didn't realize I had been squeezing him hard in my hand.

"Isabella," he growled against my chest, rocking his hips into my hand. "I shouldn't come yet."

"Right." I let go of him.

Hands now over my head, I closed my eyes and took a deep breath, struggling to keep my arousal burning when reality threatened to move in with that sudden reminder of the ultimate purpose of what we were doing here.

His chest heaved against my belly before he slowly slid down my body, peppering my skin with light, tender kisses that felt apologetic, somehow. I didn't want to blame Tairan for anything. He actually made it all better for me, making me feel wanted, cherished even.

I lowered my hands to his head as he moved down my body. Hiking the long skirt up to my waist, he kissed my belly and slid my underwear down my legs. I lifted my knees, opening up for him.

Sinking my fingers into his braids, I arched my back with a moan when he eased his tongue between my folds, already hot and slick.

This was for me, I realized suddenly.

What Tairan was doing right now had no relevance to the plan of the research team. The only purpose of his tongue darting in and out of me, swirling in tight circles with every thrust, was to make me feel good.

Waves of hot shivers ran through my body, and my thighs trembled as I panted with need, forgetting about the world around us, if just for a few moments.

"Yes." I raised my hips up for him, surrendering to his every move, as the spring of pleasure inside me coiled tight to the limit. With another firm glide of his tongue, Tairan set it free, ecstasy erupting from me in bursts of shudders.

"Oh, Tairan." I struggled to catch my breath, still fisting his braids as I was coming down from my orgasm. "Don't tell me you learned this by watching TV, too."

Moving up to me, he exhaled a small laugh.

"No, the biology of Kealan women is very much the same."

His words caused thoughts to swarm in my head, raising more questions.

"Have you been married before, Tairan?" I asked when he lay on his side next to me.

"No." He stroked my arm.

"Engaged?"

It took him longer to reply this time, I noted.

"No." He untied my belt, my dress all bunched up around my waist.

"Have you . . . made love to a woman, before me?"

He had basically admitted already he was intimately familiar with female biology, but I hoped my question would prompt him to share more about his past.

This time, the pause stretched even longer.

"Yes," he finally said, drawing me to him.

"As part of this experiment?"

"No," he replied quickly.

I held my breath, waiting for more, but he didn't elaborate.

Who was she?

The question was at the tip of my tongue, but I bit it back. Asking it felt too much like inviting someone else to bed with us. With no true commitment between us, I didn't think I could handle that right now.

Instead, I silently wrapped my arms around his shoulders when he leaned into me, rolling me on my back. I spread my legs wide for him when he pressed his pelvis into mine, and lifted my hips to take him when he entered me.

I buried my face in the side of his neck, his braids draped over my head as he moved inside me, as if in a slow dance. And when the orgasm rocked through him, I held him, until every last shudder subsided and he slackened in my arms.

Chapter 9

"CAN YOU STAY HERE TOMORROW?" I asked when Tairan came back from the bathroom.

He'd left me with my knees up to my chest again, but I released my legs the moment the entrance had closed behind him.

Now, he glared at me, noticing that I had disobeyed the instructions. Crossing his arms over his chest, he stood by the bed silently, waiting for me to comply again.

"Fine." I rolled my eyes, lifting my legs up and hugging my knees. "You know this doesn't mean much anyway? If it's meant to happen it will, no matter what position you're in. My sister got pregnant with her twins after a quickie against the back wall of a bar."

"Really?" His eyes grew wide with genuine surprise. "That was all it took?"

"Yep." I scratched my ear. "She was pretty tipsy, too. So I wish the research team would lift their stupid ban on caffeine and sugar in my food."

"Was it completely unplanned then?" He seemed to be still in shock.

"As unplanned as could be. She's never met the guy before and couldn't even demand any child support because all she knew about him was that his name was Raze and he was a biker passing through our town. I'd bet a dozen donuts that *Raze* wasn't even his real name."

"Donuts?" Tairan sat on the bed, looking somewhat over-whelmed by my babbling.

I knew I tended to talk a bit too much, both when I felt nervous around someone or comfortable with the person. The past two days I had been feeling like a fish out of water—subdued by stress and worry. Now it seemed that all the words that had been bottling up inside me wanted to come out. Having no one to talk to but a robot all day didn't help either.

"Donut." I nodded. "It's a kind of pastry. Sweet. Tell me . . ." I shifted his way a little, and he placed his hand on my ankles to steady me. "Do you have desserts on Keala?"

"Yes. Quite a few. Not pastry, though. We don't bake."

"Why not?"

"We avoid using excessive heat, including for food preparation, out of fear of causing fire in the tunnels."

"How do you cook then?"

"We don't. To preserve food, we marinate or ferment it, freeze it sometimes or dehydrate it. Many things we just eat fresh."

"How about salt? Do you season food in any way?"

"Yes, we collect underground salt deposits and use some plant and animal-based spices."

"I knew they didn't serve me bland food out of ignorance." I bit my lip in annoyance. "They did it on purpose."

"What do you mean?"

"Whatever you said about Ricread's zeal must be true. He is so overdoing it here. He must have read somewhere that too much salt was not healthy for humans and cut out any salt from my diet completely, along with sugar and coffee."

"Would you like me to smuggle you some salt tomorrow?" With a glance at his armlet, he released my ankles, letting me straighten my legs.

"Could you?" I perked up.

"I'll see what I can do." He smiled at my enthusiasm.

"Does it mean you won't be staying here through the day again, then?" My mood dropped at the prospect of spending another day alone.

"No, I will not."

"Could you, maybe, come over a little early tomorrow night then?" I sat on the bed, hugging my knees. "I mean if you do manage to get some salt for me, it would be nice to have it before dinner, right? We could eat together then. Do you need anyone's permission for that?"

"I would never get it."

"Why not?"

"Ricread derives a special kind of pleasure from denying things to me. But if *you* ask, he may let it happen."

"Why does he do that?" I asked, confused. "Does he dislike you that much?"

Tairan's eyes narrowed, his expression hardened, and the way his jaw muscles flexed told me that whatever animosity the professor might hold for him was probably mutual.

"Would you like to have dinner with me?" I asked, since he didn't reply to my previous question.

"Yes," he said simply.

"Then, I'll ask."

THE SUDDEN LIGHT BRUTALLY yanked me out of sleep again.

I cursed under my breath and threw my arm over my eyes.

"And you keep complaining about how bright our sun is?" I mumbled through the remnants of sleep and confusion from the abrupt awakening.

"It's the spectrum of sunlight, including the UV rays, that is harmful to us, not the brightness on its own," Zavis explained patiently, taking the blanket off me. "The light in the facility is different." She pointed at the lit strings along the perimeter of the ceiling.

She might have been right, but right from sleep the room still seemed uncomfortably bright. My discomfort only increased as I opened my eyes to face the crowd of Kealans once again. The four in black were already moving my way, with the obvious intention of restraining me again.

"Stop." I lifted my hand, halting them in their tracks. I found Ricread standing at the foot of the bed, arms crossed. "If these are exactly the same tests as yesterday, I'll lie still. No need to hold me down."

The procedures weren't painful, just uncomfortable, and the hands of strange males on my naked body only made it worse.

He nodded and gestured to the others to move aside.

"Could they, maybe, turn around, too?" It was a little too late to worry about modesty, since everyone in the room had gotten an eyeful of my naked flesh already. Still, I hoped there was a way to reduce the number of people idly standing by and staring at my private parts while I was being examined. "Or maybe they could leave, since I promise to co-operate?"

Ricread took a moment to consider my request then nodded again, sending the four out of the room.

"The security personnel will remain in the corridor, in case you change your mind," he warned me.

There were still close to a dozen research team members bustling about the room, setting up the divider between Tairan and me and arranging the equipment around the bed. Still, I felt better somehow at my little gain.

Stretching on the bed, I closed my eyes, letting Zavis and the others manipulate my body position for their convenience, under the cool supervision of Ricread. I held still, hoping that my co-operation would help me gain another favour in return—his permission for me to have dinner with Tairan.

The soft, barely audible groan reached me from behind the partition once again, making me tense. Worry and compassion spiked through me. There was nothing I could do to stop it, no matter what Tairan had said about the benefits of not caring.

Blindly, I stretched my hand his way along the bed. My fingers touched the rubbery material of the divider, and I slid them under by compressing the mattress down. I felt the tips brush by Tairan's skin a moment before he grabbed my hand, holding it tight, as if I had offered him a lifeline.

Peeking from under half-open eyelids, I noted the team were absorbed with probing between my legs. Ricread's attention seemed to be divided between watching them and the numerous monitors around us.

With a jolt of the mattress, Tairan's hand slipped from mine as they must have moved him to the gurney, and I missed the contact more acutely than I thought I would.

"Can you leave Tairan here today?" I asked quickly.

"Why?" Ricread's gaze snapped to my face.

Remembering Tairan's warning, I decided against telling the full truth. "I'm bored here alone, and he is more fun to talk to than the robot."

I also feel that he'd be safer here with me than wherever it is you're taking him.

"Humans are not happy if held in isolation, as I'm sure you know," I said, instead. "We are social creatures and need company."

"This is not about keeping you happy," he replied coolly while the technicians started wrapping up with their tests.

"Isn't it?" I asked innocently. "Have you done any research on the role of the overall wellbeing of a woman in successful conception and potential pregnancy?" Personally, I hadn't done any myself, but I was sure that there would be something on it somewhere if he looked. "You've done nothing but stress the hell out of me from day one, which is extremely harmful for a human body."

"You have been kept in comfort and fed a diet optimal for your species," he argued, confidently. But I noted a sign of hesitation or at least some doubt in the way his white eyebrows lifted.

Did he honestly believe he'd done nothing wrong to me?

"Intercourse has also proved to be not physically damaging to you in any way," he remarked.

I closed my eyes for a moment, taking in a deep breath to calm my rising anger.

The only reason I was not raped on my wedding night was because Tairan happened to have more honour and respect than Ricread and his team.

Instead of arguing, though, I shoved the bitter feeling aside and focused on the task at hand—negotiation—keeping my voice as even as I could.

"I'm talking more about emotional than physical wellbeing here. Surely you understand human emotions? Since we share the common ancestor and a big chunk of DNA?"

He seemed to be mulling this over, his jaw muscles moving slightly.

"Just leave him here," I urged. "Please."

"No." The divider having been removed, Ricread gestured to his assistants to take the gurney out. "We're not done with this subject yet."

Sitting up in bed quickly, I caught sight of Tairan's face, violet-rimmed eyes watching me from under the few glossy white braids that had fallen across his face as he was taken out.

"Dinner, then?" I asked hurriedly, as Ricread was on his way out, too. "Can Tairan have dinner with me? People prefer to eat in company. It'll be easier for me to force down the full *daily ration* if I have company for dinner."

He didn't seem to pay me any attention.

"I won't eat anything at all then!" I yelled at his back, in desperation. "Nothing! Unless I have Tairan to share the meal with me."

Ricread jerked to a stop, as if physically hit by my words, then pivoted on his heel slowly, his expression grave when he faced me.

"You cannot threaten me," he said slowly, staring straight at me. "I will not let you hold the success of this experiment hostage or use it as a bargaining chip to further your personal agenda. I am the Head of Research here. And you are its *subject*."

I swallowed hard under his icy glare.

"Wouldn't that mean that we should be able to find common ground then?" I said, trying to keep my voice light and soothing. "Really, there is no reason for an argument. You want this to succeed, and I'm willing to co-operate."

"By demanding concessions from me," he said, narrowing his eyes at me.

"No." I instilled as much sweetness into my tone as I was able, risking cavities. "By asking for some leniencies that wouldn't cost you anything and have the potential to improve the results you're striving for."

Again, he seemed to consider it, so I nudged a little further. "When you think about it, our goals are very much the same here. Ultimately, it is better for you to keep me happy rather than bored and miserable."

The last group of technicians filed out of the room, taking the equipment with them.

Without replying, Ricread left, too, giving me one last penetrating stare.

All I could do now was wait.

Chapter 10

I NERVOUSLY PACED THE room all afternoon. After a while, I decided even the living area didn't have enough space to walk out my anxiety and kept the door between the bedroom and living room open, pacing through both of them.

I kept an eye on the wall to the corridor in the bedroom for any sign of Tairan. It was way after lunch, and I still desperately hoped Ricread would allow us to have dinner together. The concern about what they might be doing to Tairan all this time also wouldn't leave me.

"What time is it?" I asked Gran for what seemed like the millionth time already.

From his place by the living room window, the robot pivoted on his base to face me.

"Four minutes and thirteen seconds later than what it was when you asked me last."

"Did you just make a joke?" I stared him down. By now, it was impossible to think of Gran as 'it'. "Was that sarcasm I heard there?"

"I do not know what you mean." The blue smile twinkled brightly.

"Why do I not believe you?"

I thought I heard movement in the bedroom and dashed to the sound.

The entrance to the corridor opened and closed, letting in a tall, cloaked figure. He had no goggles on, and I recognized Tairan's eyes in the shadows of his hood.

"You came!" I exhaled in relief, rushing to him. "Did you go outside?" I pointed at the cloak.

"No." He swung his arm to the side, opening it. "I wore it to hide this." He held a large, light-purple egg and a big, clear crystal in his hands.

"They are pretty, whatever they are." I smiled, taking them both from him. "Thank you."

Tairan shrugged the cloak off and tossed it on the bed, stalking to me.

"Salt." He grabbed the crystal back from me and tossed it onto the bed. "And dessert." He took the egg next and carefully set it on top of the cloak. "It's sweet, I hope you'll like it."

"Thank you," I said again, backing to the wall, as he kept advancing on me. "Are you hungry? Should we have dinner?" The last question came out a little breathy, as my back hit the wall and Tairan came flush with me.

Keeping his fascinating eyes on mine, he cupped the side of my face with his hand.

"I love your light," he said unexpectedly, brushing my hair aside, then lowered his head to kiss my temple. "The room feels brighter when you're in it." He slid his hands down, under my backside, then lifted me up. "The air around you is easier to breathe somehow."

My face heated with pleasure at the affection in his voice, even if it felt a bit sudden.

"I love your compliments." I wrapped my arms and legs around him. "No one has ever said anything like that to me before. Not even close."

"Every word is true. You make me feel things I shouldn't be feeling. I'm sure I'll be made to pay for that later, but right now I don't care."

"What are you talking about?"

He leaned in and claimed my mouth in a kiss, stopping my questions.

The glide of his lips was more confident this time. Pinning me to the wall with his hips, his hands under my butt to support me, he kissed me as if he owned me, deep and strong.

Melting into his body, I wrapped my arms tighter around him, meeting every glide of his mouth against mine. Lost in the moment, I was only half-aware when I slipped my tongue past his lips.

He stiffened briefly when our tongues touched, then resumed kissing me with renewed passion. One hand under my skirt, he tugged my underwear down and I dropped my feet to the floor, helping him remove it. Cupping my bare ass, he rocked his growing erection against me.

Anticipation rolled through me in a swell of heat, pulling low in my belly. Desire for him spiked, hot and strong.

One arm hooked around his shoulders to hold on, I eased the other between us, forgetting there was no zipper or buttons for me to get to him.

"This . . ." I kept tugging at the fabric of his suit that concealed what I wanted. "Get rid of this, please."

Quickly, he clicked his belt off, letting it drop to the ground, then swept his hand along his hips. Frantically, I shoved the fabric down as soon as it opened, wrapping my hand around his hard, ridged length.

He hissed through his teeth as I squeezed, pumping my hand up and down.

"I really have to see this up close," I whispered, running my fingers along the circular ridges.

"Not right now, please," he begged.

Badly needing him inside me, too, I slipped him in without a delay. Each hard ridge along his length tugged at my opening on its way in, sending ripples of intense pleasure through me. A long, contented moan ripped from my chest.

With a groan, Tairan thrust forward, hard enough to slide me up the wall. The sudden pressure against my core felt invigorating. Flexing both arms around his shoulders, I clung to him as he pounded hard into me, taking me with abandon. His wild passion spurring me on, an orgasm building up in me, fast and furious.

The muscles in my thighs tensed, my legs squeezing him tighter. My lips parted with another throaty moan of intense pleasure. The sweet pressure pulsated through me, exploding hot between my legs, as I came hard around him.

After a few powerful thrusts, he stilled for a fraction of a second, then I felt a violent climax rock through him, too.

Suddenly boneless, I unwrapped my legs from around his waist, but Tairan wouldn't let go of me. Leaning in, he kept me pinned between the wall and his body.

"That was . . ." I panted, struggling to catch my breath, small post-orgasmic shudders still shooting through me like tiny arrows. "*What was it?*" I shook my head with a smile, unable to find the answer on my own.

Tairan's cool composure was completely gone during this encounter. There were no attempts to follow any instructions this time, either. What had just happened felt like wild, chaotic passion, with him no longer holding back at all.

"It felt different," I murmured, nuzzling the side of his neck. His smell was the strongest here—exotic, earthy, with a hint of sweetness. "Not that I'm complaining."

"Shall we go have that dinner now?" Tairan kissed my hair, not letting me go anywhere. "You must be hungry."

"Now more than ever," I agreed.

He leaned away from me, finally releasing me, and I struggled to stay upright as my legs still felt as if made of cotton.

Tairan fixed his pants quickly and helped me locate my underwear then lifted me up in his arms. "Where to?"

"Couch. Unless you want to have a more formal dinner at the table?"

"No." He lowered me into the cushy seat gingerly, as if I were made of glass, as if he hadn't just fucked me hard against the wall.

"Your dinner is served," Gran announced brightly, rolling from the window to the compartment to get a food tray out.

Tairan glared at the robot as it approached with another salad plate in its wiry arms. With a step behind Gran, Tairan bent quickly and flipped the robotic smiley face to the side.

"What . . ." I managed, surprised when Tairan slid open a small panel under Gran's top disk and shifted a few silver rings inside.

The lights of the smiley face went out and the stringy arms dropped down limply, sending the plate with salad crashing to the floor.

"We don't need tonight's dinner recorded for anyone, do we?" Tairan muttered, taking out a small flat ring from the robot and sliding it into his arm device. A milky-white screen with black charts and characters extended from it, and he punched in something.

"Do you think the robot has been spying on me?"

"It is a part of its programming." He inserted the flat ring back into Gran then rolled the disabled robot to the closet and shoved him inside, closing the door panel behind him. "I'll make sure to get it out later."

"If he was recording, wouldn't they see that it has been interrupted?"

"Not until tomorrow morning or whenever they decide to check it. And that's only if they spot that I've added some footage on a loop to make up for the missing time." He gave me a smile. Complete with the teasing glimmer in his eyes, the expression made him look younger. "The technical skills of the security personnel on this station are not the greatest. None of them went to the Academy as I did, or have any experience with the Defense Forces."

"Sounds like you have some useful skills."

"Necessary to make life here bearable." Tairan moved his gaze to the mess of green leaves I had picked up from the floor and piled back onto the plate. "Was that supposed to be your dinner?"

"Yes." I nodded. "Now that you've disabled the robot, maybe you could use your wicked skills to order us some food?"

With a nod, he moved on to the wall with the food compartment and punched a few times into the dark glass door. Similar to the one on the closet, the door lit up, turning into a screen.

"Oh, I didn't know it could do that."

"Has the robot been feeding you all this time? It never showed you how to operate this?"

"Nope." I got off the couch and came closer, eager to learn what he was doing. "Is there something like a menu?"

Tairan scrolled through pictures with writing in English under them. "Does anything look appetizing to you?"

Steamed tilapia, boiled quinoa, a small variety of green salads—everything unseasoned, with no sauce or dressing.

"Not really." I shrugged. "But I'm hungry, so I'll eat whatever."

"Just give me a moment." Tairan punched something into his armlet, extending the screen again.

From up close, I realized that the screen was holographic, there was no hardware behind it, just the image of the white panel hovering in the air. Tairan swiped through several black-and-white diagrams that appeared and disappeared off the screen, touching some and punching something in.

The screen on the compartment door flickered, the pictures of the bland foods wavered, replaced with monochromatic images of unfamiliar items with unknown-to-me written characters lined up under each.

"Would you like to try some Kealan food?" Tairan asked, lifting an eyebrow.

"Would I?" I perked up with interest. "I'd love to!"

A smile curved up the side of his mouth.

"Let's see then." He scrolled through the pictures, selecting some, dismissing others.

"We'd better eat at the table, after all," I said, watching the amount of his selections growing.

He laughed with a nod, the sound making something light up inside me, glowing warm.

The compartment dinged, signalling the arrival of the first portion of Tairan's order.

"That was fast!" I made the table descend from the ceiling, the way Gran had showed me, followed by a pair of seats. Suspended by thin chains, the chairs reminded me of swing seats.

"Here it is." Tairan placed the first tray, laden with several small plates, on the table. "Start with this one." He put one with what looked like thick slices of salami in front of me and took one for himself before taking the seat opposite of mine.

"Do I eat it with my fingers?" I asked, not finding any utensils on the tray.

He nodded, taking a piece from his plate and taking a bite.

I picked up a disk too. On closer inspection, it looked more like a slice of orange, complete with segments, except that it had the colour and texture of smoked meat. I brought the piece to my nose.

"Smells good, like beef jerky." I bit a piece off.

The savoury taste was pleasant, the texture a little grainy but definitely that of meat. The flavour was delicious, rich and meaty.

"Really good." I stuffed the whole slice in my mouth and reached for another one.

"You like it?" Tairan gave me a wide smile, the radiance of which rendered me speechless for a moment—I'd never seen him this obviously enjoying himself.

"Do I?" I laughed, too, clearing my plate. "This sure beats the plain green leaves they've been feeding me. What is it?"

"*Bruk* worms," he said brightly. "One of my favourite foods."

"Worms?" I swallowed the piece I had in my mouth, and it went down slowly.

"These don't grow that big, just about the size of my arm," Tairan explained casually. "We marinate then dehydrate them a little, then slice the meat the way I saw in videos you slice sausage."

"I see." I stared at the half-eaten piece in my hand. It still smelled really good, and the taste of it in my mouth made me salivate despite the image of it having been a part of something that once crawled the dark caves of another planet. "You seem to have a lot of worms on Keala," I said slowly.

"Insects, worms, centipedes, and spiders are the only life forms indigenous to our planet."

"Sorry, but that does not exactly make Keala sound like a nice place to visit." Still feeling hungry, I glanced at the piece in my hand again. The mouth-watering smell was incredibly hard to resist.

Tairan tilted his head, staring at me intently. "Do you fear worms, Isabella? Or are you disgusted by them? I've seen some videos of humans eating crickets and scorpions, but I couldn't exactly figure out the common attitude towards the insects on Earth."

"It depends, I guess. There are places where people eat insects. Personally, I don't think I'm afraid of bugs unless they are venomous. I don't lose my head when I see a spider, especially if I have something hard to squish it with nearby. But I certainly never thought of eating one before."

Giving in to the appetizing smell, I took a tentative bite off of the piece I held—it was still delicious. Trying to think of it not as a worm but a slice of a deli cold-cut, I was able to finish it all.

"Spiders on Earth are not big enough to eat," Tairan nodded, thoughtfully. "The research team has a small farm here on the station if you want to try one from Keala."

"Um, thank you. Maybe later." I shook my head, a small giggle escaping me. "I'm sure it'll taste like chicken."

"The farm spiders are about the same size as your chickens." Tairan put another plate in front of me, this one with long, brown chunks, like thick noodles. "Not a spider," he reassured me. "Fungus, similar to your mushrooms."

I carefully lifted one and sniffed it. It smelled earthy, very much like marinated mushroom, in fact. I bit off a piece, chewing slowly. The texture proved to be a bit rubbery, but still enjoyable. "It's good."

"I'm glad you like it. Although, personally, it's not my favourite." Tairan reached for a plate with what looked like a fist-sized rock, covered with slime. "Sorry, you can't have this one," he warned. "This type of mould has been found to be toxic for humans." Lifting a curved utensil off the plate, he scraped the thick, greenish growth off the rock.

"Oh, that's fine," I assured him, watching him eat the green blob of mould with evident pleasure, as if it were the world's finest ice cream. "I don't think that would be for me, anyway. But you enjoy it, by all means."

After I'd tried a few other things off the newly-arrived tray, Tairan asked, "How are you feeling? Any stomach ache at all?"

"No. Why?"

"This is a lot of new food." He waved at the empty dishes. "I tried to order things for you that are closer to human foods and generally milder. The last thing I'd want is for you to get an upset stomach."

"I imagine Ricread would have a fit if that happened."

A dark shadow moved over his features at my mentioning the professor.

"Tairan." I moved aside an empty plate and leaned across the table to him. "Tell me, why are you part of this? Please."

He had never seemed to be fully behind the idea of saving the population of his planet. I sensed bitterness and even resentment in him about Ricread's work. Yet, until tonight he had been following his instructions, even making me follow them, too.

"Why? To save the race, of course," he said flatly.

"Then why don't I believe you?" I watched him closely. "They're doing things to you here." I was convinced the procedures they performed on him each morning were definitely not pleasant, even painful. "Yet you keep going along with it all. Why?"

He leaned back, stretching his neck slowly.

"Isabella . . ." he started.

I rushed in before he stopped me, "You had a career back home—"

"You've done a search on me?"

"Of course I have. You won't tell me much, and they . . ." I gestured towards the corridor, as if the whole research team stood out there. "They all view me more like a lab rat than a human being anyway, Ricread included. Especially him." I winced at how perfect that allegory was. "A lab rat in a comfy cage, fed a perfectly-balanced diet for *my species*." I rubbed my forehead. "I come from the conquered planet. It was easy enough for them to take away my rights . . ." With my gaze, I searched his eyes for a reaction to my words as his expression darkened. "But what happened to you? Unlike me, you must have had a choice? Why did you leave your job? I can see you're resentful about being reduced to—"

"Some choices are worse than none," he snapped, cutting me off. Rising from his seat abruptly, he moved away, letting his chair crash into the table in a wild swing.

"Tairan!" I leaped up, too. "Please."

He silently paced the room, not looking at me, but there was nowhere to run. No matter how either of us got here, we were both trapped now.

"We're in this together." Standing at the table, I nervously twisted the wedding band around my finger. "For better or for worse, *you* are the only one I have."

He came to me. Hands on my shoulders, he leaned his forehead to mine.

"I have no power, Isabella." His voice softened, his breathing evened out slowly. "None. The City Defence Forces lost their influence long before I left. The Science Group took over every aspect of life on Keala."

"Why?"

"Because we're dying, Isabella. Preserving the race has become the biggest political priority. Ricread has the authority to do as he pleases—bend any rule, break every law—as long as he delivers results in his research to perpetuate our species."

"This is awful." I wrapped my arms around his middle.

I understood the urgency and desperation of a dying race trying to save themselves, but it felt as if the lives and freedom of Tairan and I were being ground under the wheels of this grand purpose.

"This is our last night." He ran his fingers through the curls on my head.

"What do you mean?" I gazed up at him in alarm.

"After tonight, I won't get to see you until next month." The way his arms tightened around me, reminded me about the frantic passion he had taken me with as soon as he arrived. Was that because he knew we'd have to part?

I desperately tried to recall everything that had been said to me about this. "Ricread said three nights of *sex*," I protested, grasping at straws in denial. "He never mentioned we won't get to see each other for a whole month."

"For him, the only purpose of us getting together is sex—insemination."

"Not for me, though. Not for you either." I dared him to disagree.

He didn't. His eyes on me, violet blending with midnight blue tonight, he stroked my hair again. "For what it's worth, I'm glad it was you, Isabella."

His words curled tight around my throat, my eyes prickling with tears which I blinked away.

"Are you saying goodbye already? Because it sure sounds like it."

"No, not yet." He tucked a strand of my hair behind my ear. "We haven't had dessert yet, remember?" He smiled in an obvious attempt to cheer me up.

"Good, because I'm telling you right now, Tairan, I'm not going to sit and just let them separate us."

"What will you do?" Curiosity flashed across his face.

"I'll talk to Ricread again."

His chest rose with a sigh. He obviously didn't have much faith in that plan.

"It worked this morning, didn't it?" I reminded. "You are here now."

"Threatening Ricread has never worked for *me*." A bitter note tinted his voice. "Be very careful, Isabella. He is spiteful and can be creative at finding ways to take revenge."

"What else should I know?"

"Like I said, they don't tell me much." He paused, his forehead wrinkled in concentration. "Here is what I know from living here for over four years now. There are cameras and microphones everywhere in the corridors and public areas. One safe place to speak would be in the gardens, near the pond. There is a large blind spot to the left of the waterfall and the noise of the water covers up voices. I've tested that."

"Where are the gardens here?"

"On the other side of the landing hangar. It was made to resemble a piece of Kealan underground landscape, similar to the cave gardens we have back home." He added, "You may like it there if they let you take walks."

"Are *you* allowed to go for walks?" I asked, hope already building in me.

The prospect of spending a month completely on my own, save for the company of the robot and possibly visits from the research team, felt grim and oppressing.

"I *love* walking in the gardens," he said, a barely-there smile touching his lips. "Especially in the afternoon, just before dinner. The waterfalls are my favourite part."

I grinned wide in return, throwing my arms around his neck. "Thank you. It's a date then." Relief flooded me at the possibility of continuing seeing him during the month we were supposed to be apart.

"I may even carry a *luldai* egg in my pocket while walking," he said cheerfully. "If you tell me you like it."

"What is a *luldai* egg?"

"The dessert I brought." With a small kiss on the tip of my nose, he went to get the egg and salt crystal from the bedroom.

"I'll put the salt here." He opened one of the cabinets next to the food delivery unit. "Here is the grater for it." He showed me something resembling a cheese knife that he took from one of the trays and put in the cabinet next to the salt crystal. "Now hold this." He placed the egg in my hand and gave me a small spoon. "Crack it open. Tap at it lightly, it's pretty fragile."

Sitting down on the couch, I did what he said, breaking the shell of the egg, which seemed to be a little thicker but more porous than that of a chicken's egg. The inside had the appearance of whipped cream with a light purple tint, and I took a spoonful in my mouth.

"Oh. My. God." I moaned, closing my eyes as soon as the sweet, fragrant substance hit my tongue. The taste was unbelievably good—caramel and vanilla buttercream with the heavenly-light consistency of whipped egg whites. "This is the best!"

"You can eat the shell too." He leaned in, breaking a piece off the shell, then placed it on my tongue when I stuck it out for him.

"Just like a meringue!" The shell melted in my mouth, leaving a delicious buttery aftertaste. "Egg meringue is baked on Earth. How do you make these things, without using an oven?"

I turned the egg in my hand, admiring its perfect oval shape.

"We don't make them. We gather them off the ceilings in caves. You have to get them within two days after the mother lays them. On the third day, the eggs mature and fall into the water where the shell soaks up the moisture and forms a gelatinous mass for the larvae inside to feed on."

I paused with my spoon over my deliciousness, which suddenly didn't seem as heavenly anymore. "Larvae . . ."

"They turn into fully-grown water centipedes within four weeks," Tairan explained casually then paused, obviously catching my startled expression. "Is something wrong? You liked *bruk* worms. Is centipede unacceptable to you? Like a spider?"

"Um, no . . . I mean not really. Not unacceptable," I muttered, not wanting to insult Kealan's food culture or offend Tairan in his best intentions to feed me a yummy dessert. "It's just that, come to think of it, there *are* quite a few aspects about insects after all that I do find . . . um, unappetizing. At least initially." I stared at the spoonful of glossy, purplish-white substance in my hand, inhaling a whiff of its aroma. "But since it does taste really good . . ." I bit my lip, turning the spoon to admire the fragrant, cream-like swirl. "Who cares where it comes from, right?" I shrugged, shoving it in my mouth. The dessert melted on my tongue, coating my mouth in sweet joy. "Centipede or not, this is so freaking tasty." I quickly took another spoonful.

"It is good, isn't it?" A wide smile spread on Tairan's face at my delight.

Promptly getting off the couch, he moved to the food compartment and punched something in. "I've used a small loophole in the coding of your food unit. Now, you can order Kealan desserts or other foods you like. Just don't do it too often and take care not to eat too much at once to avoid sudden changes in your blood content, which may trigger their alarm."

He took a small bowl from the unit and another spoon from the cabinet then returned to me on the couch.

"Since you liked the *luldai* egg, you may like this, too." Sitting next to me, he offered me a spoonful of cream-coloured substance with small brown balls mixed in.

The smell lured me in, and I took a tiny bit off the spoon. Sweet and crunchy, the dish turned out to be just as good as the egg, even if of a slightly different flavour.

"These here are—" Tairan started, but I didn't let him finish.

"Nope." I quickly shushed him, covering his mouth with my hand for good measure. "I really don't want to know."

He just laughed, and I picked up the spoon, digging into the dessert in peace. "As far as I'm concerned, this is extra crunchy, puffed coco rice in vanilla yogurt. And I'm sticking with that."

THE WHOLE EVENING ENDED up being bittersweet for me. Tairan was here, the dinner was great, and there were moments when I almost forgot where we were. Except that the minutes kept ticking by, bringing the morning closer.

In bed, Tairan rolled to me. Curled in his arms, the sad feeling overtook me again.

"You know I'll miss you," I whispered quietly.

He raked his fingers through my hair, holding me close.

"I'll miss you, too, Isabella. When they told me they found a match, I had no idea how this would go. At most, I hoped I would be able to make it through without hurting you in any way. I never thought it would be *me* hurting to leave you at the end."

I slid my leg between both of his and snuggled tighter.

"Promise me you'll come to the gardens, Tairan. I can't wait for a whole month to see you again. Maybe," I added carefully, "together, we could figure something out?"

Like what? An escape plan? Would Tairan agree to help me with that?

Where would I go if he did?

Earth's government had given me to the Kealans. Even if I some-how managed to survive the harsh Antarctic winter and make it to any of the other continents, there would be the populations of two planets searching for me to bring me back.

"Beware of false hopes, Isabella," Tairan cautioned me.

Would he consider coming with me, away from his own people and into the unknown?

There was hardly any place on Earth outside of this facility where he wouldn't be blinded and burned by the Sun. And Keala was too far away, even if I was willing to share a cave with chicken-sized spiders on that planet, just to be out of reach from Ricread's prodding equipment.

"Oh, trust me," I sighed, "I'm really struggling here to have any hope at all." I leaned my forehead into his chest. "What kind of a future is there for us, Tairan? I was told there is hardly any chance of a pregnancy during this *phase*, whatever that is. How about after?

Since a pregnancy is the ultimate purpose of this whole thing, will they keep *breeding* us until it happens?"

Stroking my hair gently, he didn't reply, which was probably for the best anyway. Continuing this conversation held a real chance of plunging me into despair and ruining whatever little time we still had together.

Instead, I made an effort to shove the gloomy thoughts aside as far as I could.

"Well," I said, keeping my tone lighter this time, although some sarcasm seeped through. "At least I'd be guaranteed a chance to see you regularly. We'll have dinners each month and maybe even get to have some walks in the gardens."

He kissed my hair with a chuckle. "You have the ability to turn dark into light somehow."

"Oh, but that's why you like me—I make you smile." I giggled in reply, playfully shoving at his chest. "Admit it, you like me," I teased.

"I do." The smile left his face. "As hard as I've tried *not* to like you, I failed way too quickly."

My heart skipped at his confession. I opened my mouth to reply, but he didn't give me a chance, bringing his lips to mine.

The kiss was slow, unhurried, as if he tasted me, savouring every second. Pressed tight against his chest, I closed my eyes, melting into this moment with him.

He slid his hands down my back, and I felt him grow hard against my thigh. Breaking the kiss, he moved his lips down my body, but I stopped him. "My turn."

Before he could protest, I pushed him to his back, then trailed light kisses down his belly, following the ridges of his abs. The thin line of fine stubble on his stomach below his navel let me know Kealans were not naturally hairless in their pubic area. He must have been groomed the way I was before coming here.

For ease of access for the technicians and their equipment.

I resolutely shoved the bitter thought to the background. The experiment had nothing to do with what I was up to right now. Diverting all my attention to the man who was here with me, I licked down that happy trail all the way to his rising erection.

I slid the tip of my tongue along a raised bump under the silky skin of his shaft then took him in my hand, sitting up.

"Night light," I ordered the strip mounted into the top of the headboard to turn on then stroked Tairan's arm. "I've got to see it up close. Do you mind?"

"Not at all." He shifted on the mattress, stretching his tall, muscular body, awash in the soft light. "Just . . . keep touching as you look," he added, with a wicked smile.

Still at half-mast, his shaft was already considerably longer than my hand. His skin, white as bleached paper, seemed to be decorated with swirling designs in silver-grey running along his length.

"What is this?" I marvelled as the pattern seemed to swell and bulge in a raised relief the harder he got in my fingers. The silver lines thinned and paled until he was fully erect, like a magnificently carved piece of ivory in my hand. "This is real art, Tairan!"

"It better be," he laughed. "It cost me a fortune to get it done back in the day."

"So, you weren't born with this pattern?"

"Of course not. A lot of us went through a phase in the last couple of years at the Academy." He shrugged with a chuckle. "They said girls liked it, and we were young and stupid enough to believe that, wanting to impress them."

"Well, I am impressed. And I definitely loved the way it felt. But how could it even be done? I mean . . ." I traced along one of the thick lines curling around in an elegant swirl. "It's so detailed and absolutely perfect."

"A harmless substance is injected under the skin in the pattern of your choice. It reacts with blood flow and temperature . . ." He trailed off with a grunt, lifting his hips to thrust into my hand, as I kept stroking along the pretty lines of his body art.

"Does it react to moisture, too?" I wiggled my eyebrows and licked where my finger had touched.

"*That* definitely gets the blood flow going," Tairan's voice sounded strangled.

I hummed in agreement, taking the tip in my mouth then sliding my lips up and down the raised pattern.

Lying on his back, Tairan bent his knee with a groan, pressing the heel hard into the mattress as he thrust his hips up, fully invading my mouth. I tightened my lips around him, swirling my tongue along the hard ridges.

My palm flat on his lower belly, I felt his abs tense, hard as stone. His hand fisted in my hair, as if he needed to hold on when the climax surged through his body.

With a few last swirls of my tongue, I released him the moment he sagged on the mattress, his chest rising and falling with heavy breaths.

"I definitely like what you did to your penis," I announced, licking my lips.

His hands on my waist, he dragged me up to him. A teasing glint danced along with the shades of purple in his eyes as he stroked my bottom lip with his thumb.

"That was a waste of prime genetic material, you know."

"It was, wasn't it." Eyes wide, I faked an expression of horror. "Ricread would totally lose his shit if he knew I swallowed his precious research resource!"

I giggled and Tairan followed me with a chuckle.

Wrapping his arms around me, he rolled us both on our sides, facing each other.

Slowly, he drew me closer, his hand brushed by my breast then slid down along my side, and I stopped him, by grabbing his wrist.

"You don't need to return the favour. I don't want it right now."

"What *do* you want?" he asked softly. "Anything?"

I draped his arm around my waist. "Can you just hold me, please? While I fall asleep?"

Silently, he hugged me to him, tugging the blanket over us, and I snuggled into his warmth and scent.

Tomorrow I'd be alone.

IN THE MORNING THEY took him away, right after the tests.

Lying in bed, with my hand clenched into a fist, as if that would preserve the lingering sensation of Tairan's fingers held in mine just moments ago, I only had one thought bounce through my brain.

Now what?

A long and lonely month lay ahead of me.

Chapter 11

"I WILL NOT HAVE YOU dictate to me how to do my work." Ricread's eyes had narrowed to slits, his voice as cold as ice.

"Yet *you* dictate to *me* how to live every moment of my life!" I yelled, jumping off the bed.

God knew, I'd attempted to reason while trying to convince him to let me out of these rooms. Every time he showed up here for whatever tests they needed to do on me, I asked him for permission to go for a walk.

I'd used honey, begging him sweetly.

After having done some research, I'd presented him with facts on the benefits of exercise for human health.

When none of that worked after nearly a week of trying, I realized it might not be entirely about logic or science to Ricread. Standing over me, hands crossed, legs in a wide stance, he regarded me with detached interest, making me feel like nothing more than a lab rat, indeed. And he obviously enjoyed every moment of having that power over me.

"Your life is no longer your own," he tossed at me on his way out. "It belongs to Keala, just like mine does. For as long as my planet has no future, you have no right to have one either."

THE FOLLOWING DAY I stayed in bed for hours. What was the point of getting up if I knew there was nothing but another empty day ahead of me? Nothing to look forward to and no one I wanted to see.

As the new week started, they fitted me with my own armlet, similar to the one they all wore around their forearms. Zavis was the one to put it on me. She demonstrated the features I was allowed to use. However, from her explanation, I realized the main purpose of the device was to continuously track my vital functions.

Apparently, they had been getting my heart rate and body temperature through the translator installed in my ear, but now needed more detailed and varied data, including my blood pressure and composition.

"Why?" I asked her, glad that someone was actually explaining to me what was going on.

"We have been tracking the progress of the embryo traveling through your fallopian tube, but it's in the uterus now and we don't want to miss the moment of implantation," she explained casually, fiddling with some raised buttons on my armlet. "We need to do continuous scans for that."

"What embryo?" I blinked at her, hoping I had heard her wrong.

She tossed her short braids over her shoulder, darting a glance at the wall leading to the corridor as if expecting someone to burst through it at any moment.

"There have been no explicit instructions on not sharing this with you, although no directive to share came in either," she sounded as if debating with herself, excitement clearly ready to erupt in her expression. "This is an incredible advancement for us. It is the first successful insemination in years." Her eyes wide with delight, she leaned into me. "The first human-Kealan embryo ever!"

I stared at her in shock. It felt like she was talking about some event that was happening outside of my body.

"You mean it worked? Already?" I pressed my hand to my stomach through the fabric of the white dress I'd started using as a nightgown after they took Tairan away. "Am I pregnant?"

I'd been told the chance of it happening was miniscule, and I had believed them. The news blew all my thoughts and feelings into disarray, as if a hurricane swept through my mind.

"Yes!" Zavis nodded her head vigorously, sending the braids flying wildly about her head. "We went all the way to sixteen cells before it entered the uterus," she said proudly, as if she had personally added all those cells together. "The implantation will be happening anytime now. This is so incredible to watch!"

"I bet it is," I mumbled, barely able to form words, the revelation still floating through my brain in a cloud of shock.

"Of course, the pregnancy is not expected to last long."

"It's not?" I jerked my hand away from my stomach, as if even that slight contact had the power to attach me to what would be inevitably lost. "How long will it last?"

Zavis shrugged a shoulder.

"There is no way to tell for sure." Her face brightened again. "But at this point, every day is a gift. This stage has been a success beyond belief."

"Does Tairan know?"

Her expression shut down immediately. "The focus of the entire experiment is solely on you at this point."

"That doesn't answer my question."

"There are instructions to keep you away from the male subject for the time being. Some risks have been identified from engaging in certain physical activities, and intercourse has been deemed undesirable at this point."

"I'm not asking for *intercourse*." I drew in a measured breath, forcing myself to remain calm in hopes of getting some more information from her. Although, anger and frustration seethed inside me.

"I've been asking to *see* him, not begging to jump his bones." The calmness was swiftly evaporating, despite my best intentions. "Can you at least tell me how he is? And whether or not he knows what is happening here?"

Zavis drew her thin white eyebrows together, a frown of concentration settled on her delicate face.

"Well, there are procedures being conducted on the male subject, parallel to the main course of the experiment, to continuously improve the compatibility of his genetic material with your—"

"How *is* he?" I repeated slowly, my voice vibrating low in my throat.

"I'm not authorized to provide the details on his status to you. With your level of clearance—"

"Oh, God, not this again!" I jumped off the bed, yanking my arm out of her hands. "All I'm asking is for you to tell me how Tairan is doing. Do you know what it's like to sit here alone, day after day, wondering how much suffering you all are putting through the only person who's ever showed any kindness or understanding to me in here?"

"Um, Isabella . . ." Zavis rose from the mattress. The screen of her armlet extended as she rapidly shuffled through charts and graphs flickering through it. "Please, calm down."

"You want me to calm down?" Unable to stay still, I stomped into the living room, and she followed me like a shadow, punching things into her screen.

"It is imperative that you do so," Zavis insisted, only annoying me further. "The readings of your vital signs and the body functions that we're monitoring are highly volatile. The numbers have been barely within the acceptable range since the day you got here, but now they're crossing into an area of concern . . ."

"Are they? So that's what makes you concerned? The *numbers*?"

"And the extreme fluctuations between them." She nodded. "Our research has shown that we need to keep the readings even, in order to ensure the best environment for the embryo and, hopefully, the soon-to-be fetus. The risks are extremely high."

The air left my lungs with a long sigh as I sank onto the couch, feeling suddenly deflated.

"I'm not a doctor or a scientist, Zavis, but I've talked to Ricread about the benefits of my wellbeing. I've begged him to let me out of here . . ."

"The instructions are to keep you in a controlled environment. While you are in these rooms, we know exactly every particle of the air you breathe, the food you eat, the amount of energy you exert, and the waste you expel."

"And how has that been working out for you, Zavis? It doesn't help in keeping my *numbers* even, does it?" I grabbed a flower-print cushion off the couch and hugged it to my chest. "Do you think *you* would feel calm and serene, locked in a 'controlled environment?'"

I hoped Kealans were close enough to humans for Zavis to understand my stand on forced confinement. Tairan seemed to have emotions I understood. But then again, Ricread appeared to be void of any feelings whatsoever.

Zavis swept the room with her gaze, as if considering something.

"Well, this is, by far, much more space than I've ever had back home," she said slowly. "But we knew that people on Earth are generally used to having more room to move around, so we made it spacious. We got some Earth plants in here." She pointed at the shelves, lined with greenery. "And do you like the cushions?" She pointed at the one I kept crushing in my arms.

"They're nice," I mumbled, and she beamed at my reply.

"I ordered them from a shop on this planet and had them delivered by a drone."

"Really?" I stared at the bright roses printed on the cushion in my arms.

"Yes. It said 'colourful' in the description, and I figured you would like them. I'm so glad you do."

Still staring at the cushion, I took some time to rearrange my understanding about this place and the people here.

On one hand, decorating the place for me with 'local elements' reminded me way too much of the way I once set up an empty jar with grass and flowers for a caterpillar I found in the garden when I was little. I made it pretty, and was very upset to find the caterpillar dead in my beautifully decorated jar the next morning.

The efforts of the Kealans to keep me well seemed to be there, but very misguided. The six-year-old me didn't put the right leaves for the caterpillar to eat and closed the lid of the jar a little too tight, essentially killing it at the end. And I was beginning to worry that if not my body, then my mind and spirit could end up being irrevocably damaged with me locked up here.

On the other hand, this woman seemed to care enough to go through the hassle of getting these cushions here for me . . .

I turned to Zavis. "The plants there." I gestured at the shelves. "They need sun, right?"

"Not really," she objected. "These are indoor plants that do well in artificial light."

"Well, humans do need sunshine in order to thrive. Vitamin D?"

"You're given all the nutrients and vitamins you require through your meals and supplements," she assured me confidently.

"Okay. How about the exercise?"

"Extreme physical activities are harmful in your state."

"Again, I'm not talking about anything *extreme*." I brushed a hand over my face. This conversation was beginning to feel *extremely* exhausting. "All I'm asking for now is to be let out of these rooms and for you to explain to me the purpose of separating me from Tairan. It makes no sense other than a power trip on Ricread's part—"

"Your vital signs . . ." she leaned in and lowered her voice, as if sharing a secret with me. "The readings were off the charts during your insemination process. Especially, the last time. If that relatively mild level of activity resulted in spikes of that sort—"

"Zavis," I interrupted her softly, my heart filling with something sweet and painful. "Not all strong emotions are negative. In fact, many are positive. I really like Tairan. I wish I had a chance to get to know him better or that I had met him some place other than this. But even the way it happened, I truly enjoyed being with him, every minute we got. Surely, as a woman you would understand." I pointed at her armlet. "Check your readings now if you want. I bet there was 'a spike' in my numbers when I simply mentioned his name." I exhaled a long breath, my voice low, "It doesn't take much . . ."

She didn't check the screen. Her head down, she said, "I'm afraid those spikes may be a part of the reason behind the instructions of zero contact between you and him now."

"So, if I'd lain there unmoving and emotionless while he *inseminated* me, it would have improved my chances of getting to see him now?"

"No, of course not . . . Well, maybe? Anyway, that's not the only factor." Lifting her gaze to mine, she tugged at her braids anxiously. "Professor Ricread is a brilliant scientist. His studies give our race hope. And now that he has successfully bred two interplanetary specimens—"

"He'll be unstoppable," I finished for her.

With a deep inhale, she rose from the couch.

"No one would want to jeopardize his incredible progress by demanding changes to the protocol he'd established, Isabella. Definitely not I."

"I understand."

"What I *can* do," she added softly, "is to present to the professor and the team the correlation between the fluctuations in your readings and your emotional instability, as well as suggest possible improvements through regular, mild physical activity like walking and possibly exposure to the open space you call 'outdoors.'"

"You would?" Dropping the pillow, I jumped off the couch, hope flooding me with excitement.

"Remember . . ." she spread her arms in the air, palms facing me. "We need to keep those numbers within the acceptable range if and when these changes happen to be allowed."

"Absolutely." I nodded earnestly, pressing both hands to my chest. "Thank you."

"No need to thank me yet."

With a smile and a brief nod, Zavis left me alone once again.

Chapter 12

A FEW DAYS LATER, THE implantation was confirmed and I was officially pronounced pregnant.

Ricread had personally delivered the news during a set of tests the research team did that week. In an uncharacteristic move, he even shared that the purpose of the tests at this point was to monitor every miniscule change in my body as well as to continue tracking the development of the embryo—now a fetus—on a cellular level.

I sat on the bed long after he and the team were gone and stared at the grey walls surrounding me.

An intense feeling of warm tenderness threatened to rise from low in my belly to my heart and flood the emptiness that reigned there.

I struggled but fought it.

Nothing belonged to me, and I forbade myself to *feel* anything at all, desperately holding on to that emptiness instead.

This was not about bringing a new life into the world, not about Tairan and me. It was all about Ricread and his ambition.

And it might be gone soon.

APPARENTLY, ZAVIS TURNED out to be better at persuasion than I had been.

Nearly a week later, Gran rolled into my bedroom with a black cloak draped over his wire-arms.

"You have mild physical activity on your schedule today—a thirty-minute walk through the facility—provided you finish your morning meal."

Eating had been a struggle lately. Mild but persistent nausea turned me off food. It also proved nearly impossible to work up any appetite while lying in bed most of the day. The less I moved, the less I felt like eating or doing anything at all for that matter. Now I wondered if my regularly unfinished meals had aided in Zavis's persuasion efforts.

In any case, I rushed to the table as soon as Gran put my food tray on it, and wolfed down the watery oatmeal, tepid chamomile tea, and a cupful of fresh blueberries, which were actually delicious.

"I'm ready," I said moments later.

"Your instructions are to move at the pace I will set for you and strive to keep the distance between me and you of no more than one metre."

"Right." I swung the cloak over my shoulders. Bringing the two ends together made them fuse at my collarbone without any visible closures like buttons or clasps. "I'll walk slow and keep close. Let's go," I urged him, impatiently.

Once we left my rooms, I asked Gran to take me to the gardens.

Tairan had spoken of visiting in the afternoon, just before dinnertime, and it was morning right now. But some wild, unreasonable hope drove me there anyway, making me realize how desperately I wanted to see him again.

"Would you prefer to visit the Kealan section of the gardens or the one from Earth?" Gran asked, taking me around the landing hangar at a snail's speed.

"There are two sections?"

"The Earth portion was added to conduct studies in the environment of this planet, such as the work on improving the material used in protective clothing. It also houses a variety of Earth plants, including those used in your meals. The light inside this section is exactly the same spectrum as sunlight. It is therefore not a comfortable area for the Kealans."

"Let's go to the Kealan gardens today. The one with the waterfalls."

"There are waterfalls in the Earth section, as well. Both areas were designed with aesthetics in mind."

"Why?" I retorted bitterly. "I am the only one on this station capable of fully appreciating the *aesthetics* of the Earth gardens here, without feeling the discomfort from the light. And I wasn't allowed to walk in there anyway?"

"You are now," Gran chirped, his wide smile shining cheerfully.

After we had circled the landing hangar, Gran whirred right and I followed him. The corridors here became wider, and the colour of the walls changed from grey to dark-brown. The ceiling gradually curved into an arch as we entered the Kealan gardens.

The corridors now were shaped like tunnels. They were much smaller than those I imagined the giant *ure* worms would dig, still my heart skipped as I found myself in a world I had learned about.

As we moved along the tunnel. More of them branched off in every direction, not all perfectly aligned or horizontal, some were slanted, running up or downhill. The floor on the one I walked in seemed to be made from the same rock as the rest of it, slightly uneven yet still smooth and even enough for the robot to roll along beside me.

Soft lighting came from the plant life on the walls and under the ceiling—some shaped like mushrooms or flowers, others sprawled like moss or mould—all glowed in various colours and intensity. My breath caught in my throat at the beauty of the warm yellows and pale pinks of the glowing plants. Delicate pulsating blue and violet streaks ran in swirls along the rock.

"It's a shame Kealans can't see the colours to fully appreciate it all," I muttered.

"They don't need colours to appreciate the beauty," Gran replied. "Kealans cherish their lighting plants."

I gave him a side glance. "You know, despite being a robot and a spy, you say profound things sometimes, almost poetic."

"Thank you."

After a while, the sound of running water alerted me that we must be close.

"Waterfalls?" I asked Gran.

"This way, please." He turned off into a tunnel to the right, leading me into a wide-open cavern.

I spun around, taking in the high domed ceiling with stalactites hanging from it, long vines of glowing vegetation draped between them like strings of pulsating lights.

"This cave was built to imitate the naturally formed cavities in Keala's mantel," Gran explained. "The *ure*-dug tunnels often connect them in the fashion simulated at this facility."

"How were all these plants brought here?" I bent to touch a delicate, glowing purple flower. Its eight petals moved under my fingers, like the soft brush of suede, they then bent down to the rock it was on, and the 'flower' scurried away. Surprised, I jerked my hand back.

"*Edhie* spider," Gran said calmly. "They are non-toxic and harmless."

"That pretty thing was a *spider*?" I gaped in the direction, in which the 'flower' had disappeared.

"Most of the life forms here have been transported as eggs, spores or seeds during the past nine years. Although some were in their adult form when they arrived on Earth."

"How long does it take to get from here to Keala."

"Using Kealan technology, anywhere from six months to a year, relative to Earth time. Keala would be impossible to reach if using the space travel technology available on Earth."

"That's why they found us first," I remarked softly.

Gran took me around a bend in the wall, and I spotted the waterfalls in the distance. The glow of the surrounding plants shimmered through the dark water, making it look as if the falls themselves were illuminated.

The air grew rich with moisture the closer we got. Tearing my gaze away from the wondrous plant life, I surveyed the surrounding walls and their rocky protrusions to locate the blind spot Tairan spoke about. There was an indentation in the wall, like a shallow grotto, partially hidden behind a rocky protrusion on the left side of the pool.

I stepped into the alcove, hiding behind a wall. The stream of the falls misted me from the opposite side. I exhaled a long breath, wishing Tairan was here.

"May I come back here this afternoon, Gran?"

"There are no more walks on your schedule for today."

"Well, can we put one on it? I know for a fact my schedule is not *that* packed."

"You cannot plan your daily activities yourself," he replied coolly. *Didn't I know that.*

"How about tomorrow?"

"There is a thirty-minute exercise slot after breakfast."

Well, at least I could leave my room on a daily basis now. *Thank you, Zavis.*

"You have sixteen minutes to explore the gardens before we need to start on our way back," Gran reminded.

I left the grotto and followed the robot around the spacious cave.

Several tunnels branched out from it here and there. I stopped in front of a short one that turned into the grey corridor further in the distance.

"Where does that go?"

"It leads to the clinical wing of the facility."

"A clinic?" I stepped into the short tunnel. "Meaning this is where 'procedures' would be performed?" Zavis's words about Tairan came to mind.

"Yes, but you're not authorized to visit any of the rooms there." The robot hurried after me.

"How about just walking along the corridors? You said I still had sixteen minutes . . ."

"Only fourteen now, and it will be a long detour to get to your rooms through here, with no time left to spend in the gardens."

"Well, I'll have lots of time to explore the gardens tomorrow, won't I?

The robot seemed to be scrambling for an answer, so I just kept walking. "Let's take the detour, Gran."

The matte grey corridors were wide and empty. With my gaze, I traced along the strings of light running along the walls under the ceiling, noting the breaks most likely indicating entrances to rooms. Many of them were marked with symbols, too.

"What are these?" I pointed at them to Gran.

"Room numbers, along with a brief description of each room's function."

I felt the limitation of my translator acutely. As wonderful as it was for interpreting the spoken language, it did nothing too help me understand the words glowing on the walls.

"Can you read what it says to me?" I asked Gran.

"Learning the functions of the rooms in this section is not in your level of clearance."

"I wonder why," I mumbled sarcastically, moving from one glowing sign to another.

"I have no access to the reasons behind this decision."

Following the curve of the corridor, we turned, and I stopped in my tracks, suddenly coming upon an arched opening in the wall—the entrance to a room that seemed to have been left open.

The light coming from behind it was brighter than that in the corridor, but I heard no voices or any other noise coming from inside it.

Keeping to the wall, I crept to the opening to take a peek inside. The room seemed completely empty. Bigger than my living area, it had no visible furnishings or equipment. Taking a step in, I noted screens of various sizes on the wall to my right.

"You're not authorized to be inside," Gran chimed in from behind me, but unless he was about to physically stop me, I was ignoring him—my attention fully turned to the screens.

The images on them were not transmissions, I realized as I came closer. These were biological samples, preserved in liquid, illustrating each stage of conception and fetus development—from slices of tissue, to invisible embryos, complete with magnified images of their cell clusters, to fetuses of increasing size and limb definition. The last one could have been a newborn.

Not a *human* newborn, though, I noted, staring at the last exhibit of a fully-formed baby with papery-white skin and long, colourless filaments of hair fanning in the liquid around its head.

Kealan.

"The exhibit of our losses and accomplishments," a male voice stated calmly behind me, jolting me with surprise.

Pivoting on my heels to face him, I nearly crashed into the wall with the glass containers.

"I do not believe you are supposed to be here." Valran narrowed his lavender-rimmed eyes at me, moving into the room from the entrance. A black cloak was draped over his wide shoulders. However, like mine, his hood was off.

"I'm . . . um, I was on my way back from the gardens." I attempted to sneak past him along the wall, but he pinned me with his gaze, keeping me in place.

"This is not the best way to your quarters from the gardens."

With his penetrating gaze on me, I had no idea what to say next and kept quiet.

"Did the robot lead you astray?" he asked unexpectedly.

"Yes," I said quickly, though it felt like throwing Gran under a bus.

"I must disagree—" Gran protested.

Bending at the waist, Valran quickly reached behind the robot's top disk that was turned upright as the smiley face. Gran's lights faded, having been switched off.

"I'll report the malfunction," Valran informed me, straightening up.

"Um, thank you."

"However, I must escort you back to your rooms myself, now."

I ventured a glance at his face, his expression unreadable.

"Thank you," was all I could say, feeling weighted down by his stare on me.

"This exhibit," he said, without moving from the spot, "represents a decade of hard work."

"Okay," I replied, wondering why he wasn't taking me back right away. Despite the bright lighting in the room, the atmosphere inside was gloomy. A heavy darkness seemed to spread from the glass wall, and I couldn't hold back the question. "How did they all get here?"

"These are the results of the earlier stages of the experiment, when we still hoped to procreate on our own, without the use of human genetic material."

He moved along the wall with the glass compartments, pointing at the beginning of the lineup. "These arrived from Keala during our earlier years here. And this stillborn is from eight years ago." He splayed his hand on the glass with the fully formed baby, the last in line. "Our hope for a live birth of a pure-blooded Kealan is dead. Now, we *need* you."

Valran walked to the entrance, and I followed, anxious to leave this room with its crypt-like atmosphere.

"I was told *this* is unlikely to last long, too," I said, placing my hand to my stomach.

"Right." He nodded calmly.

I had been desperately resisting any feelings about what was happening inside me. In this room, I got a visual of how it all would end—displayed on the wall under glass, the only unknown being its exact position in this lineup. Valran's cool confirmation drove it in, slicing me with pain I had tried hard to avoid.

The heavy dread threatened to suffocate me, and I swallowed hard.

"Why go ahead with this at all if you already know it's hopeless?"

"Hopeless?" He stopped in the corridor, regarding me with confusion. "Isabella, this fetus is viable. There is a solid three percent chance of a live birth. Do you realize what that means?"

"Yes," I retorted bitterly, fighting a hard lump in my throat. "You'd better get another glass container ready for your wall. As there is a ninety-seven percent chance you're going to need it."

He shook his head, staring at me in bewilderment.

"It means that for the first time in eight years, we finally have hope again."

His was a species on the verge of extinction, with a long and painful quest to save themselves at all cost. The problem was that my life and my future, as well as those of the man I had grown to care about, were all part of that cost.

And I could see no way of stopping this.

Now, there was a three percent chance of another life being brought into this world. To what future? To also be fed into the grand machine of The Experiment?

"What would happen to the baby? *If* there was a live baby at the end?"

"Protocols have been put in place for every possible outcome long ago. In case of a live birth, the fertility potential of the offspring is expected to be the same or better than that of the parents—"

"So, you'll just keep on breeding all of us?" I didn't really need his answer. Ricread had outlined the big picture of his plans on my flight here, weeks ago. One child may hold the hope, but what came after it that was the actual result. What I hoped to gauge from Valran's reply was his personal attitude to it all.

"As soon as it is possible to perform the first analysis without the risk to the subject, the population of both planets will be evaluated to find the most suitable genetic match for your offspring. The long-term focus of the program is to eventually reduce the content of human DNA in the new species and to bring the ratio back to what Kealans currently have. This will take time—"

"So, this . . . child will be *the subject* from the moment it is born until its last days. You have already separated me from its father. Will you take the baby away from its parents too when it's born? Its entire life has been sacrificed to your cause before it has even begun."

"All of us have dedicated our lives to saving our race, Isabella. Every resource we have has been diverted to support Professor Ricread's research. We've lost so much to it. We need to rebuild, start anew, and grow again."

"Do you, personally, believe that it would be possible to *start anew* after everything that you have done for this, Valran? After what you're still planning to do? Do you think you could just move ahead into the bright tomorrow after grinding my future, Tairan's, and the future of all those who'd come after us for your big purpose?" I pointed at my stomach. "Tell me, what exactly are you trying to preserve here? Is a race that has already lost its values, its morals, and its kindness still worth saving at all?"

BACK IN MY ROOM, I had a hard time settling down for a while. Simply taking one day at a time seemed to be harder than ever.

For reasons unknown, Valran had shared with me some information I suspected was way above my *level of clearance*, bringing to the surface the emotions I had struggled to bury deep.

In a desperate attempt to distract myself, I ended up searching the communication system for any information on Valran. With Gran being gone, I used the screen of my armlet to pull up pictures of the members of The Science Group.

Nine times out of ten, any group photo containing Valran also had Ricread in it. They seemed to have had a long career together. At least ten years younger than Ricread, Valran had been just a step behind him in every position they had held.

Unlike the City Defense Forces, however, the members of The Science Group didn't wear the signs of distinction much. Instead, the Group commemorated their members with plaques around the walls of the central facility in Atal.

'These are our losses and accomplishments.'

I thought back to the wall of samples marking the long and painful journey of Kealans on their quest to survive. Despite some sympathy for their situation, I had meant every word I said to Valran.

In their struggle to procreate, Kealan society had forgotten about the lives of individuals like myself. Worry about Tairan hadn't left me, nagging me from the inside day after day.

Pacing the floor, I forced myself to take long, measured breaths, then found some calming music on the screen of my armlet.

Now that I had finally got permission to leave my rooms, I couldn't risk losing it. Stretching out on the bed, I recalled the pleasant images of the Kealan gardens in an attempt to bring my 'numbers' into the acceptable range for Ricread.

Chapter 13

DAYS MOVED BY, NEARLY identical and monotonous. The cells inside me kept multiplying, the fetus seemed to be holding on for now. Although, I refrained from asking anyone about the details of its progress, stubbornly struggling to distance myself from what was happening.

The day after I spoke with Valran, Gran was returned to me with no recollection of my ever going to the clinical wing. Despite, his unwavering smile, though, I couldn't help but feel guilty, as if I had betrayed the robot, and I made an extra effort to be nice to him now.

We went for a walk to the gardens every morning. I made it to the section with Earth plants and found the waterfalls there, too. The grotto there looked identical to the one in the Kealan part, and I wondered if it was in a blind spot as well.

To my bitter disappointment, I never saw Tairan in any part of the gardens or in the corridors of the facility on my way to and from them.

Sometimes, I would run into personnel, though. They seemed to wear the cloaks and often their goggles, too, as a precaution whenever they had to come anywhere near the spacecraft landing hangar. Even despite the twenty-four-hour darkness in Antarctica this time of the year, any chance of exposure to the outside seemed to make the Kealans nervous, as if the sunlight still lingered out there somewhere.

One day, about two weeks after I first started visiting the gardens, I ran into Valran again, although I was nowhere near the clinical part of the facility this time.

He was walking swiftly through the corridors, in the company of another Kealan. Barely inclining his head my way in greeting while passing by, Valran said to his companion, when he must have thought I was out of earshot, "Move the subject X-001 to room SR04 tonight. He is post-surgery."

It took me a moment to absorb what I'd heard. As if frozen in place, I stood in the middle of the corridor, Valran's words bouncing through my mind.

'He.'

How many male subjects did they have in this place? Or even female, for that matter? To my knowledge it had been just Tairan and me.

Even if the research team had acquired more people for any other purpose by now, the feeling that Valran had specifically been referring to Tairan wouldn't leave me.

"Gran, where is the room number SR04?"

"In the clinical wing."

"What is its function? Post-surgery recovery? Never mind." I waved my hand at him. "I know, I know 'not my level of clearance.'"

"I am not authorized to confirm the room's function," the robot replied, his blue smile stretching wider. "But I have complete freedom to *state* that individuals generally require a recovery period after surgery."

His words made me pause.

"Granny?" I crouched in front of the robot, staring at him as if I could read behind the glowing lights of his 'eyes.' "Would you also 'state' for me how long the individuals could be *generally* expected to stay in the recovery?"

"Two to six days depending on the surgery."

"And what kind of care would they receive?"

"Around-the-clock recording and transmission of vital statistics and regular analysis by a group of technicians, with the purpose of monitoring the progress of recovery and assessing medication requirements."

"What time of the day do the technicians' visits happen?"

"The time has been recently amended to nine thirty in the morning. Right after your breakfast."

My heart began to race faster, and I rose to my feet, breathing in deeply in an attempt to calm down.

If it was indeed Tairan who was being transferred to that room tonight, then I could be there when the technicians left tomorrow morning. At best I could hope for a glimpse of him through the open door, but maybe I would overhear something about his condition or the surgery he just had.

All I had to do was to find a way to stay out of sight and, if that failed, feign ignorance and claim I had gotten lost. That could mean losing the privilege of going for a walk in the future, but I needed to use this chance to find out what was going on with Tairan.

"Gran, can you show me the numbers X-001 and SR04? How they're written in Kealan?"

"Certainly." The smiley face melted into the screen with the glowing set of characters representing the numbers.

"Thank you so much." Opening the drawing screen on my armlet, I quickly copied them over.

BACK IN MY BEDROOM, I paced the floor once again, this time thinking of the best way to accomplish what I had in mind tomorrow.

Opening my screen again, I stared at the room and subject numbers I had copied, trying to memorize them. It was hard to focus. I thought of a way to mark the room when I found it, so it would be easier for me to find it again if needed, and I remembered the nail file I hid when I first got here.

Crouching down by the bed, I searched in the narrow gap between it and the floor with a thin kitchen utensil I had brought from one of the cabinets in the living area. With another sweep of the utensil, the long nail file slid out, and I tucked it in my pocket quickly.

I needed it to scrape a part of the light strip over the room SR04 to mark it. However, having a 'weapon' in my pocket, no matter how inadequate it might be against anyone at the station, gave me some confidence, too.

Chapter 14

MY HEART WAS POUNDING wildly in my chest, and I'd given up on attempts to calm down. With Gran on my heels, I was heading to the tunnel leading from the gardens to the clinical wing.

"I am required to remind you that you're not authorized to enter any rooms in this corridor," the robot stated.

"If I confirm that I am completely aware of that, would you not repeat it ever again? Especially, not within the next twenty minutes. In fact, could you promise me to say absolutely nothing for the next twenty minutes?"

"You're not authorized to shut down my inputting functions." I believed Gran's voice sounded a bit grumpy. "However," he continued, "there is no instruction against your temporarily turning off my output device."

"Really? How do I do that?"

"There are several ways. Voice command is one of them—"

"Is it?" I cut him off, anxious to keep going. "Shut up, Gran."

He immediately went quiet. Although, the lights on his round 'face' shifted, forming into a sentence.

There was no need to be rude.

Pinching the bridge of my nose, I said, actually feeling ashamed, "Sorry. Can we go now, please?"

Heading through the tunnel, with the soft sound of Gran rolling behind me, I opened the screen on my forearm device and pulled up the number of the room I'd recorded.

Silently moving through the corridor of the clinic, I referenced the numbers on the wall to the one on my screen. The progress was slow, as I had no idea whether I was moving in the right direction because I had no way of telling if the numbers were increasing or decreasing as I went along, simply searching for the exact one I had on my screen.

A noise in the distance made me flatten against the wall. I frantically waved to Gran to roll to me as I curled my fingers around the nail file in the pocket of my dress.

"Leave it open," I heard a male voice. "Someone is bringing in a gurney."

"Are they going to transfer him again? They just moved him here last night."

"No idea. That information is above my clearance level . . ."

To my relief, the voices faded—the people talking were obviously moving in the opposite direction from me.

I snuck after them quickly. If they were talking about an open door, I didn't want it to close before I got to it.

Turning around the corner, I spotted the backs of two male figures as they moved away. Light spilled into the corridor from the open door to my right. Not waiting for the technicians to disappear from view completely, I quietly ran to the door and into the room, anxious to get out of their line of sight as soon as possible.

"You *are* entering . . ." Gran's cranky voice followed me in, but I stopped paying attention to him at the sight of the Kealan spread on his back on a high, narrow bed in the middle of the room.

His eyes closed, his features sunken, he was naked, save for the wide bandages across his hips that covered his crotch completely. Wide straps of plastic or rubber crossed his thighs and chest, strapping his torso to the cot he lay on.

I took a few tentative steps to him. The man seemed leaner than I remembered Tairan being. Although just as broad-shouldered, his ribs protruded distinctly and the bindings couldn't hide how sharp his hip bones were.

As I came closer, though, the familiar exotic scent filtered through the clinical air of the room.

"Tairan," I whispered, and bit my lip to stop it from trembling. Even his tangled braids seemed less lustrous somehow.

I gently touched his arm. His eyelids moved, the white eyelashes fluttered like snowflakes. Then his violet-rimmed eyes met mine. The expression in them seemed unfocused, disoriented.

"Isabella?" His voice sounded rough, but the tone of it was so warm, it melted my heart.

He shifted in an attempt to turn to me. His body jerked, his face distorting into a grimace of pain as he clenched his jaw with a strangled groan.

"What have they been doing to you?" I blinked away the tears that were threatening to spill over and carefully took his outstretched hand.

The reply to my question didn't come from Tairan.

"A series of necessary procedures to improve his performance and compatibility with you," Ricread's voice came from the direction of the door.

Startled, I turned around quickly, keeping Tairan's hand in mine.

Arms across his chest, black cloak open, Ricread glared at me from the entrance. A number of research team members flanked him, along with a group of security personnel in black uniforms.

I spotted Valran behind Ricread's shoulder. Visibly calm and collected, he didn't seem surprised to see me.

Was it a trap?

Come to think of it, my plan of getting here had gone exceptionally smoothly. Had Valran set it up?

"It doesn't look like he is *improved* in any way." I returned Ricread's glare.

"He will fully recover by the time the next insemination is required."

"Next insemination?" I flinched. "You *really* are planning ahead. This fetus is still in me."

"I must foresee every possibility and devise an appropriate response to every possible outcome. Faced with a multitude of unpredictable variables, it is paramount for all involved to behave exactly as I expect, including you. *Especially* you." He spat the last word through his clenched teeth before turning to Zavis. "Adjust her daily schedule immediately. She no longer has the privilege of a morning walk."

Zavis nodded, vigorously punching into her screen.

"Sikril." Ricread gave a sign, and two of the security personnel in black uniforms moved my way.

"No." My spine snapping straight, I got a firmer hold of Tairan's hand behind my back. "I'm staying here."

Ricread shrugged, brushing me off then turned to leave.

"Listen to me!" I yelled, getting his attention. "You have married us. He is my husband. It may mean nothing to you, but it hurts me to see him suffer."

"No one invited you here to *see* him," Ricread retorted coolly. "And I have no time to waste on appeasing your cultural expectations anymore. The rules are in place for a reason. They're meant to control what we can, and that means you. You need to be in your room, right now."

"I'm staying here." The idea of being locked away again was appalling. But the thought of leaving Tairan, strapped to the table and subjected to Ricread's cruelties, was simply terrifying. I might not be able to protect him, but now that I'd found him, I simply couldn't leave him. "It is important for me to have the support of a husband in my condition." I attempted to use the previous tactic of persuasion. "We need to be together."

"It's time for you to understand the importance of the work we all do here!" Ricread raised his voice, his composure melting away. Impatiently, he gestured to the two Kealans who now flanked me. "Take her and put her in her place."

"No!" Letting go of Tairan's hand, I moved out of their reach, desperately trying to delay the inevitable. "I'm not going to be locked away again! I'm not your lab rat. I'm not spending the rest of my life alone in a cage."

"You have no say here!" Ricread exclaimed with force, hands fisted at his sides. "You will do as you're instructed. And if not, you will be *made* to comply. You are the property of Keala, which means you are *mine* to do with as I please, for the future of our planet."

With the two men moving on me from both sides, I fervently searched inside my pocket for the nail file. I realized the moment I pulled it out that my weapon was simply ridiculous against two strong, fully-grown Kealans.

"No," I repeated, shaking my head. "I am not property. I don't care how much you've paid for me, because I was never for sale in the first place. Stop!" I ordered to the men reaching for me and pointed the nail file at my own belly. Every muscle in my body tensed. Every nerve vibrated, strung tight like a string. "You just don't want to listen," I addressed Ricread again. "You refuse to understand. See how you'll feel if I kill *your* hope and *your* future the way you've killed mine."

"You wouldn't dare." His eyes on my hands, Ricread's voice turned hollow, his expression guarded.

"Would you bet your entire career and the future of your race on that?"

My hands shaking, I gripped the nail file as hard as I could, pressing it into my dress a few centimetres below my belly button.

"You would die, too," he hissed. "You will bleed to death, unless I decide to stop it."

"My death is the whole point here, *Professor*." I stared at him, unblinking. "If you want me to live, you'll have to give me something worth living for."

His eyes burning with fury, he threw his hands up in the air, spinning on his heel, which sent the ends of his cloak flying in a twirl around his shoulders.

"This is unbelievable! You cannot keep blackmailing me into concessions."

"I've asked for little and got even less," I argued.

"The protocol is there for a reason." He ignored my words. "It took me years to establish it. Decades!"

"And now, if you want your experiment to continue, you will have to change it," I replied as calmly as I could muster, with the tip of the nail file piercing through the fabric of my dress. "I want my husband with me, at all times. I want you to stop all surgeries on him. We both should be free to walk where we want and to eat whatever we like. No more spying. Let us live in peace. In exchange, I'll promise not to cause any deliberate harm to myself and treat my body with the utmost care to ensure the results of your experiment remain in my uterus for as long as possible. Deal?"

"This is unacceptable. Your physical activities and your nutrition have to be strictly regulated—"

"You'll have to trust me when I say I'll treat my body with care."

"You are not the one in control here!"

"No. But I'm trying to change that."

Ricread stopped right in front of me, his eyes flicked to the nail file in my hands then to the men on both sides of me, who appeared ready to pounce on me at his signal.

"I cannot agree to that." Ricread shook his head, his eyelid twitched. "I've put my life into this research, I cannot let an emotionally unstable female ruin it now."

"Then I'll fight." I sighed. "Every moment of every day. To *ruin* it for all of you. Even if you stop me now, I'll find another way. You take sharp objects away from me—I'll refuse to eat. I'll keep finding ways to make myself sick, and I promise your head will spin at how fast and how many ways I'll come up with, no matter how great you think you are at *foreseeing all outcomes*." My hands cramped from gripping my 'weapon', and my chest felt tight. I panted to draw enough oxygen in, but I kept an eye on them all, watching their every move. "Look. Like I said before, ultimately, our goals are the same. You want me well and healthy, and I wish for nothing more."

"Except that the list of your demands to achieve that state of *wellbeing* keeps growing, exponentially," he snarled. The way his body seemed to deflate a little told me he might be losing steam. "You are holding my work hostage."

I nodded. "Literally."

He rubbed his face with both hands. "This will delay the whole process," he groaned.

"How?"

"I'm running out of time." He ignored my question. "You're leaving me no choice." He raised his head, meeting my eyes straight on. "I'll go with what you demand, but only for the duration of the pregnancy."

I stared at him, trying to process what seemed to be a victory for me but didn't feel as such. With the high risk of my pregnancy, it already felt like living under a suspended anvil, expecting it to drop any minute.

"This is the reassurance I need for your co-operation during this time." Ricread crossed his arms over his chest, regaining his calm composure once again. "This way, I believe it really would be in both our interests for the pregnancy to continue for as long as possible."

"Tairan is staying with me." I swallowed thickly, my throat dry and sore. "No more surgeries. If you need to check on him, you'll do it in my room, with me present." For however long it was going to last, I'd got my way for now. "No invasive procedures on either of us. And we both need to know what's going on."

"You need updates?" Ricread squinted at me, incredulously.

"Yes. Daily." I had intentionally stayed away from knowing anything about the way my pregnancy was progressing before, but now, since it had been made a vital condition of our deal, I had no excuse to avoid the updates. "I'll also need an explanation before any test or exam you decide to put us through. Deal?"

"Fine." Ricread's jaw flexed.

"Get it in writing." Tairan's rough, quiet voice reached me from behind. "He needs to sign it."

"What he said." I flicked my thumb over my shoulder.

Zavis rushed to Ricread with her screen aglow. "I got all the points of the verbal agreement right here."

Ricread threw her a glance. "Add the condition of no intercourse between them." He levelled a glare at me. "None, until another insemination is required."

Zavis nodded, hurriedly punching into her screen before shoving her arm his way again. Ricread scribbled his signature on the screen. The weight of resentment in his eyes when he stared at me again was much easier to bear this time.

"Is this good?" I grabbed Zavis's wrist and yanked her screen closer to Tairan's face. He slid his gaze along the text quickly and nodded, letting me know I could sign it, too.

"Done," Ricread bit the word out then spun around and stomped out of the room.

The nervous energy that kept me upright, vibrating through my every bone and muscle, left me with his departure. My knees buckled, and I propped my ass against Tairan's bed, lest I collapse to the floor. His arm immediately went around my waist, as if he were strapping me to his side.

"The subject can't be moved for another twenty-four to forty-eight hours, at least," one of the team technicians pointed out, gesturing at the tubes and wires that were attached to Tairan's waist, thighs, and bandages. "Her rooms don't have the necessary equipment."

"His name is Tairan." I glared at the man who spoke. "Does referring to him as 'the subject' help you sleep at night after all the shit you've done to him through the day?"

The technician blanched, and Valran stepped forward.

"We'll move him within forty-eight hours."

"Then I'm staying here until then." My voice was steady and firm, even as my body trembled from exhaustion.

"Bring another bed in for Isabella," Valran instructed the team. "And arrange for her meals to be delivered here until the commander can be moved."

I paid no attention to the commotion resulting from his words. Staring at the wall while the research team rushed to comply with Valran's orders, I sat on the bed, my back to Tairan, his arm around my waist keeping me grounded.

"Would you have done it?" he asked quietly, as soon as everyone left and the entrance wall solidified behind them. "Would you have hurt yourself?"

The nail file slipped out of my weakened fingers and slid to the floor along the skirt of my dress.

"I honestly don't know." I shook my head. "I'm just really glad it didn't come down to it."

Feeling completely and utterly exhausted, I climbed into the narrow bed they had placed next to Tairan's. He lifted his arm, letting me lie on his bicep, then drew me into his side.

Finally, it felt like a safe place to have a meltdown, and I stopped holding back the belated fear and tears. His arm tight around me, I pressed my forehead into his shoulder and cried.

"I'm so sorry, Tairan," I sobbed quietly, unsure of what I was apologizing for. "I'm just a girl from a small town, practically a nobody. I have no real weapons and no power, but I need to fight somehow. I simply can't let them keep getting away with all of this."

He kissed my hair, rubbing my shoulder soothingly.

"You're doing good, Isabella. Better than good." His voice was rough and sombre, with a hard note of steel I had not heard from him before. "And you have strength, so much of it, it astounds me. From now on, I'll be your weapon and your power. We'll fight together."

Chapter 15

I DIDN'T LEAVE TAIRAN'S side, except to use the bathroom. We took all our meals together, and I was present at all his examinations. I watched them closely as they changed his bandages and reapplied the neon pink blobs of the Kealan healing gel to the puncture wounds along both sides of the hard V of his lower abdomen and at the top of his inner thighs.

I demanded painkillers, which had apparently been denied to him by Ricread, on the grounds that any 'secondary' medication risked interfering with the main objective of Tairan's participation in the experiment—his fertility and level of 'performance'. I suspected, however, that the true reason for keeping Tairan in pain had to do with Ricread's personal dislike of the subject of his experiment, resulting in this unnecessary cruelty.

For a while, Tairan remained apathetic, bracing against the pain. However, when my struggle to get him painkillers finally registered with him, he grabbed by the throat the first technician who had the misfortune to step too close to his bed.

"Give her what she wants," he gritted through his teeth, the lean, ropy muscles bulging in his arm.

The female attendant also present in the room spoke rapidly into her armlet, requesting authorization for the use of painkillers, as Tairan continued to hold the choking, gasping-for-air male technician by the throat.

Eventually, we managed to get the mildest analgesic for Tairan. It wasn't much, coming at the point when the pain from the surgery had already started to recede, still, it felt like a victory for us.

"I am required to remind you," the female attendant said before leaving the room that day, "that Commander Tairan Saryal has agreed to every procedure we have ever performed, including the most recent one. We have his written permissions on file. And I am told to advise you to keep this in mind before making any more demands or using violence against our team members."

"You agreed?" I turned to Tairan the moment she was gone. "But why?"

He lay still, his features hard. Silent.

"Does he torture you into signing things? How can it even be legal? Do Kealan laws allow coercion and duress?"

"The Science Group has more power than the Kealan government now," he replied gruffly. "Ricread *is* the law."

He looked exhausted and worn, tired beyond belief. And I wondered what it must have taken from him, having to fight this battle alone for years now.

TWO DAYS LATER, THEY disconnected Tairan from all support systems and allowed him to be moved to my rooms. Placed in a gurney that had been folded into a seat, he was taken down the corridors, with me following closely behind.

Once in my rooms, he asked for a shower.

I started to unbraid his hair, while he sat in the gurney-chair hovering above the floor.

"Who braids it this neat for you?" I asked, carefully placing each of his hair rings into a velvet-lined tray.

"It's done by robots now."

I continued to undo his braids. Each strand slightly thicker than that of a human, his hair sprang perfectly straight as soon as it was released from the ring, without any wave left from the pleats.

"You look different." I ran my fingers through the snow-white silk of his hair, brushing it away from his face.

"Gaunt and scary?" He gave me a faint smile.

His white skin had an ashen undertone, and he still had a long way to go in regaining his former body mass. Regardless, I found him very handsome.

"Far from scary," I disagreed.

There was a kind of poetic beauty in the suffering imprinted on his face and body that filled me with sadness. I wanted to erase every single shadow under his eyes and in the hollow of his cheeks, brighten his skin again, and return the lustrous glow to his hair and eyes.

"You are beautiful." I traced the side of his face with my fingers.

He caught my hand in his, pressing it to his lips. "I don't believe anyone has ever called me that." He chuckled against my skin.

Arm around my waist, he yanked me into his lap.

"Be careful," I warned, tensing to keep away from his surgery site. "You're going to hurt yourself."

"I *am* hurting whenever you're near," he stated matter-of-fact, and I spotted the movement of an erection under his bandages.

"Tairan, this must be painful," I said softly and made a move to get off his lap. But he flexed his arm around my waist, keeping me where I was.

"It hurts," he said simply, sliding his other hand up and down my bare thigh under my skirt. "And there is nothing I can do about it yet—that part of my body is not healed enough to be useful." He moved his arm higher, cupping my nape to draw me closer. "But I *need* you close, Isabella. I want to feel you, breathe you." He nuzzled the side of my neck with a deep inhale. "Touch you." His hands roamed over my body as his lips captured mine in a kiss.

Perched on his knees, I leaned into him. Sinking my hands into his hair, I deepened our kiss, every stroke of his lips, every brush of his tongue against mine reassuring me again and again that he was really here now. I'd got him back.

"You know." His breathing was deeper when he broke our kiss. "Before I met you, I ordered myself not to care about you. But you crawled in here," he pressed his fist to his chest, over his heart, "curled up like a baby *edhie* spider in there, and refused to leave."

"I saw that spider in the gardens. It's pretty." Head on his shoulder, I played with a long strand of his hair. "And I care about you, too, Tairan. Very much."

"In this place, emotions are a weakness." His tone sobered, prompting me to glance up at him. "Caring, sympathy, love—all can be used as a weapon against you."

"Is that how Ricread has been forcing you to comply all this time?" It dawned on me. "Is he threatening someone you love?"

The moment stretched into eternity as he hesitated. Our marriage came with no commitment. And there has always been a part of him that I felt had been closed for me.

"You left someone on Keala?" I asked quietly, moving away.

Was there a woman he loved?

The thought was more agonizing than I could have imagined. Without having any confirmation of him being single and unattached, somehow I had allowed myself to believe that he was.

He drew in a long breath.

"The last live birth on Keala . . ." he started.

"I know, I've heard about it. It was a boy."

"Erix. My son."

I shrank back in shock, letting my hands drop from his shoulders.

"Your son?" I stared at him blankly for a moment.

"I was twenty-two when he was born. The Science Group took him right away, but I used all my influence in the Forces to allow him to be raised at home. And for a while it was possible . . ." A shadow crossed his face, his forehead furrowed.

"Where is Erix now?"

"Back in our home, in Atal on Keala, with my friends. I have an agreement with Ricread. He won't touch him, as long as he has me."

"You traded his future for yours."

"Except that Ricread is getting impatient. He is determined to see tangible results of his work before he dies. Erix is ten, heading into puberty soon, and I don't know how long I can keep Ricread's eager hands off him."

SITTING ON THE COUCH in the living area, I waited for Tairan while he was taking his shower. He had refused my help, and I didn't insist when he explained that my presence there would result in another painful erection for him.

Instead, I sat alone, staring at the dark, snowy landscape outside of the huge window as I tried to process what I'd learned.

"Tell me everything," I asked as soon as he was back in the room in his chair, freshly showered and dried off, wearing a loose white caftan instead of the usual grey uniform.

"What do you want to know?" He manoeuvred the chair to the couch, and I helped him take the seat next to me. "Where shall I start?"

"From the beginning. Who is Erix's mother?"

"Adrids, she was two years older than me. We met in the Academy and started seeing each other as a couple shortly after graduation."

"You were never married." I remembered him saying that once.

"No. Marriage no longer exists on Keala. My grandparents were the last of my family who had a real wedding ceremony. My parents lived most of their lives together but never made their union official. Many couples of their generation started to split. Now, many prefer living on their own, having short-term, casual relationships. With the chance of procreation at zero, no one cared about forming a family unit any longer. Adrids and I used to spend time together, sometimes like a couple, other times with a group of friends. We never shared a home, never even talked about living together until she went for a routine medical check-up one day and discovered she was pregnant."

"What happened then?"

His jaw flexed, his throat moved with a hard swallow.

"Adrids never came home that day. The Group kept her in the clinic at their facility. They came for me the day after."

"Was that when you learned you'd be a father?"

He nodded.

"Were you happy?"

"Initially? Scared." He shook his head. "I'd never seen a baby up-close in my life, but I'd heard about pregnancies ending early, fetuses dying in the womb. Maternal mortality rates were high, despite our advances in medicine.

"On Keala, Ricread is lauded as a hero. Back then, he was already well on the rise. His team put Adrids under round-the-clock supervision, promising they'd do everything to keep her and the baby alive and healthy. I agreed to whatever testing Ricread wanted to put me through, thinking I was helping Adrids in some way. I realized later that Ricread was simply evaluating me as his next subject at that point."

"If he is such a miracle maker, why doesn't he increase the fertility of other men, instead of focusing on you?"

"Ricread may think himself a God, but he is not," Tairan scoffed. "Despite his genius, he cannot create life from nothing. He cannot revive dead cells or conjure non-existing sperm. For his experiments, he needed a starting point—a specimen with viable genetic material, which men on Keala don't have."

"Except for you."

He nodded slowly.

"The conception of Erix put me on Ricread's radar. And once I caught his attention, it proved impossible to get away."

"Wouldn't that also have made Adrids exceptional? It takes two to make a baby. Where is she now?"

"Adrids died the day Erix was born. The pregnancy was extremely difficult. She slipped into a coma and would have passed away two months before she did if Ricread hadn't kept her vital functions going. As soon as they got Erix out, they turned her life support off, without asking or even informing me. Ricread declared her body too damaged to maintain even as a living womb."

"Would he really do that?" I gasped, utterly appalled. "Continue to use her as an *incubator*?" I couldn't imagine anyone doing that, even Ricread.

"Knowing him the way I do now," Tairan replied. "I don't doubt he would have."

A rush of cold shivers spread through me at the grave tone of his voice. Wrapping his arm around me, Tairan drew me into his side.

"What did you do then?" I asked.

"After I buried Adrids, my life became a constant race for power against Ricread. The City Defence Forces were still one of the most influential organizations in Atal. I used whatever power I could gain from being in it to wrestle Erix from his hands. I moved my parents in with me, afraid to trust anyone else to look after him while I was at work. I earned the rank of the commander at twenty-six. Ricread and his core team had departed for Earth by that time, and I thought I could keep my boy safe, away from him."

"What changed?"

"There was a power shift about a year later. Ricread made it to the top of The Science Group, and his organization received unlimited authority to act as deemed necessary to preserve our race."

Closing his eyes, he rubbed his forehead.

"Within months of this happening, Ricread's people broke into my home while I was at work and took Erix. My father passed away from heart failure shortly after. I fought for nearly a year to get Erix back, using every legal avenue available. Once it all failed and Ricread personally came back to Keala to take Erix to Earth with him, I walked into his office and offered him a deal."

"You instead of your son?"

He nodded as his chest heaved.

"I signed my body away for the use of science, effective that day, under the condition that The Group left Erix alone." Hands clasped behind his head, he leaned back against the couch. "That was the only thing I asked for. And so far, it's worked. Erix was living in our house with my mother. When she passed away a year ago, a couple of my friends moved in to look after him. He goes to school like every other child did before him. He is the youngest one by five years there. And no matter what, he can't escape the status of a celebrity being, literally, the last Kealan born. But aside from the regular, non-invasive medical checkup once a year, he is not going through any tests or procedures."

"When was the last time you saw him?"

"More than four years ago. They let me see him before I left Keala."

"Have you had a chance to speak with him since then?"

"No." His mouth thinned into a firm line, and his eyes glistened in the light of the room.

I took his hand in mine, stroking it lightly. Keeping Tairan away from his son seemed absolutely unnecessary to the purpose of the experiment. I couldn't come up with any logical reason to do that except it being simply another chance for Ricread to assert his power over Tairan.

"This is incredibly cruel."

"I hacked into the facility communication system." Tairan said, meeting my gaze. "I can't use it too much or risk being caught and stopped, but I've been sending letters to my friends in Atal every month and getting updates on Erix from them. Do you have anyone back home you would like to send a message to, Isabella?"

"Me?" I straightened in my seat.

I'd only been here for several weeks, although it seemed like a lifetime had passed since my nerve-wracking wedding day. My family was not one you'd call close-knit. My mom had never been particularly close to any of us. And my sister and I had our share of disagreements. Still, when I thought about home right now, my heart squeezed with longing. Realizing I might never see any of my family again and not know how they were doing was devastating.

"Wouldn't that mean that you won't be able to send *your* letter this month then?" I asked, careful not to give into hope yet.

"I can wait until the month after. You just got here, I'm sure your family members are losing their minds over what is going on with you."

"The little ones must be missing me," I agreed, thinking out loud. "Mom and Mary are probably wondering, too. Tony will definitely demand some answers once he gets home. And Dad will, too."

"Think about what you want to say to them. I have no access to the English alphabet for you to type it on my arm device. But since it's a much shorter distance, I can send a voice message from you. It will still need to be brief."

Chapter 16

AS PROMISED, TAIRAN sent a message to my sister the very next day. I told her where I was and that I was alive and well. I did not say I was happy.

Neither did I say anything about being pregnant.

Whenever I had imagined having children, my friends and family had always been a huge part of that experience in my mind. But just like my wedding, my pregnancy now was not my own. Instead of feeling joy I would want to share with the world, I was wracked by worry, anxiety, fear, and anger. No matter how hard I pretended to feel nothing at all on the surface as time went by, these emotions wreaked havoc on the inside, wearing me down day after day and week after week.

I caught Tairan gazing at my stomach one day, the soft expression of wonder on his face set an explosion of anger inside me—although not at him.

Any woman, I imagined, would cherish the time spent with her husband, the father of her child, waiting together for the happy arrival.

I was robbed of the chance to appreciate it or the right to enjoy it.

"Don't." I placed my hand over his eyes, unable to stand it. "No matter how long it'll last, it'll never be more than a subject number in a catalogue somewhere, dissected under Ricread's microscope the moment it leaves my body, then placed in a jar on display . . ." My voice broke under the swell of ice-cold dread and sorrow.

I said the cruel words out loud to remind myself what was to come, to keep any hope from rising, to stop any feeling. Yet they cut me sharp from the inside. There was no escaping this pain.

I closed my eyes, struggling to listen to the voice of reason, but the more I actually *felt* pregnant, the harder it was to pretend or ignore. My stomach grew, my breasts felt sore and tender, and the morning sickness got more intense.

Still I resisted allowing the being growing in my uterus to find a way into my heart, because I had no idea how to mend the void it'd leave behind when it was inevitably gone.

Even if this fetus managed to beat the odds and become a baby, I knew it would never be allowed to belong to me, and I had no idea how to prevent that from happening.

ONE DAY AFTER BREAKFAST, Zavis showed up in our rooms, the screen of her arm device glowing.

"There has been some slight modifications to your daily schedule," she addressed me, beaming almost as bright as her screen.

"What kind of changes?" Tairan rose from the couch where he had been showing me more videos of Kealan life—the cave system he had visited while still in the Academy.

With all testing and procedures cancelled for the time being, Tairan had been allowed to recover in peace, regaining his strength and body mass.

I hated to see him tense at Zavis's statement now. My own hackles rose—I rather liked our simple existence of late, and changes weren't always for the better in this place.

"Walking outside has been added to your list of permitted activities," Zavis announced, excitement bouncing in her pretty pink eyes.

"Outside?" It was Antarctica, with temperatures well below zero this time of the year. Still, any chance of getting some fresh air—even if frozen—and seeing the open sky again—even if dark—felt exciting.

"And, Commander . . ." Zavis turned to Tairan. "Your health has been found fully restored. You are allowed to resume your regular level of activity."

He nodded, without saying a word.

I'd noted that Zavis, along with other members of the research team had been abandoning the term 'subject' in reference to us. More often than not, they referred to me by name—which Zavis always did anyway—and to Tairan by rank.

Except for Ricread. He still preferred to address me by nothing at all and often spoke about us to his team as if we weren't present.

Since the confrontation in the clinic, we hardly saw Ricread at all. He seemed to be dealing with us through directives to his people, which I greatly preferred.

"Would you like to go outside now?" Tairan asked, after Zavis left.

"How cold is it out there?"

"Around zero Celsius in the walking area." He went to get our cloaks from the closet.

"Zero? How can that be—is it heated?"

He wrapped the cloak over my shoulders then put his own on and reached for his goggles. "Come, I'll show you."

"THIS IS LIKE A PLANETARIUM!" I tilted my head all the way back to take in the night sky through the high glass ceiling.

We stood in a large, round room, right before the exit to the outside.

"Come," Tairan urged. "We may see the aurora australis if we're lucky. I've read it's active this time of the year."

With his cloak wrapped tightly around him and the goggles firmly on his face, Tairan looked every bit the alien I remembered when we first met.

He checked the entire length of the closure seam of my cloak, from my neck to my ankles, and showed me how to regulate the temperature inside it by sliding my fingers along the hexagonal pattern. Despite the cool air in this room, I felt nice and toasty in my clothes.

The glass entrance opened, and we stepped outside. Cold air touched my face, but it was far from being freezing.

"The walking area runs along the perimeter of the facility." Tairan pointed at the wide path, lined with what appeared to be thin mesh on the packed snow by the wall on both sides of the glass entrance. Outside of the mesh, the snow piled high in drifts.

"The walking area is heated," Tairan confirmed my guess.

The outside walls of the facility were of smooth grey, with a soft glow at the bottom to mark the way. We moved along the path, side by side.

"Is there an invisible fence here?" I examined the edge of the mesh on the ground as we walked. "Anything that would stop us from running out there?"

"No." He turned his head to me, lights streaking his goggles in hexagons. "Just the freezing cold of the Earth's Southern Pole, icy ocean, and vast distance to civilization."

No fence was necessary to keep us in place.

"There is also an electronic barrier," Tairan continued. "In the shape of a dome around the facility. It's not a fence, more like a warning system. The security team gets notified if anyone crosses it."

"Humans?"

"Yes. There are scientific expeditions on this continent. Ricread doesn't want anyone near here. His orders to Earth's government were to keep away from the facility, and the warning system is there to let him know if humans disobey his instructions."

After walking for a couple of minutes, we turned around a corner into compete darkness, with not even the illumination at the bottom of the wall.

"We should see the lights better from here." Tairan slid his hand out through the opening in his cloak and took my elbow.

"Did you turn the lights off in this section somehow?" I ventured a guess, well familiar by now with some of his creative ways of getting around rules and barriers.

"Just for a little while," he admitted, the corner of his mouth lifted in the cheeky smile I loved. "Watch."

With my gaze, I followed in the direction he pointed. A wing of neon green silently swept through the dark sky just over the horizon.

"Wow," I exhaled, watching another wave rise and ebb in the distance. "I never realized they can be this quiet." The eerie silence combined with the stunning beauty of the lights was astonishing. Somehow, I'd expected natural beauty of this magnitude be accompanied by some spectacular noise to match, like thunder and lightning.

"What colour are they?" Tairan asked.

"Green, with a tint of aqua blue right there, this time." I pointed at the curling waves as the Southern Lights moved through the sky in a spectacular lightshow. "Why do you ask?"

"I've read they could also be purple-pink."

"Would those two colours look any different to you?" I moved my gaze to him.

"No. Depending on the saturation one may seem a little darker than the other, but both would remain grey. How different are they for you?"

"Me? To me, green and purple are very different." I paused, wondering how to explain colours to someone who'd never seen them. "If you think about colours like sounds," I started, "the light intensity could be compared to the sound volume. Right? There is the two-dimensional range from darker to lighter, just like volume moves from quiet to loud. Now think about all the multi-faceted variations of the sound intonations, individual tilts, accents, and cadence. They all mix and blend together in various combinations, creating something entirely new, like songs and music."

I watched his face carefully to see if my explanation was making any sense to him. The goggles proved it difficult to figure out his expression, though.

"So, according to that logic, the voice of each person would have its own colour, too?"

"I guess it would." I smiled. "Yours would be purple, like your eyes, I imagine. Although I've heard your voice sounding steely grey, cold and dangerous, at times."

Sliding his cloak open, he reached for me.

"Yours would be a tangerine orange then." He drew me closer.

"Orange?"

"Warm and bright. Sweet and strong. I've read it is the colour of your Sun, late in the afternoon. When it no longer burns your skin, but gives warmth and life."

"Is that how I sound?" I leaned into him.

"That's how you *are*. To me." He brushed the side of my face with his fingers.

Needing to touch him, I opened my cloak, too. Cool air snuck through the opening right away.

"Stay warm, Isabella." Tairan came flush with me. Sliding his hands along the open ends of our cloaks, he merged them together, like a tent, with the two of us inside.

I wrapped my arms around his middle, leaning into his large body.

"You remind me of the *ila* flower," Tairan said softly. If I had to describe his voice in colour at that moment, I'd say the purple had been saturated with warm pink and coral.

"Do they have that flower in the gardens here?"

"No. It's very rare. But I've seen it while cave exploring. It senses any movement nearby and opens up to attract life forms for pollination."

"Hmm, how does it remind you of me, exactly?"

He cupped my face between his hands.

"When the *ila* flower opens, it emits light, so bright it can illuminate a large cave all on its own." He leaned in, brushing his lips against mine in a tender Kealan kiss. "For me, you brighten any room you're in," he whispered against my mouth, then kissed me hard, like a man from Earth would.

His lips parted mine as he searched for my tongue with his. I responded, and he pressed me tighter against him, deepening the kiss further, as if he had been starving for me all this time.

I missed this, I realized, hungrily devouring his mouth. Tairan held me close at night, and I got hugs and kisses from him during the day. But now I desperately needed more.

"What is the cologne you wear?" I murmured when he let me come up for air to nibble at my neck. "I can't get enough of your scent. It makes me want to lick you all over." Burying my nose in his braids, I traced the shell of his ear with my tongue.

"No cologne." He breathed against my skin, prickling it with pleasure. "Just *olmerberry* soap." He walked me backwards and gently pressed my back to the wall. "And you can lick all you want," he added, with a smile in his voice.

I giggled into his neck, the sound coming out a little breathy as Tairan roamed his hands along my body. He slid one inside the low neckline of my dress, cupping my breast and rolling the nipple under his thumb.

Hooking my leg around his hip, I drew him closer. "We're not allowed . . ." I panted, remembering the deal I had made with Ricread and the condition of no intercourse he had added. Alarm rose in my brain through the hazy fog of desire.

"No one needs to know," Tairan growled low, lifting my skirt.

"What if they do the tests?" I hated this—having to worry about *them* when all I wanted was to lose myself in Tairan completely. "They will take you away from me again."

I hugged him tighter, as if someone was already ripping him out of my arms.

He halted the frantic movement of his hands on my body, and I felt the intensity of his gaze on me despite the goggles he wore.

"We won't let that happen, my *ila* flower." He slid his hand up my naked thigh under my dress "There'll be no evidence."

Slowly, I rocked my hips against him, rubbing myself against his erection through the smooth material of his pants. My body responded immediately, starved for his touch, a hot flush of arousal rolled through me.

"I love your resilience," he murmured against my lips, before kissing me again. His chest rose with a deep inhale as he pressed close to me again. "Your fierce loyalty . . ."

I realized he was adding to the list of the things he liked about me again, and I added to mine about him, too.

"I love the way you make me feel, Tairan. When I'm with you, no one else exists." I slid my hands up to his back. Still leaner than he was when I first met him, he had been gaining his former strength back, hard muscles pushing against the material of his suit.

He eased his hand between us, slipping a finger inside me, and I shifted my hips to the side to take more of it in. My hand at his waist,

I traced the line of his suit connecting the top and the bottom parts together, feeling it open under my fingers.

"It worked?" I whispered in surprise.

"I've changed the code for my clothing and added your fingerprints."

"You did?" I smiled, slipping my hand through the gap.

"I liked you undressing me that night and hoped for more of this." With a small groan, he rocked his hips into my palm as I wrapped my fingers around his erection, his hand moving faster between my thighs.

No one needed to know.

This was between Tairan and me, only. At this moment no one else seemed to exist.

Clinging to his shoulders with one hand, I kept sliding the other one up and down his hard length, as he pumped his fingers in and out of me, our breath mingling together in another frantic kiss.

I exhaled a sharp moan into his mouth when the orgasm hit me, hard and strong, and felt him pulse in my hand a moment after.

"Tairan . . ." I trembled in his arms as the last waves of our climax rocked through my body and his. "God, I've missed you." I pressed myself tighter to him, wishing we could just stay like this, outside of the station and everything that was in it.

Chapter 17

DUE TO THE SHARP SPIKE in the numbers on my vital signs chart and whatever else the research team had been tracking during our walk, the time I was allowed to spend outdoors was cut in half. Not that it made me regret our brief intimacy. Besides, now that we both were free to walk anywhere inside the station, Tairan helped me explore the amenities this place had to offer.

In addition to the expansive indoor gardens, the station also had a huge pool area. Here the Kealan plant life had been made to coexist with some of the Earth plants that did not require sunlight to thrive, creating a truly unique piece of landscape, complete with colourful rock formations around the space and along the walls.

The water from the lagoon-style swimming pool placidly flowed into the tunnel-shaped canals that connected the garden waterfalls and a few other water features at the station.

"Tairan, would you teach me to speak Kealan?" I asked one day when we were getting ready to go to the exercise hall also located inside the facility.

"Are there problems with your translator?"

"No. But I want to be able to read and write in your language. Also, I don't want to depend on the translator forever." Ricread could order it taken away any minute, just like he had Gran taken away shortly after Tairan had moved in. I actually missed seeing the blue smiley face. Although, having the robot nearby often made me feel like I was being watched.

Without the translator, it would be like being mute and deaf for me here.

Tairan nodded, unclipping his belt to get ready for his workout. I could see how excited he was about being active again. The energy seemed to radiate from him with his every move.

"Alright, we'll start after lunch today," he agreed. "Just don't mention to anyone what we're doing."

"Do you think they'll object to my learning the language?"

"By gaining a skill that Ricread has obviously not intended you to have, you get potentially more power. If he finds you're doing something like that behind his back, I wouldn't put it past him to forbid it, if only to remind you who is in charge here."

His features hardened, something cold and sharp flashed through his eyes.

Knowing Tairan as well as I did now, I realized how painful it must have been for him to submit to someone like Ricread and to remain in that man's power for years, shackled by his love for his son.

I also understood now why it had been so hard for Tairan to let me in. From the moment we met, he was placed in a situation where he had to act against his own instincts and obey orders against his better judgment. All because Ricread held his son's freedom as collateral. By beginning to care about me, Tairan must have felt he was giving Ricread another weapon to use against him. No wonder, he viewed the affection between us as a weakness.

"Is there any chance for you to ever renegotiate your agreement with Ricread?" I asked quietly. "At least to allow you to speak with Erix regularly?"

"He would never admit there is no chance for a re-negotiation, because he needs to dangle that morsel of hope in front of me every time I rebel." He raked his fingers through his braids, on the way to the exit. "The only way to stop this is to kill Ricread," he muttered under his breath unexpectedly, and I froze in shock at his words. "I swear, I'll do it one day."

"Tairan."

He turned to face me, his expression grim.

"Is there capital punishment for murder on Keala?" I was surprised at myself. Apparently, I did not question the potential murder, just the punishment for it.

"Yes, there is. And that is the only thing that has been holding me back at times." Something raw and painful flashed across his features. "The thought that if I'm gone, Erix would have no family left."

"Oh, Tairan, honey . . ." I wrapped my arms around his middle and pressed my head to his chest.

I could never forget that my current deal with Ricread had an end, and what lay after that was scary in its uncertainty.

THE EXERCISE HALL TURNED out to be a gigantic cavern, with the walls and dome-shaped ceiling made of a material resembling roughly hewn rock. Instead of any known-to-me exercise machines or equipment, various-size cylinders had been placed along the walls, all the way to the ceiling in some places. The rubber-like cylinders seemed to rotate at different speeds.

Without having any exercise clothes and mindful of my condition, I only ventured to use the lowest cylinder, which rotated at a low speed and had handle bars for me to hold on to.

Using it as a sort of a treadmill, I walked slowly in my long dress, holding on to the handles and watching the Kealans climb the walls.

Despite a relatively large number of personnel at the facility, I rarely ran into many of them during my daily routine. Right now, though, there must have been close to a hundred of them in here.

Dressed in their sleek uniforms, some grey for the maintenance people and research team, some black for security personnel, all of them seemed incredibly fit. They climbed the walls of the cavern by using even the slightest protrusion in the rock or hopping from one rotating cylinder to another. I imagined it required a certain degree of skill and coordination not to fall from the constantly rotating cylinders.

Tairan had explained that despite different modes of transportation available on Keala, many excursions outside of homes or city centres still required a hike through caves and tunnels, not all of which would be perfectly horizontal or smooth.

I wondered if this was what gave the Kealans their athletic build. Even Ricread seemed to be in excellent shape—his straight posture and broad-shouldered figure were definitely not how I would envision an aging scientist.

Sweeping the open space with my gaze, I searched for Tairan and spotted his lithe form as he climbed high under the ceiling of the dome. Hanging by his fingers and toes, he went from vertical to being almost horizontal as he progressed higher.

As if sensing my watching him, he glanced my way then let go of the rock to wave at me with his right hand, making my heart skip a beat with worry that he'd plummet to the ground.

The expression on his face, though, was joyous, his smile as wide as could be. And I grinned back, waving at him in return as he started his descent.

As soon as he moved back to the wall, though, Tairan leaped off the rock onto one of the rotating cylinders, positioned high, then quickly hopped to another. Jumping from one cylinder to the next, he descended to the floor and jogged to me.

His body radiated power and energy. Kealan skin never got any colour. Even after exercise, Tairan's remained snow-white, with only tiny beads of sweat glistening on his brow along the hairline.

"How was it?" I let go of the handrail and nearly tripped, skipping a step.

"Come here." He swept me off my cylinder and into his arms. "We don't want Zavis rushing in here with her screen to chastise us about your elevated numbers again."

"You have to be more careful, too. My numbers must have gone through the roof, when I thought you'd fall from under there." I gestured up at the ceiling before hugging his waist.

"I am severely out of shape." He sighed. "But don't worry, I wouldn't fall, this hall is not that difficult in terms of equipment." He drew me in closer. "We need to keep your *spikes* for other occasions." He kissed my hair.

Leaning into his large body, warm from the exercise, I felt as if his strength and vitality seeped into me, flooding me with joy.

All my numbers must have jumped whenever Tairan hugged me like this, but I wished Zavis's equipment were sensitive enough to capture this feeling of peace and security that filled me when in his arms—the happiness I felt with him. Maybe then I'd have strong enough evidence to convince them all once and for all that we were better together than apart.

Chapter 18

ANOTHER AMENITY THE Kealan station on Earth had to offer was a movie theater. Zavis took me there one day and introduced me to two of her friends—Yaee, who seemed to be in her early thirties like Zavis, and Ires, who was older, possibly well into her forties.

Both greeted me in a friendly way and made an obvious effort not to stare at my belly, which had become fairly noticeable by now, even the loose dresses I wore were no longer hiding it.

"Do you have popcorn here, too?" I asked, taking in the large room with circular rows of seating, like in an amphitheater. "To snack on while you watch the movie?"

"Come." Zavis waved me to a glass screen door on the wall, similar to the food compartment in my rooms. "Show me how it looks, the food that you're talking about."

I scrolled through the list of Earth foods, surprised to actually find a picture of a bowl of popcorn on it. Although the description below was in Kealan, by now I had learned the written language enough to understand that there was no salt or butter on the popcorn.

"Here." I pointed at the picture to Zavis, and she quickly made the selection.

"I ordered double," she said to me. "It looks interesting, I want to try some too."

"It won't taste the best without the salt or butter," I warned her. "You guys don't let me have any flavour on my food."

"Most if not all food additives you use on Earth have been found damaging to your health. This is actually mind-boggling." She spread her arms apart in a gesture of confusion. "Why do you deliberately add harmful substances to wholesome foods and ingest them?"

"'Cause it tastes good." I shrugged, not feeling like getting into an argument about human nutrition at the moment.

Since part of my current agreement with Ricread was me eating whatever foods I wanted, the restrictions on salt, coffee, and sugar for me had been lifted. Remembering my part of the deal, though—my promise to take care of my body and health—I had those in moderation. I was keeping an eye on my *numbers* now, too, not wanting to give Ricread any excuse to break our agreement early.

"What movie are we watching today?" I asked.

"Oh, it's a little old but one of my favourites." Zavis took two small bowls of popcorn and handed one to me as we walked back to our seats next to Yaee and Ires. "I find newer movies depressing, to be honest. This one is funny, and it still has live child actors in it, not the computer-generated characters."

"What is this?" Yaee asked, pointing at the bowls in our hands.

"Try some," Zavis offered her bowl to her, after taking one popped kernel into her mouth, too.

"It's popcorn," I explained, stretching over Zavis's seat with my bowl for Ires to try. "People in many places on Earth like to eat it while watching movies."

"Interesting," Ires muttered, sniffing the kernel first.

"The texture reminds me of the *ziboo*, the woodsy mushrooms we have growing in some of the drier caves," Yaee said, taking some more popcorn from Zavis's bowl.

"A little dry," Ires declared.

"Well, it's better with butter," I muttered. "But you'd need a drink either way. I'll get us some." I started to get up, but Yaee stopped me quickly.

"You sit, I'll go," she said firmly, basically jumping out of her seat.

"Is she worrying about my vitals, too?" I asked, watching Yaee rush to the food compartment, her long braids whipping behind her.

"Everyone is," Ires said matter-of-factly. "I check your status first thing every morning, before I even get out of bed."

"It is so exciting to watch her grow." Zavis nodded with a huge smile on her face.

"Here you go." Yaee returned, with four narrow containers of water in her hands. She handed them to us and took her seat.

The theater had filled with Kealans fairly quickly. I knew that everyone had a chance to watch the very same movie on their personal devices in their rooms. Their purpose to be here was the same I had—socializing, even as we all were about to sit quietly for an hour or two.

A tall figure walked past us and crossed the aisle to take a seat in one of the top rows to the right. I recognized the man.

"Valran comes to the movies, too?" For some reason, he seemed out of place here.

"Pretty often." Zavis nodded, staring in his direction.

"Maybe because he works with Ricread," I said quietly, "but he doesn't seem like the kind of man who'd enjoy watching a funny movie. Honestly, he appears to be more of a robot than a man at times."

"Oh, Valran is very much a man." Zavis giggled, stuffing her face with popcorn.

"Yes," Yaee agreed. "I can attest to that, too."

"What do you mean?" I moved my gaze from one to the other, in bewilderment. "Are you saying you . . . um, dated Valran? Both of you?"

"I believe all of us *dated* him at some point. Right, Ires?"

"I can't be sure," the older woman said casually. "I know I didn't have sex with him here on the station, but Valran and I worked together on Keala for a long time before this expedition. I believe we did sleep together once or twice then, but I can't recall it. It must have not been memorable."

"There is no marriage in your culture." I remembered what Tairan told me about Kealan customs.

"No, not anymore." Yaee shook her head. "Personally, I find the concept of marriage fascinating and scary. It seems so very romantic to be with one man all your life. But this is exactly what scares me out of my mind." She laughed. "Having the same person in your space, every day. Why would anyone do it nowadays?"

"Marriage is an archaic concept," Ires agreed. "It only works in primitive cultures where the economic factors force two people to stay together and raise their offspring jointly."

Zavis glanced in the direction of Valran's seat again, with a wistful glimmer in her eyes.

"I've never tried to see anyone on a regular basis," she said quietly. "Never felt the need, before . . . Lately, I've been wondering, though, what it would be like."

Ires followed her gaze then leaned in so that only the four of us could hear. "Valran's pride has been bruised badly. Professor Ricread demoted him in rank and greatly reduced his access level."

"Demoted?" Zavis gasped.

"Who has been promoted to his place then?" Yaee whispered quickly.

"No one." Ires shrugged. "The truth is there simply isn't anyone more qualified to be The First Assistant Professor than Valran on this station. So he is still performing all the duties, but with lower rank and at reduced pay."

"Knowing Valran, you're right, that must have been bruising to his pride." Yaee nodded, a thoughtful expression on her face.

"Why did he get demoted?" I asked, and all three turned to me, staring.

"Um . . . this is way above what you're allowed to know." Yaee frowned.

"Well, I know now," I replied.

"For allowing the administration of anesthetics to the commander, post-surgery, among a number of other violations that have recently come to light," Ires said, her voice firm, her eyes on mine. The way she stared at me made me wonder just how 'unintentional' her revealing this information in my presence was. "He's done a few things without the professor's permission."

"It was Valran who approved the painkillers for Tairan?" I asked.

Ires nodded. "And now he no longer has the authority to do so again. Not anymore. So, when you're no longer pregnant—"

"Ires . . ." Zavis touched her friend's arm as if to silence her.

The round stage in the middle of the room lit up at that moment. Figures rose from it. The clarity and quality of the hologram was good enough to make me believe I was watching a play, with live actors on the stage.

Except that I had a hard time focusing on the storyline of the movie, playing in 3-D in front of me. My brain was still going through the information Ires provided.

I believed I had glimpsed some understanding in Valran before, during our one and only conversation in that crypt of a room. Learning that he had assisted us in some way filled my heart with gratitude. Knowing that he had been penalized for his act of kindness was disheartening and disturbing. Ricread obviously was discouraging his team from displaying sympathy towards us.

Zavis was right to worry about her friend telling me too much—anxiety already crawled through me, like a colony of ants.

Our lives had been relatively calm lately, thanks to the agreement I forced on Ricread, but the time kept ticking by. I splayed my hand on my rounded belly. Sooner or later this would end. No one could tell me when or how, but whenever I dared to think of the future, it was always with dread and fear.

Chapter 19

BY THE END OF SEPTEMBER, the sun had inched up, ready to peek over the horizon, and already lighting the edge of the sky. The long night was about to be over in Antarctica.

Tairan would still come with me for my brief walks outside, but he made sure his cloak was securely sealed at all times, his goggles firmly in place, and his hood drawn low over his face. I sensed that seeing the greying sky with the golden edge over the horizon of the weeks-long sunrise had made him increasingly anxious about going outside.

Twilight was about to set over the Arctic, though, and the entire staff of the facility were getting ready to move from the Earth's South Pole to the North.

"Believe it or not, I think I'll miss this place," I said to Tairan as we walked down the corridors to the landing hangar. "The life here at the station can be enjoyable once you're allowed to explore it. I'll miss the gardens and the swimming pool."

"There are exactly the same gardens and swimming pool in the northern station as they are here." Tairan found my hand through the layers of our cloaks.

"Completely identical?"

He nodded, sending the hexagons flashing across his goggles.

"Both stations were built using the same plans so that the semi-annual moves wouldn't disrupt the life or work of personnel. The biggest difference is the way the two buildings were constructed.

Since the North Pole is not located on a continent, the whole facility there is actually suspended in the air by a forcefield and anchored to Earth-bound coordinates. It basically floats about a metre over ice that is moving constantly." He squeezed my hand. "Once inside, though, I promise you will hardly notice the difference."

Tairan was right. When our flying craft landed in the northern facility a few hours later and we exited into the landing hanger, I couldn't shake the feeling that we'd come right back to where we started.

The hangar, the corridors, the plants, even the cushions on the couch in my rooms seemed exactly the same. The only difference I noticed was the 'unlived in' air in the rooms.

As soon as we settled, our life here closely resembled the one we led in Antarctica, the only difference being that the sky during my walks outside was slowly turning darker now, twilight turning to polar night.

Then one morning, I felt the fetus kick inside my growing belly.

I was in the shower and couldn't believe what I felt at first. Shocked, I watched the soapy streaks of water run down my stretched skin then I actually *saw* the second kick.

Until now, I had attempted to distance my heart from what was going on inside my own body by forcing myself into the mindset of a surrogate—trying to view my body as simply a temporary vessel, a living incubator.

I placed my shaking hand on the spot where the little foot or the elbow had just shoved against my belly from the inside—all my logic and reasoning now torn to pieces at once.

The walls I had been desperately building around my heart all these months shook and crumbled to the ground, knocked down by that one tiny kick.

My knees gave in and I sank to the floor, the soapy water plummeting on me from the above.

I could no longer pretend to be simply a surrogate, because the baby inside me was mine—mine and Tairan's, the man I cared deeply about. But there was also an arrogant, ambitious scientist, cold and ruthless in his drive to succeed, who waited for this baby to be born so he could get his hands on it. And I had no idea how to stop him.

Sitting on the floor in the shower, I shook with tears as feelings of terror and helplessness overcame me.

That was how Tairan found me a while later. He rinsed the soap off me and wrapped me in a blanket from the bed instead of waiting for the hot air to dry me, then carried me to the couch in the living room.

"What are the chances of a live birth now, Tairan?" I asked through tears the question I hadn't dared to ask for months.

"Well into double digits at this point, I've heard," he said somberly, stroking my wet hair. "And inching up with every day."

"Oh God." I exhaled a shuddered breath, struggling to draw air into my lungs. "It *will* be a baby one day. And Ricread will take it away . . ."

Zavis rushed in, her thin white eyebrows drawn into a tight frown of concern. "What is going on? Her readings are—"

"Leave," Tairan ordered gravely, his tone that of a commander, not the powerless subject of an experiment.

"If the numbers turn critical, I'll have no choice but to report it back to the team," she warned, visibly taken aback by his tone.

"I'll handle this."

Still, she lingered.

"Is Isabella okay?" she asked softly as I pressed my face into Tairan's shoulder, struggling to get my tears under control. "I'm concerned about the baby, of course, and her development."

"Just go." Tairan waved her off. "I've got her."

Quietly, Zavis exited the room, but her words still rang through my brain like a bell.

Her development.

I realized the research team must have been able to identify the gender of the fetus by now. They probably knew it all along, since they had been tracking the development on cellular level from before the implantation took place. They had probably tested the chromosomes right away.

Now I recalled a number of references to 'her', thinking at the time they were talking about me, when in fact they must have been referring to the baby.

"It's a girl, isn't it?" I exhaled into Tairan's shoulder. He just stroked my back, without replying. "I've always wanted a baby girl. I even had a name picked—Elizabeth . . ." My voice broke as I spoke about another dream that had been stolen from me. "Not that we get to keep her . . ." Tears choked me anew. "Or even name her."

His arms around me tightened, but he remained quiet, and his silence felt scarier than words. I lifted my head up, needing to see his face. His expression terrified me—every feature appeared hard as rock, a dark storm brewing deep in the violet of his eyes.

Afraid he might do something irreversible, I made a frantic effort to pull myself together, forcing the tears to subdue.

"All is well, darling." I wrapped my arms around his neck, kissing his cheek. "At this very moment, all is still well."

Chapter 20

BY FORCING OUR AGREEMENT on Ricread back in Antarctica, I had managed to protect my daughter from being tested excessively while still in the womb. But with her defying the odds every day, I could not ignore the fact that I would have no agreements to protect her when she was born.

As weeks and months continued to go by, each seemingly passing faster than the one before, worry about the baby grew stronger as she grew bigger.

Tairan had been spending a fair amount of time in the exercise hall. Every muscle in his body felt hard as rock now, his shoulders getting wider and his arms and thighs even thicker than when I first met him. I wondered if making himself physically stronger helped him combat the worry and helplessness I was sure he shared with me.

While he was working out his fear and frustration by climbing the walls in the exercise hall, I walked in the gardens, pretty much for the same reasons. Lately, I favoured the Earth portion—the familiarity of the plants and landscape there seemed to help me manage my anxiety.

One morning, in my last trimester, I entered the open cave with the waterfall and spotted a cloaked figure near the wall. It was very rare to see a Kealan in this part of the gardens.

When the figure stirred and moved my way, I wondered if the person came specifically to speak with me, knowing they would likely find me here at this time of the day. However, I couldn't recognize who it was right away, aside from judging by the shape and height the person was male.

"Bella," the loud whisper came from under the hood, as he came closer and grabbed my arm.

His eyes were hidden by goggles. But I recognised the shape of his chin and his tanned skin, with the familiar shadow of dark stubble that never seemed to go away, no matter how often he shaved.

"Oh my goodness," I whispered, pressing my hand to my chest to calm my racing heart. "Tony! What are you doing here? How?"

"Like I would let the fucking aliens get away with taking my little sister," he scoffed, cocky as ever.

I dragged him into the alcove beside the waterfalls.

"We can talk here, it's a blind spot," I explained, reaching to shove his hood back.

He yanked his goggles off, staring at me with his dark-brown eyes, the same as my father's—and mine.

"Oh, God. Tony!" I threw my arms around him, hugging him tight. "How on earth did you even get in here?"

"It wasn't as hard as I'd feared." He hugged me back. "Apparently, the aliens are super interested in your genetic material and since you and I are related—"

"Oh no." I shrank back, staring at him in horror. "Please don't tell me they've taken you, too."

"No, not like that. They did some testing on me, while I was still locked up. Now that I got out, they brought me here for some more thorough . . . examinations. They're taking me back home tonight, though. Apparently, I am not as valuable as you are." He shrugged easily.

"Consider yourself lucky," I muttered, relief for him flooding every cell of my body.

"I'm not going back with them."

"What?"

"I'm getting you out of here."

"How, Tony?" I asked in disbelief.

"You have their coat." He adjusted the cloak on my shoulders. At this point, I only wore it inside when I had to pass close to the hangar where the air could be chilly. Right now, my cloak was open, the ends of it thrown behind my shoulders. Tony straightened it, closing it in the front. "It will keep you warm outside."

"Where are we going?" Even the shock of finding him here paled in the light of the sudden hope of freedom, so unexpectedly close to me now.

"There's an aircraft waiting for us, just outside of the warning barrier. I can sneak you out of here, following the tunnel of the water canal. See this?" He tossed the end of his cloak back, revealing what appeared to be a clumsier version of the Kealan arm device over his wrist. "We reverse-engineered this, I can scramble the signal of the warning barrier for a few seconds, just enough time to cross it."

"Who is 'we', Tony?" I asked, my head reeling from all of this.

"The resistance group I'm with."

"There is such a thing?"

"We're small, but there are some pretty smart guys with us. We've intercepted one of the Kealan drones, and the guys were able to replicate their DNA tracking function. That's how I've found you here. We'd better hurry." He tugged me further under the waterfall where the channel tunnel began.

"They will look for me, Tony," I warned. "They'll want her back." I placed my hand on my swollen belly. "And they will get violent when they find me gone." I did not doubt that Ricread would stop at nothing, even resorting to violence against humans again, to get the results of his precious experiment back.

Tony's gaze flickered to my belly, his expression darkening. "The assholes bred you."

"A baby girl." I nodded. "She is due in just a few weeks. The first ever Kealan-human child." I paused, Tony did the same, staring at me.

"What's her name?" He asked, finally.

I swallowed hard, clearing my throat.

"I call her Elizabeth. They've arranged for a human doctor, who specializes in high-risk pregnancies and deliveries, to be here for the labour," I explained quietly. "Some complications are expected." I felt her stir inside me and petted the side of my belly soothingly. Drawing a lungful of air, I rushed it out, as if jumping off a cliff, "I'm afraid I can't go with you, Tony."

"Well, we could . . ." He rubbed the back of his neck, hesitating. "We could get a doctor, too."

"A human doctor wouldn't have the Kealan expertise, though. I'm afraid both will be necessary here." My heart sank, as hope left it. "That's not the only thing," I added. "The truth is, Tony, I wouldn't be able to leave her father behind either. He is a subject of the experiment, too. Without me, his life here would be miserable. I'm afraid the head of the research team would take it out on him if he found me gone."

"Bella," Tony gaped at me as if I had suddenly grown a tentacle. "Are you worried about some fucking alien?"

"He is my husband, Tony." I twisted the wedding band that I never took off. "I care about him."

I love him. The realization exploded in my chest, warming my heart.

Even if it weren't for the baby, I wouldn't be able to leave Tairan behind. Grim and silent, cheerful and caring, he had been my rock through it all, my support and comfort. Through the months, he had increasingly become a bigger part of my life, until I could no longer imagine a life without him.

"I love Tairan," I said with certainty. "If I leave, he needs to come, too."

"He is a freaking Kealan, Bella." Tony shook his head, a grimace of disgust on his face. "One of the dirty aliens who took over the Earth."

"Tairan wasn't a part of that." I rolled my shoulders back. "He wasn't even here when the invasion happened. And Tairan has been very good to me, Tony. Better than anyone has ever been before—human or alien."

Stepping away from the entrance to the tunnel, my brother sat on the rock protrusion within the alcove.

"So, you want me to get him out, too?"

"I honestly don't know if it'd be possible for him to leave," I admitted. "Kealan skin and eyes are extremely sensitive to sunlight. Back on their planet they live underground."

"What if we got him a cave?" he suggested, as if it was as simple as getting a real estate agent to find suitable accommodation for my husband.

Still, hope stirred in me anew.

"Maybe if it's deep enough, and at least somewhat habitable, we could make it work?" I said tentatively.

Tony nodded thoughtfully. The active brain of my restless brother must be hard at work already.

"Ricread, the head of research here, would never rest searching for us, though," I pointed out. "The Kealan race is dying, Tairan and I are the only match and Ricread's best bet for continuation of their species."

"I see." His chest rising with a deep inhale, Tony stared at my belly again. "Well, I'll tell you what. You have a way to send messages now. Mary got the one you sent earlier. How about you let me know through her if and when you're ready to get out of here. I don't think I'll find another way to sneak in here again. But I can arrange for the aircraft to land just outside of the barrier. It would take me a week after I get your message, so keep that in mind. You'll have to hike out there yourselves, but we'll pick you up and find a place to hide you two . . ." he glanced at my middle again, "or three, as may be."

"Tony," I stopped him as he rose from the rock. "Thank you so much for thinking of me, for making it here . . ."

"It wasn't that much trouble." He waved me off with a lopsided grin. "Just a few handfuls of sperm . . ." He pumped his fist in the air, laughing at my embarrassment as I placed my hand over my eyes with a groan, shaking my head. "The aliens can have it."

"God, you're simply incorrigible." I gave a slight shove at his chest then grabbed his arm, lest he leave already. It was so good to have someone from back home here. "Listen, tell me, how is every-one there? Mary, Mom, Dad, all the little ones?"

My lip trembled, as the sudden desire to see them all again shot through me.

"They're good." Tony shrugged. "Mary bought a house, right in town. She and the twins have moved out, although she brings them over nearly every day. She's been looking for a job since they turned one, but now that she's got some of your money, I don't think she is in that much of a hurry to start working again."

"Is Mom okay? How is Dad?"

"Yeah, Mom is good. She cut down on the hours she works quite a bit, but is afraid to quit completely, always worried about money running out any minute. The usual, you know."

"I don't think she'll ever retire," I agreed.

"Dad has been home for a while now," Tony continued. "He's doing better on the new meds and even started helping out in the garage again, tinkering with cars about once or twice a week. Johnny is the main mechanic there now."

"Johnny?" A faint echo of a long-forgotten feeling struck a note inside me at this name and vanished quickly, without resonance.

"He is getting married, too," Tony continued. "To Jen Stratton. Remember her? The wedding is this summer. Not sure how long it'll last though, knowing Jen."

"I guess he has finally saved enough to buy a ring."

Tony gave me a long look. "He wasn't good for you, Bell. I wish I saw that sooner."

"It really doesn't matter now. Wish them my best," I said sincerely. "And please say hi to everyone."

"You take care of yourself, you hear me?" He drew me into a bear hug. "I'd better go. Since you're not coming with me, I may as well hitch the ride in their flying saucer and let them take me back home. Those things are cool."

I smiled. "I love you so much, Tony." I held my brother one more time before letting him go.

Chapter 21

WITH TONY GONE, I SAT on the rocky ledge by the waterfall and wondered for a moment if I had made the biggest mistake of my life. This was my one chance of freedom, and I let it go.

Still, the decision to stay felt like the wisest choice, especially with the baby nearing term.

Somehow, against my will, the little being inside me had found a way into my heart, taking her place in it as if she'd always belonged there. Within a very short time, I'd fallen in love with her—completely and unconditionally.

My Elizabeth was what I called her in my mind, because right now, she was truly my own, closer to me than she would ever be again. As long as she stayed inside me, she was safe.

Once she was born, though . . .

My job as her mother, the main purpose of being her parent was to keep my child safe and happy. Now, more than ever, I understood Tairan's sacrifice. Without ever laying eyes on my daughter, I would gladly exchange my future for hers, the way he had done for Erix.

Except that I didn't even have that to bargain with. Everything I had—my life, my body, my future, and my freedom—Ricread already owned. I had nothing else to offer.

There was the very real threat of Tairan being taken from me as well, as soon as the baby was born and my deal with Ricread ended.

Tairan had avoided any direct discussion about the future with me. At times, I even wondered how he really felt about our relationship. Despite the wonderful things he had said to me when we were alone, he had never professed his love to me or voiced any long-term commitment.

I feared expecting anything of the kind from him might be setting myself up for heartbreak—the commitment of marriage hadn't existed in his society for generations. Having recognized my love for him, I wondered what that would mean to him.

Sitting there, lost in my thoughts, I had no idea how much time had passed, until a

cloaked figure turned the corner, heading my way.

"Isabella," Tairan's voice sounded concerned from under his hood, safely pulled low over his face. "Are you alright, my *ila* flower?"

The softness of his voice when he crouched in front of me blew away my doubts like last year's leaves, filling me with the warmth and tenderness I always felt in his presence.

"I'm fine."

"I knew I'd find you here when you weren't in our rooms."

Getting up, I walked to the alcove by the waterfall and behind the protruding ledge to obscure us from view.

"My brother Tony was here," I said softly as soon as Tairan joined me. "He came to take me home."

"What?" He turned around quickly, as if expecting to find Tony hiding nearby. "Where is he?"

"He's gone."

"He left you behind?"

"I couldn't go, Tairan. The baby . . . she'll need the help of the research team to be born healthy. No human ever delivered a Kealan baby, let alone a Kealan-human one. You know there may be complications. She will need all the help there is."

"You could have been out of here. Free." He shook his head, as if not hearing me. "Today."

"And what about you?" I grasped his arms, wishing I could see through his goggles. "You would have been left here all alone."

Circling me with his arms, he slid his hands up and down my back.

"That's not how you should be thinking, Isabella. You have to worry about yourself first—you and the baby."

"It's impossible for me not to think about you, honey. No matter what, we are all in this together—you, me," I placed my hand on my stomach, "and she."

Chapter 22

TAIRAN

Not counting solely on the information provided by the research team, Tairan had read everything he could get his hands on about human pregnancy and delivery. Before Erix was born, he had learned a lot about the Kealan process, too.

Still, he wasn't prepared for the moment it actually started happening. He had thought there'd be some noise—a huge commotion from the research team started by screams of pain from Isabella. He dreaded the time when the pain of labour would hit her.

Instead, it all started rather quietly.

Early in the morning, Isabella turned in her sleep with a faint grunt, a few seconds later the door to their bedroom opened, letting Ricread in, accompanied by the core of the research team.

The lights flicked to life, making Tairan blink. For a moment, the dreadful memories of the morning tests came to mind, tightening his stomach with apprehension.

Today was different, though.

"We'll need you to get out of bed, Commander," Zavis addressed him softly, tugging at the cover.

As always, he winced inside at her calling him by the rank he held in his old position. Technically, the rank stayed with a person to their death unless they'd been dishonourably discharged. But he didn't feel he'd earned the honour of keeping it, since he'd abandoned his job. No matter what the reasons for that were, no matter that he'd do it again, over and over if necessary, he'd left, and he had no right to be called *Commander* now.

"I'm not leaving the room," he warned, getting out of bed. "Isabella?" Moving to her side, he squeezed past the attendants who had already swarmed her.

"I'm good. Honestly." She smiled at him from the headrest, seemingly calm and collected in contrast to the quivering mess he felt inside. "Just some little cramps for now." Grabbing his arm, she pulled him down to her. "Go, put some pants on, honey," she whispered in his ear, sparks of humour bouncing in her dark eyes. "This whole thing may take a while."

Like most Kealans, Tairan slept naked. Getting dressed didn't seem like a priority right now.

"There is nothing here that they haven't seen," he muttered.

"Still, I don't want all these girls to ogle that pretty penis of yours." Her tone was light, teasing. And he realized what she was doing. Facing the pain and uncertainty of labour ahead of her, Isabella was trying to ease *his* worry, thinking about him before herself.

His chest tightened, and he swallowed a huge lump in his throat. Placing a kiss on her smiling lips, he gave her what she wanted—he smiled back, no matter how hard it felt to stretch his mouth and to force his brow to smooth over.

"Don't go anywhere," he said, making an extra effort to match her light tone of voice, then walked to the shelf on the wall where his clothes lay.

Quickly putting his suit on, Tairan closely watched the technicians as they took off the dress Isabella wore to bed then applied a number of sensors all over her body. Combined with the readings that were constantly sent through her arm device, now Ricread could literally monitor and record every twitch of her muscles and every slight change in her blood content, along with those of the baby.

The normalcy of getting dressed helped calm his nerves some-what. When he came back to the bed and met Isabella's gaze again, he was sure his expression was relaxed, his fear hidden securely behind a smile.

"Come here." She reached for him, and he took her hand. "Just stay here, please."

"I'm not going anywhere," he promised, loud enough for everyone in the room to hear, then sat on the bed beside her. "I'm with you."

AFTER HOURS OF LABOUR, Isabella was still working hard. Her gorgeous hair slick with perspiration, her face flushed dark, she clung to his hand like to a lifeline as he watched the energy drain from her over time, helpless to do anything about it.

The bed had been raised, the headboard was removed, and the part with the headrest elevated to place her in a more suitable position.

Their spacious bedroom seemed way too small now, packed tight with personnel and equipment. In addition to the research people, the Head of Security, Sikril, was also present, along with several of his team. Silently, they lined up along the perimeter. Tairan was sure they were here to keep an eye on him.

Doctor Saroyan, a human medical professional, who reportedly had vast experience in deliveries of high-risk newborns and had been highly recommended by Earth's coalition, was allowed to work alongside Ricread today. Her jet-black hair was slicked under a hairband similar to the ones all of the research team members wore. Unlike their grey uniforms, however, she had a white coat on.

And none of all these highly trained, experienced professionals could do anything to ease Isabella's suffering. Gasping for air, during the moments between contractions, she panted hard, her eyes closed.

Something was going wrong. No one had said a word to him to give any updates, but he sensed the tension in the air by the drawn facial expressions of the attendants and by the overall atmosphere in the room that had changed from busy excitement to that of grim focus.

"How is the baby?" Doctor Saroyan asked someone quietly.

"The heartbeat is still there," Ricread confidently replied instead of the person she'd asked.

"It's weakening," one of the Research Assistants, Ires, added quickly.

"I know your goal was a vaginal birth, professor," Saroyan spoke to Ricread. "But I would get ready for an emergency caesarean section at this point."

"You have been made aware, doctor, that Kealan babies have practically no chance of survival unless they travel through the birth canal," Ricread replied, his voice unwaveringly calm, arms crossed on his chest.

"It's been taking too long with hardly any progress. Their condition has been getting worse, you may be risking losing both the mother and the baby," she uttered softly, but the words reached Tairan, piercing him straight through the heart.

A decade-old flashback exploded through his memory—a different room on another planet. But the situation quickly turned similarly frightening.

Another violent contraction rocked Isabella's body, tearing a strangled groan from her throat. She had been denied pain medication out of concerns it might disturb the delicate balance during the labour.

His hand long numb in Isabella's grip, Tairan leaned to her ear, wishing he could absorb her pain for her, and whispered all the things he'd often told her, listing everything he loved about her, hoping that he could help her separate herself from the pain.

"We have a partial abruption of the placenta, Professor." Urgency vibrated through Ires' voice. "She's hemorrhaging."

Unlike Kealan's pale blood, Isabella's was dark. Tairan knew the name of the colour was *'red'*. But to him it seemed to be the same as the grey surgical pad they had placed under her. Flowing out in a pulsing gush, the blood soaked the pad and seeped into the sheets around it, as if the life itself was draining out of Isabella and was absorbed by the bedding.

"You brought me in for my advice, Professor." The stern voice of Doctor Saroyan reached him, a brittle note of genuine fear ringing through it. "I strongly *advise* performing a C-section on this woman. The baby is half-human, she may have a better chance than a full-blooded Kealan. Otherwise, you'll kill her and the mother."

"The baby's heartbeat is faltering," Ires called out.

"Make sure all life-support equipment is connected and functional," Ricread ordered to his team.

"Life-support?" A frown of utter confusion set over the female doctor's face. "This is highly unnecessary right now."

"Trust me, things can change at any moment, considering the circumstances," Ricread retorted, his voice sharp as a laser blade. "I've seen more stillbirths than I care to count. No matter what, I'm prepared for it—I'll be able to collect some excellent data through a full post-mortem analysis."

"I don't understand." Saroyan shook her head, her eyes wide as she stared at Ricread. "Do you actually *want* the baby dead?"

"No. Of course, I'd prefer it alive. However, I find a stillbirth acceptable. It still offers plenty of opportunities for post-mortem data collection and analysis. This is just a first step, doctor. And I am satisfied with the results of this stage."

"Will you deliberately let the baby suffocate rather than do a relatively simple procedure like a C-section and give it a chance?" Sariyan demanded, raising her voice.

Moving his gaze from Isabella, Ricread regarded the doctor with cool disdain. "I will not let you damage the uterus. It is necessary for my future work. I need it intact."

"What do you mean by 'damage?' Women on Earth routinely proceed to have vaginal births, following a C-section. If the possibility of another pregnancy is of concern to you—"

"Just *one* other pregnancy will not be sufficient to complete my research. Neither will *a few*. A scarred uterus has a much shorter useful life."

"But the scars will heal," the doctor protested, her cheeks darkened and her chest rose in quick shallow breaths. "Even with *our* current medical advances, women can still have a number of pregnancies after a C-section. And I've heard Kealan technology for tissue healing is phenomenal."

Tairan felt grateful to the doctor for fighting this fiercely on behalf of his wife. However, the dreadful premonition that she was losing this battle sank heavily into his chest. He froze, keeping quiet so as to not attract any attention to himself while he considered the options for action that needed to be taken.

"We can make it heal faster," Ricread agreed. "However, the strength and elasticity of a scarred organ is permanently compromised. I have at least forty more pregnancies planned for this particular subject. Can you guarantee me that the scars of her uterus won't rupture before she has gone through them all?"

"Forty?" The doctor gasped. "That's scientifically unrealistic."

"For *you*, certainly," he scoffed. "But *I* can and will make it happen. By using my techniques of tissue rejuvenation and maintaining hormonal levels, I can extend her reproductive age well into six decades of her biological age. But I need an uncompromised organ."

"With all due respect, this woman is hemorrhaging, Professor." Saroyan threw her hands in the air, visibly exasperated, then pointed at the screens around them. "Her other systems are in distress. You are in danger of losing your *uterus* altogether."

The grip of Isabella's hand in Tairan's weakened. Her skin felt cool, with a sheen of sweat. Her chest rose and fell rapidly. Tairan threw a glance at Ricread, who turned to his team. "Monitor her vital functions. If any of them fail, replace them by turning the life support on."

"She may not even need the life support if we hurry," Saroyan protested. "I believe, the baby is contributing to the mother's condition. Let's get the baby out now, then we can work on stopping the bleeding and stabilizing the woman. Professor, it's criminal to let this continue. Without the C-section, she'll be brain dead within hours or even less."

"I don't need her brain," Ricread bit out, turning away from the doctor, as if to shut her out completely. "In fact, I would be able to achieve more with the subject being comatose. Her *free will* has caused nothing but interruptions and delays in my work."

"Listen," the doctor wouldn't give up, stepping around Ricread to make him face her again, "you've said before that Kealan sperm does not survive outside of the body. Are you planning to force this man to have sex with his clinically dead wife in order to further your experiments?"

Ricread leveled her with his stare, unyielding in his arrogance.

"If that is what it takes . . ."

Tairan had stopped listening. One thing was perfectly clear to him, Isabella had been mistaken ever believing that Ricread's objective could be aligned with theirs and that he could be reasoned with.

Any trace of kindness or empathy in the man had been killed by cold ambition.

Isabella was frighteningly still now, her chest barely rising in small shallow breaths, her eyes closed.

Carefully letting go of her hand, Tairan quickly scanned the room for any possible weapons, noting the exact location of each member of the security team.

All the medical tools were slim and delicate, securely attached to the robots as parts of bulky equipment, useless to him.

His gaze slid along the belt of the security man closest to him—a laser blade and a stun gun—both were for hand to hand combat. Not pausing to decide which one would do better, Tairan went for both.

Leaping across the short distance that separated him from the guard, he tackled him to the ground. The element of surprise and intense physical training he'd been putting himself through came in handy now.

Easily overpowering the guard, Tairan snatched the stun gun off the man's belt and clipped it to his, then grabbed the laser knife, squeezing its handle to release the hot-white blade.

"Get him!" Ricread cursed under his breath, but Sikril was already rushing across the room to Tairan, a stun gun in his hand.

Another guard jumped onto Tairan's back. With his free hand Tairan grabbed the wrist of the man's hand that held the stun gun, forcing it away—he could not afford to be knocked unconscious. Without his help, Isabella was as good as dead.

With a hard punch of his elbow in the guard's stomach, Tairan shook him off, then reached Ricread in two wide leaps.

"Saryal . . ." Ricread grunted as Tairan fisted his hand in the braids on the back of his head and yanked back, pressing the handle of the switched-off laser knife to Ricread's exposed throat.

"Silence," Tairan gritted through his teeth, giving another firm tug at the Professor's hair. "Stand back!" he ordered the guards and glanced around the room, noting their positions as he backed up to the wall with his hostage. "He dies if anyone moves a muscle."

The research team seemed frozen on the spot. The hands of the guards twitched, though, as they glared at him, obviously going through ways to neutralize him in their heads.

"Sikril, get out." Tairan jerked his chin in the direction of the entrance mark on the wall. "Take your pawns with you. Doctor," he addressed Saroyan as the security team moved to the door. "How many assistants do you need to save my family?"

"Um . . ." She blinked, recovering quickly. "An anesthesiologist, a nurse, an assistant . . . Someone who knows exactly what all of these are." She waved her hand at the robots aligned along the bed.

Tairan swept the research team with an assessing stare. He knew all of them and quickly tried to assess their skills and level of integrity before making a selection.

"Ires, Zavis . . ." He gestured to the women to join Saroyan then faced the remaining members of the research team. "The rest of you, out."

"You'll never see your son again, Saryal," Ricread croaked against the knife handle shoved at his neck, as his team was exiting.

"I won't let you kill her," he replied, his voice eerily calm even to his own ear. *Steel grey*, he recalled Isabella describing it, and his throat tightened.

"She is as good as dead already. And soon, I'll make you wish you were, too."

"That's enough!"

Letting go off Ricread's hair, Tairan unclipped the stun gun with his free hand. Taking a step back, he quickly shoved the gun in the other man's neck and pressed the trigger.

With a jerk, Ricread collapsed to the floor at Tairan's feet.

"Much better," Tairan muttered. "Valran." He stopped the man on his way out of the room. "You'll stay. Seal the door and show your screen to me once done. Doctor . . ."

Already bringing her small team into action, Saroyan glanced at him over her shoulder.

"I want both the mother and the baby alive. Please."

She nodded briefly and turned back to Isabella. The doctor seemed collected and in control, he noted with relief.

Tairan dragged Ricread's motionless body to the corner. Intimately familiar with the effects of the stun gun himself, he knew it would take Ricread at least a couple of hours to come to.

Standing tall, he then surveyed the room again. Following the quick commands of Saroyan, the women were busy. The scanner sensors on Isabella's belly transmitted grey images to the white screen by the bed. Ires put a mask over her face, delivering the anesthetic. Tairan also spotted thin tubes attached to one of the medical robots, guessing these were in preparation to stop the bleeding and provide blood supply.

He caught the confusion on Saroyan's face as she glanced at that and some other pieces of equipment, obviously not familiar with them.

"The entrance is secured," Valran put the screen of his arm device in front of Tairan.

"What's your clearance code?" Tairan demanded, punching the numbers in when told, then coded the door with his own DNA imprint. Now, no one would be able to enter for at least a few hours until they would figure out what he'd done then find a way to override his instructions. He hoped this would give the doctor enough time to complete the surgery. "Shall I neutralize you, too?" He narrowed his eyes at Valran. "Or will you be willing to assist her?"

Valran met his gaze straight on. "I will assist."

"If she dies, I'll kill you all." Said in a calm, quiet voice, the threat came out more like a promise—one he fully intended to keep if anyone hurt Isabella. "Go, do your work."

Tairan watched Valran join Doctor Saroyan as she was getting ready to make the incision. Feeling suddenly exhausted, he fought to stay upright instead of sinking to the floor, next to the motionless Ricread.

It wasn't over yet.

Chapter 23

TAIRAN

The cry was nothing like he remembered. Not even a cry but a soft whimper. It took him a few moments to realize their baby was born. And she was crying.

As if a string immediately formed around his heart, reeling him in, Tairan inched to the bed.

"We're doing well," Saroyan gave him a brief update, immediately turning her attention back to Isabella, as Valran began sealing the incision low on her belly. "I need some help with . . . this thing here." The doctor touched one of the tubes descending from a robot, and Ires squeezed by Tairan to assist her.

Zavis emerged from the group around the bed, with a tiny, pale, whimpering being in her arms. With a wide-eyed expression on her face, she placed his daughter into a niche in one of the robots. Lights flickered, scanning the baby, several sensors roamed over her, some touching her papery-white skin lightly to administer necessary immunity boosters and other drugs that would help her to survive.

"She is moving," Zavis whispered, her expression that of stunned wonder as she tried to catch a tiny leg kicking in the air. "I've never seen a live one before—I was not with the team when Erix was born."

"I've forgotten how small they are." Tairan reached to touch a miniature foot but jerked his hand back when the baby kicked, afraid he might break it—the delicate toes seemed too fragile in their near translucency. "Will she live?"

No one in the whole of the Universe would be able to answer his question with certainty, he was fully aware of that. Still, he longed for some reassurance, anything to be able to allow himself to love this tiny being without debilitating fear. Although, love for her had already flooded every corner of his soul.

"So far, so good." Zavis kept her voice low, as if speaking out loud would invite some evil in. "Her vitals and all other parameters are nearly within the range. Most are rapidly improving." Her fingers tapped with quick efficiency over the control screens of the robot holding his baby. "We'll just make sure she is warm and comfortable . . ." Zavis muttered, adjusting the controls.

The baby didn't seem to be comfortable, though. Her pale little face scrunched into a grimace as she continued to kick wildly.

"Can I hold her?" He asked, on impulse.

"Yes," Doctor Saroyan threw his way over her shoulder. "Can you just open your shirt first?" Hand in a bloody surgical glove, she gestured in front of her chest, imitating opening her clothing. "Skin to skin is the best."

"How is Isabella now?" He made a move towards the bed, but the doctor gestured for him to hold back.

"I'll give you a full update in a minute." She waved him off.

"Commander?" He heard the soft voice of Zavis at his back and turned around.

She stood there, holding his baby in her arms.

"Your suit." She tipped her chin at his chest, and he quickly slid his finger along the centre, opening the top part.

"Here we go," she murmured, helping to place the baby onto his bare chest. "It may be easier if you sit down."

Zavis walked with him to the wall and held his elbow as he sat on the floor, too distracted by the feather-light weight in his arms to bother with looking for a chair.

"I know she has a number assigned already," Zavis said, sitting next to him, too, her gaze not leaving the baby. "But have you thought of giving her a name?"

"Elizabeth," he replied quickly, pressing the baby closer. Turning her to face him, he found she seemed to prefer this position better. Tucking her legs under her belly, bum up in the air, she finally settled—her whimpering stopped—seemingly content. "Isabella wanted to name her Elizabeth."

"I like it." Zavis agreed.

Hand under the baby's soft bottom to hold her in place, he leaned back against the wall, mindful to support her head, too. Gently, he stroked her damp hair—white and straight, like his own.

"She looks just like you," Zavis pointed out. "Although her skin seems just a touch darker than Kealan. I'll have to run some more light-sensitivity tests." Opening her screen, she punched some notes in. "I wonder if her tolerance to sunlight is better than ours."

Doctor Saroyan approached them at that moment. Pausing in front of him, she also lowered herself to the ground, sitting down on the other side of him.

"Sorry, we haven't been introduced. I don't know your name." She stretched her legs in front of her—her white pants and canvas shoes generously splattered with dark blood. "I'm Doctor Anahit Saroyan." She offered him her hand, now gloveless.

"Tairan." Shifting the baby to free one hand, he shook hers firmly. "How is Isabella? Can I see her?"

"She is out for now. I want to keep her under for at least a day, to give her body time to recover. She lost a lot of blood. The Kealan heritage of the baby has added to the complications during the labour and delivery . . . To be honest, all of this wouldn't have been survivable had we been in one of our hospitals. Thank goodness for Kealan technology." She rubbed her face, seemingly exhausted, then slid her headband off. "Of course, no human doctor worth his license would have ever let it go this far." She shot a deadly glare to the corner where Ricread lay. And Tairan followed her gaze.

Dark anger rose in him, making all other emotions fade.

Clenching his jaw, he got up. Shifting Elizabeth to the crook of his elbow, he clasped the laser knife and swiftly moved to the man lying on the floor. Kneeling at Ricread's side, he pressed the handle to extend the lethal blade. The hatred that had been building up inside him for years flared hot, guiding his hand to Ricread's throat.

"Commander," Zavis spoke softly, although no one made a move to physically stop him. "At this point, his murder will bring you more harm than good."

"Right now, he is a national hero," the calm voice of Valran sounded nearby. "Sikril is just outside the door. You will be detained and executed swiftly."

"I must keep this monster away from my family," Tairan gritted through his teeth.

Everything inside him rebelled against murdering an unconscious man, even if the man was Ricread, but he forced himself to focus. He had to protect Isabella and his children. "This may be my only chance to end him."

"With you gone, what will happen to them?" Zavis crouched in front of him.

"As long as Ricread is not here to hurt them—"

"There is still the rest of The Science Group to consider," Valran said, coming closer, too. "Those of them on Keala still trust Ricread. It'll take some hard work and definitely more time to shake their faith in his character. Right now, there will be serious consequences to your actions."

"You'll turn Erix from the son of a respected Force Commander into the offspring of a convicted murderer." Zavis reached out and lightly touched his hand. "Your execution would crush Isabella. There has to be another way . . ."

"My life is already off the table, Zavis. Ricread won't let me live to see another day if I allow him awake."

"He needs you," Valran objected. "You are still an essential part for his research to continue."

Tairan recalled Ricread's words.

'I'll make you wish you were dead.'

"He doesn't need to kill me to make me regret leaving him alive a million times over. He wouldn't hesitate hurting my wife and children either."

"No one, not even Ricread, would dare to harm Elizabeth now," Zavis stated confidently.

"He almost killed her already."

"Not anymore." Ires came closer, the screen of her arm device open. "Yaee has just sent the media package with the live birth announcement to Keala. There is no way to stop the transmission. In a few hours, this baby will be a celebrity—our hope, loved by all. Hurting her in any way would turn Ricread from an interplanetary hero to a publicly despised criminal. He wouldn't risk that."

Tairan didn't come up from his crouch, but his hand relaxed on the knife handle, extinguishing the laser blade.

Zavis was vigorously punching into her screen. "I'm requesting her to add a note to the media release that your commendable actions saved the lives of both mother and child. That would put you into the public eye again and should keep Ricread at bay in his personal vendetta against you." She finished sending her request and met his eyes again. "As long as you stay alive, you and your family have a chance at a better future."

In his mind, he quickly went through the options. The best solution was to get Isabella and Elizabeth away from here and out of Ricread's reach. Thanks to the contact made with Isabella's brother, there was a real chance for that to happen now.

Zavis was right, he needed to be alive to accomplish that, even if it meant leaving his sworn enemy live, too.

"Did you say the baby would be able to withstand sunlight?" he asked Zavis.

She flicked her short braids back. "The early tests aren't conclusive enough, but her skin is slightly darker than ours. She could only get the pigmentation from her mother. In which case it may be assumed that the ability to withstand sunlight has passed on to her as well, at least to some degree."

"When can you confirm that?" A plan had been forming in his head, but he needed to be certain.

"She'd need to be a little older for further testing."

"How long until you can do that?"

"A few weeks. I'll make sure to find a way to get the results to you when I have them."

"Thank you." He rose to his feet, facing Doctor Saroyan.

"Tairan. I'm expecting to be taken off this station the moment this one wakes up." She tipped her head in the direction of Ricread, without sparing the professor another glance. "Your family will need some care to recover and thrive. I'll leave some instructions, especially in regards to the care of the baby, since Kealan knowledge on that subject is lacking practical experience. Which one of these individuals do you trust with looking after your loved ones?"

Tairan swept the room with his gaze, briefly pausing on each face, looking for a person with compassion and decency, who would think twice if ordered to harm a woman or a baby. He had no authority on the station himself, and he needed someone who did.

His gaze caught Valran's. The other man didn't waver under his scrutinizing stare. Nevertheless, Tairan's skin crawled with suspicion, when he thought about seeing Valran's face at every procedure that had ever been done on him. For years, Valran had been Ricread's right hand in everything, standing in his shadow.

He'd heard that Valran had been demoted and therefore lost some of the authority and power he needed him to have. That said, the reason for Valran's demotion was his authorization of painkillers for him, when he lay blinded by pain, post-surgery.

"Can you promise to keep my wife and daughter safe in my absence?" He asked Valran straight up. After what he had done today, Tairan harboured no illusions—he would be separated from Isabella and the baby just like he had been separated from Erix. But he needed some time to organize an escape for when Isabella and the baby had recovered enough.

Valran inclined his head.

"I give you my word."

Zavis moved into his line of view. "I had been made the lead of the team appointed to take care of Elizabeth. If you let me, I'll promise to take the best care of her."

For one long moment, he examined her expression, searching for anything that might make him refuse her request. Not finding it in her open, eager face, he nodded, and she faced Saroyan.

"Doctor, I'll gladly listen to any information you have on how to best keep Elizabeth happy and healthy."

"Can I see Isabella now?" he asked Saroyan before she started with the instructions.

"Yes." The doctor nodded.

He went to the bed and sat at Isabella's side.

Her skin seemed lighter than usual, except for around her eyes where it sank into dark shadows. The tangled mess of her wild hair sprung from under the hairband the team had put on her before the surgery. Resting Elizabeth in the crook of his arm, he lifted a dark, curly strand that had fallen across his wife's face and moved it behind her ear. Her eyelids fluttered, but she didn't wake up.

"I love your strength." His own words filled him with hope. No matter what the future held, he trusted Isabella's resilience. He believed she'd cling to life the way he'd seen her cling to joy. "I love your stubborn persistence and optimism."

Isabella had shown up in this gloomy place, like a ray of warmth and light, breaking through the darkness. She revived his senses and gave him back his zest for life. Whatever their reality had been, she lightened it and lifted him up.

"I love *you*, my *ila* flower," he whispered in her ear, desperately wishing she could hear him.

He'd never said these words to her, afraid that uttering them out loud would make them both weaker and their enemy stronger. The feelings for her had been growing inside him, to the point that it was impossible to keep them to himself now. Astonishingly, voicing his confession made him feel more powerful than ever before. There was nothing he wouldn't crush if it stood between them.

"I'll get you out of here. Promise." He kissed her gently.

"The professor is moving." Ires warned from across the room.

"They're attempting to hack the door code, too." Valran stared at the screen of his device.

Tairan got up, turning to Zavis. "I want to see Isabella when she wakes up."

She cleared her throat. "With Elizabeth's birth, Isabella's agreement with the professor has ended—you won't be allowed to stay together. The next insemination is scheduled for three months from now."

"Three months?"

"It's too soon, considering her situation," Saroyan objected.

"Ricread is accelerating the whole process," Zavis explained. "The protocol to stimulate ovulation cycles in Isabella is to begin in a month, along with some procedures scheduled for the commander around the same time."

"Three months is a long time for me to wait, Zavis." Tairan stared at her, trying to gauge how much he could count on her, if at all. "I'll need to see her sooner."

She shot a quick glance in Ricread's direction then took a step closer, lowering her voice. "The instructions were to move you back to the clinical wing. But there were no *explicit* orders to strip you of the privilege to walk about the station."

"Thank you." He inclined his head in genuine gratitude. Having some freedom to move inside the facility gave him a better chance at bringing his escape plan to life.

Tairan harboured no illusions about Ricread getting his revenge on him sooner or later. He had overstepped the man's authority, humiliated him in front of his team. Well familiar with the moods and the character of his adversary, Tairan fully expected some grim consequences.

Valran was right, however, Ricread still needed Tairan alive. At least for a little while, as the Head of Research, he'd have his hands full with the impending media storm.

That should give Tairan some time to get everything ready. Getting Isabella and the baby out of the facility was now his top priority, no matter the price.

An alarm came from Valran's device, alerting of a series of attempts to break the door code.

"It's time." Tairan kissed the soft fluff of his baby's hair and handed her to Zavis, heading for the sealed door.

Touching his hand to the entrance sensors, he opened it, coming face to face with Sikril. The Head of Security held up a set of restraints, his expression cold.

"I'm ready," Tairan nodded.

Chapter 24

FOR A WHILE, I HAD no idea where I was. Then awareness slowly returned and with it the soreness in my lower belly. With a groan, I threw my arm across my middle, searching for the source of pain. My body felt smaller than it should—lighter. The weight that used to compress my spine, preventing me from sleeping on my back, was no longer there.

Elizabeth!

Fear jolted me fully awake, although I still struggled to open my eyes completely—my eyelids seemed unnaturally heavy.

Where was she?

Slowly, the memories started coming back, like a stack of images and sensations, sliding in one by one.

The concern on Tairan's face, no matter how hard he tried to hide it.

The sensation of his hand in mine, anchoring me to him, as the swells of breathtaking pain rolled through me.

"Tairan . . ." I managed, my voice sounding strangely distant as if it wasn't my own.

"Can you open your eyes, Isabella?" A soft, female voice asked. I had a feeling I knew the person speaking, but couldn't think of her name or recall her face at the moment.

"Is the baby . . . well?"

"Yes, she is right here. You can see her."

Relief rushed me in a warm swell.

"Yes, please, I want to . . ." I stirred, struggling to gain full control over my unruly limbs in an attempt to get up.

"Here, let me help you."

With a soft whirring noise, the surface behind my back rose, slowly putting me in a sitting position.

"Better now?"

I blinked, finally opening my eyes, the light no longer seemed to be directed straight at me.

"Zavis?" I stared at the smiling face that finally merged with the name in my mind.

"Yes!" She nodded enthusiastically. "I have Eli . . . um, the baby right here." A shadow crossed her face as her eyes momentarily flickered to the side.

Following her gaze, I stared straight at Ricread, standing at the foot of my bed.

"Status?" He snapped, not taking his stare off me, the expression on his face even more severe than usual.

This time someone else gave him the numbers, as Zavis had her hands full with a small bundle.

"Here you go," she whispered quickly, pressing the baby into my chest.

Automatically, I lifted my arms to accept.

My baby.

Mine and Tairan's.

Her father's heritage was prominent—Elizabeth had his pale skin and long, white hair. The hooded blanket she was wrapped in couldn't completely hide her downy strands that extended past her shoulders, much longer than any hair I'd ever seen on a baby.

Her eyes were closed. She appeared to be sleeping peacefully, but her stillness alarmed me.

"Is she okay?"

"Just a little sleepy." Zavis smiled.

"She needs nourishment." Ricread's voice, cold and resentful, was out of place in the room with my sleeping angel. "Human milk is the optimal sustenance to ensure her survival."

"Is she in danger?" I pressed the small bundle closer to my chest, as if that alone would keep her safe.

"The risk is always there," he dismissed my concern. "The feeding schedule is every two hours, around the clock, to stimulate milk production and build a sufficient supply. Her first meal is due now." Ricread glanced at one of the two security guards standing silently by the wall. "They will be present at every feeding."

"Where is Tairan?" I asked quickly.

He threw over his shoulder on his way to the door, "I've told you all you need to know."

Ricread fixed his stare on Zavis for a moment. She blanched, fiddling with the end of one of her braids, then sank into a chair by the bed as soon as he left.

"Where is Tairan, Zavis?" I immediately turned to her.

"Your level of clearance does not allow for status updates on the male subject," she said loud and clear. By the way her gaze jerked to the direction of the guards, I understood the statement was for their benefit.

"Has he seen his daughter?"

She didn't answer out loud, but the barely discernible nod of her head, combined with a tiny smile let me know that he had. I exhaled a long sigh, fighting the tightness in my chest as worry for him descended over me.

The baby squirmed in my arms, bringing both of our attention to her. Her eyes firmly closed, only the tips of the snow-white eyelashes visible, she seemed to struggle against the blanket, which restricted her movements. The little face scrunched tight, turning a faint shade of pink, which brought out her white eyebrows in contrast.

"She must be hungry," I said softly, stroking the side of her face gently.

"Must be," Zavis chimed in, enthusiastically. "She slept for hours. It was such a beautiful sight to watch her."

Shifting the baby to one arm, I tugged down the cover, freeing my breast. Acutely aware of the stares of the guards by the door, I lifted Elizabeth higher, trying to shield myself with her tiny body.

"Let me help you," Zavis said quickly and moved to the bed, placing herself between me and the guards.

Trying to remember how Mary did it, I held up my breast, pressing the tip to Elizabeth's mouth. She eagerly moved her head, searching with her parted lips, then latched on to the nipple quickly.

"She looks like she knows what she is doing." Zavis laughed.

"That makes one of us." I huffed a laugh, too, amazed to feel the rhythmic tugs of the baby's mouth on my breast. "I don't even have any idea if my milk has come in yet."

"Well, she is working on getting something," Zavis pointed out.

As if knowing that we were talking about her, Elizabeth opened her eyes, gazing up at me.

"She has your eyes!" Zavis gasped, bringing a hand to her mouth.

"It can't be," I shook my head even as the evidence was literally staring me in the eye. "The irises of human newborns are almost always blue at first. They normally change weeks if not months later."

"Well, she is only *half*-human," Zavis argued.

That was true. The first ever human-Kealan baby, Elizabeth was one of a kind, truly unique. Who was there to tell how my baby should look and grow? There had never been anyone like her before in whole of the Universe.

Staring up at me with her dark-chocolate eyes, which seemed eerily out of place yet so wonderfully fitting under her snow-white eyelashes, the baby kept sucking, an expression of intense concentration on her tiny, pale face.

An all-powerful feeling of love flooded me from head to toe. There was absolutely nothing in this world that I wouldn't do for her.

"I love you, baby," I whispered, stroking the small fisted hand that she had worked out of the blanket. Immediately, she grabbed on to my finger, holding tight. "I'm not going anywhere." I smiled. "I'll always be with you, for as long as I live."

At that moment, I didn't care that we were both prisoners in this place, vulnerable to the whims of an evil man. I made her a promise, and I fully intended to keep it.

Chapter 25

IT HAD BEEN WELL OVER a month since Elizabeth's birth, with no news of Tairan. In some truly dark moments during that time, I doubted he was even alive.

Pleading with staff for any information on his health and whereabouts got me nowhere. And I believed that was part of the plan to keep us apart, devised to torture me in retribution for the agreement I had forced on Ricread earlier.

Tairan was absolutely right when he warned me not to show any signs that I cared about anyone, my love for him was now used against me. After weeks of not knowing, I was ready to do anything for any piece of information about him.

The grim expression on Zavis's face every time I mentioned his name terrified me. My mind swung from one horrific scenario to another—from dreading he was dead, to being afraid to think in what state he might be kept alive.

The scar on my belly healed to nearly invisible within days, but because of it being there in the first place, I knew that Elizabeth was born by C-section. Although, no one gave me any details about her delivery, either.

Nursing Elizabeth continued to follow the same feeding schedule—every two hours, day and night. Zavis was always the one who brought her to me, accompanied by the two guards from the security team.

Both Zavis and I were sleep deprived after the six weeks of waking every two hours, but Ricread refused to change the schedule even when Elizabeth started skipping meals, especially at night, obviously more in need of sleep than food as she grew.

For me, the days and nights had merged into one. With perpetual darkness outside the huge window in the living room, I had to closely follow the clock if I wanted to track the time, which I cared less and less about.

Sitting on the bed one day, with a bowl of 'crispy rice in yogurt' I was still able to get a couple of times a month thanks to Tairan's rigging the food unit, I lost track of time and didn't realize it was another feeding until the door opened and Zavis walked in with Elizabeth in her arms.

"What is that?" She stared at my bowl, catching me red-handed—a spoon full of creamy substance with chocolate-coloured balls in my hand. "Those are *ecoot* beetle chitin sheddings, aren't they? In *garula* moth yolk protein. I don't believe either are on the list of approved foods for you."

"Great." I dropped the spoon into the bowl. "I knew it had to be something nasty, but really didn't care to know exactly what. You just couldn't let me keep believing it was crispy rice, could you?"

"Um . . . okay." She sat on the bed, placing Elizabeth in her lap. Having eaten well two hours ago, the baby appeared to be in a deep, contented sleep. "It is *crispy rice*, if you want it to be. How did you get it, though?"

"Well, it's too late now." I frowned at the offensive brown balls in my bowl. "I already know what they are. Some beetle waste . . ." Picking up the spoon, I stirred the creamy mass in my bowl. A whiff of delicious aroma reached my nostrils, making my mouth water. "Ugh, whatever." I took another spoonful. Enjoying the fragrant sweetness on my tongue, I tried not to think about where it came from. "I've already eaten a whole bunch of gross-sounding things. Who cares what it is as long as it tastes good, right?" I shrugged, quickly finishing the bowl. Now that Zavis had caught me, this would surely be my last time eating it.

"Did the commander do something to your food unit?" Zavis asked, narrowing her eyes at me. "Kealan foods are not on your menu list."

"What difference does it make now?" I sat the empty bowl aside and reached for my baby. "I'm not even pregnant anymore."

"Still, you shouldn't—"

"How is Tairan?" I asked, not expecting her to answer, but wanting to stop her before she delivered some lecture on optimal nutrition for nursing mothers or worse—potential perils of violating Ricread's rules.

Snapping her gaze to mine, she rattled out quickly, "You don't have the clearance to receive this type of information."

The words I'd heard at least a thousand times before. The expression on her face, however, was different. Staring at me, with a wide smile, Zavis appeared excited—happy even—making relief spread through me. I took this as her way of reassuring me that Tairan was alive and well, which was the best news of him I'd gotten since the birth of our baby.

"Oh, my goodness," I breathed out, pressing Elizabeth to my chest. "Thank you. Thank you so much," I whispered, barely audible. Still, she glanced cautiously at the guards, as if warning me to tone down my gratitude. I dropped my gaze to my baby, in an attempt to hide the enormous relief that must be plain to read on my face.

A dark-brown gaze greeted me. Seeming fully awake now, Elizabeth squirmed in the blanket, as if struggling to free herself.

"I think she wants this off." I tugged at the blanket, unwrapping her.

"Did she poop, maybe?" Zavis leaned over my lap.

The white stretchy shorts Kealans had for babies were designed to fully absorb and process any liquids and smells. However, some residue after a bowel movement could still irritate the baby's skin, which made changing them still necessary from time to time.

"Don't take her away, you just got here," I asked, not ready to part with my daughter whom I never could get enough of no matter how frequent the feedings were. "Let's just change her here quickly."

Shifting on the bed, I made room to put Elizabeth down, and Zavis opened the shorts on the sides then slid them off for an inspection.

"No," she said thoughtfully, examining the inside of the shorts closely. "These are still clean. She must have just wanted to stretch her legs."

Her arms and legs in the air, Elizabeth kicked with abandon, moving her wide-eyed gaze from Zavis to me.

"Does it feel nice?" I cooed, pretending I was trying to catch her fists and feet. "What a butt-naked cutie pie you are."

One small leg stretched with a kick, and a tiny blob of pink on her belly caught my eye.

"What is this?" I held her other leg down, finding another pink drop, identical to the first—both positioned low on her belly, opposite of each other. "This is healing gel." My stomach dropped at the dreadful realization of what that must mean. "Zavis, why are there two puncture wounds on my baby?"

"I—I'm not sure." She faltered under my glare. "I'm not always with her—"

"Then who is?" I jumped off the bed, my hands shaking as terror and rage filled me at once. "Since I'm not allowed to keep my child with me at all times, who is responsible for looking after her when she is not here?"

"I am the lead," Zavis explained, seemingly confused. "But there are six of us on the team. I must have dozed off . . ."

"*Who* did this to her?" I shouted, anger taking over every other emotion in me. Although, I already guessed the answer to my own question. "Get him in here now!" Grabbing the baby off the bed, I rushed for the entrance wall. "Open the damn door!" I yelled at the guards then pivoted back to Zavis. "I want to speak to Ricread, *now*."

"I'll let him know." She clicked her screen open. "But I can't promise he'll see you—"

"Oh, he'd better," I gritted through my teeth, pacing wildly along the wall, Elizabeth pressed to my chest. "I want answers, and I swear I'll find a way to get them!"

Fury burned hot in me, fuelled by the frustration of the last weeks. Even the guards took a step back, letting me pace to my heart's content.

"He already has *me* to do with as he pleases," I kept raging, addressing no one in particular. "God only knows what he has been doing to her father all this time. He *cannot* touch her!"

"Yes I can," came the cool reply from behind me, prompting me to turn on my heel to the open entrance in the wall.

Ricread stepped into my bedroom, Valran right behind him—a shadow of his boss, like usual.

"What was the reason to take me away from my analysis?" Ricread inquired calmly. "It better be a valid one."

"What are you doing to my daughter?" I moved on him, but the guards stepped between us.

"She is the subject of my research, first and foremost." He crossed his arms over his chest, taking his usual wide stance.

Mindful of Elizabeth in my arms, I didn't launch for him, although the urge to hurt him burned through me.

"She is six weeks old! What can you possibly be *researching* in a baby?"

"I have absolutely no obligation to give you any explanation whatsoever. Our agreement has long ended, and it never applied to the baby in the first place. She is the result of *my* experiment and is the newest subject of *my* research.”

“She is only a baby, for goodness sake.” Pressing Elizabeth to my chest, I backed away from him, as if I could take her far away from this monster.

“To me, she is a female, with over a million eggs in her ovaries and a brand-new uterus.”

“What are you talking about?” Horror pressed heavy on my chest, making it harder and harder to breathe. “What are you planning to do with her?”

“Again, I’m not obligated to share anything with you. However, I feel inclined to give you a glimpse into the future, if you insist.” A cruel glint in his eyes alerted me to the true reasoning behind this sudden sharing of information—he knew it’d hurt me and derived pleasure from that. A highly vindictive man, Ricread surely couldn’t forget my win over him that one time. “Since my previous plans have been severely impacted by the actions of your so-called husband, I was forced to make some adjustments to the course of the experiment.”

“What adjustments?” I whispered, dreading his answer.

“So far, the new subject’s eggs have tested perfect.”

“You’re testing my baby’s eggs,” I muttered, staring at him blankly, my outrage frozen by shock for a moment.

“I have put a protocol in place to accelerate the process of her maturity. In six to eight years, she will experience the onset of puberty and will reach full sexual maturity by the age of twelve, ready to be bred—”

“Stop it . . . You can’t . . .”

“The main objective has always been to breed the human portion out of the subjects’ DNA, bringing the ratio back to what it currently is in Kealans—thus essentially re-creating our race.” His face lit up more and more as he spoke. Stunned, I realized he truly, passionately believed in what he did. For Ricread, this experiment was larger-than-life, any life. And all of us—myself, my family, even the staff—were but a means to get him the results he strived for, nothing more but *resources* to fulfill his ambition. "For that, the new subject will have to be bred with a pure-blooded Kealan."

"There is no male, capable of reproducing on Keala . . ." I whispered. "Except for her father. Surely, you wouldn't . . ."

"I would, if I had to. Although, her father may be past his prime by then, with his reproductive functions diminishing. There will be another, younger male, however—"

"Erix."

"Exactly."

"He is her brother!"

"*Half*-brother. I am able to block the harmful genes, thus eliminating the negative effects of inbreeding. Their offspring, however, will be significantly more Kealan than human."

"You can't touch Erix. His father gave up everything to make sure you would stay away from his son."

"I still have at least a decade to figure out the details. However, the recent success has opened doors for me that may have previously been closed. I'm confident I can get access to any resources I need if I can present my case to The Group in a compelling way."

Horror shook me to the point that I was afraid I'd drop Elizabeth. I clutched her tighter, making her squirm in protest.

These were not just some delusional ramblings of a lunatic. Ricread had the means and the power to bring his plan to life. He had been unstoppable in his ambition. By successfully breeding two sentient species, he had become untouchable.

"This is so wrong." I shook my head. "Can't you see how many lives you'll ruin during this process? Including the lives of children yet to be born?"

"I've given my own life for this cause. I will not stop now over the concerns of the lives of others. Besides, what are a few individuals if I give a future to an entire race?"

"A race that demands sacrifices of children does not deserve to have a future."

MY KNEES GAVE UNDER the burden of the horrible picture that Ricread had painted for my family. Zavis grabbed Elizabeth out of my arms, as I sank to the floor when he exited the room.

"This can't be happening," I muttered, feeling gutted. "You know this isn't right," I said to Zavis, searching her face as she avoided my gaze. "He may have tricked the rest of Keala into lauding him as a hero, but you *must* see him for what he is." I glanced around the room, pausing to stare at everyone in turn. "Is this how you want to bring life back to your planet? I'm sure deep inside you *know* that what he is doing is wrong."

With an apologetic expression on her face, Zavis slowly backed to the door with Elizabeth. Valran stopped her by putting his hand on her shoulder.

I addressed him. "If you know he is wrong, you can't obey his orders and remain true to yourself. Every time you agree to follow his rules, it chips away at your integrity—little by little—until one day you will no longer recognize the person you have become."

Valran gave me a long stare before replying, "It is not easy to stop a rolling boulder. One risks being crushed, accomplishing nothing."

He turned away and left swiftly.

Before following him, Zavis paused. She caught my attention then directed her gaze upwards, pointedly, as if trying to show me something.

I stared up, too, as the wall between us solidified. There was nothing but the entrance mark.

A sudden thought occurred to me. Rising on my weakened legs, I moved to the wall. Leaning my forehead to it, I counted down to give Valran and the guards sufficient time to walk away then stepped back and ordered, "Open."

My heart skipped as the wall in front of me shimmered and thinned forming an opening into the corridor. With a quick glance to make sure the space was empty of guards, I dashed to the closet to grab the cloak I hadn't used in weeks.

Wrapping myself quickly, complete with the hood fully drawn over my face, I slipped out of my bedroom and ordered the door closed behind me.

Chapter 26

I HAD LESS THAN TWO hours before the next feeding when Zavis and the guards would be back in my room. And that was only if security hadn't caught the image of a cloaked figure leaving my room and decided to investigate.

Without pausing, I headed straight to the clinical wing, determined to search for Tairan. I believed there was a reason why Zavis left the door unlocked. She knew I wouldn't run away from the station without Elizabeth, but she gave me a chance to exit my rooms. And I hoped it was because Tairan was also out there somewhere where I could meet him.

Passing through the gardens, I made a turn to the Kealan waterfalls first, just on the off-chance Tairan was there. Not finding anyone by the waterfalls in the Kealan portion of the gardens, I decided to check the part with the Earth plants, too.

A black curtain separating the two sections had a warning in glowing letters in Kealan on it—cautioning about the harmful effects of sunlight. Reading it was easy for me now, I'd spent hours practicing my Kealan when on my own. Before Elizabeth was born, Tairan used to scramble the signal of my translator for about an hour a day, during which time we would speak his language in order to work on my pronunciation, too.

Slipping under the curtain, I entered the wide, brightly-lit tunnel, with walls covered by green vines. A short distance farther, the tunnel opened into a spacious cavern, with a blue ceiling, imitating the sky.

I inhaled deeply—even the air here had the quality of that outside on a warm, sunny day. Spending weeks locked in my rooms, this now felt very much like being in a summer meadow somewhere.

Savouring the warmth of the 'sunshine' on the exposed parts of my face and hands, I moved along the stone path in the tall grass, crossing the open space to the waterfalls. The air here was thick with mist.

"Isabella."

I barely heard his voice through the crashing noise of the water, yet I recognized it right away.

"Tairan?" I rushed to the niche beside the falls.

A tall, cloaked figure dragged me behind the stone ledge.

"It is you!" I shoved his hood off, touching his face. His goggles were on, but I recognized the hard line of his jaw, the sensual curve of his mouth, the rise of his cheekbones.

"Are you well? Healthy? How are you feeling?" I kept asking, peppering his face with kisses.

Slipping his hands under my cloak, he yanked me to him, hungrily kissing me back.

"I'm fine now, with you," he groaned against my neck.

"God, I've missed you," I murmured, nuzzling the skin just above his ear, my heart feeling ready to burst from the pure pleasure of being in his arms again. "I've worried, so much . . ."

"I love you, Isabella." He leaned back, yanking his goggles down, and I met his intense stare in the shade inside the alcove. "I should have told you sooner. I should have said it to you every day."

Sliding my hands under his braids and around his neck, I drew him close.

"I love you, too." My breath caught in my throat, suddenly depriving me of words. Instead, I rose on my tiptoes, reaching for a kiss.

Eagerly, he covered my mouth with his, parting my lips. The kiss was fervent, hungry, passionate, and messy, yet absolutely perfect.

Finally, he let me come up for air, both of us panting.

"How is Elizabeth?"

Ricread's words rose in my mind, spreading a chill through my insides.

"Tairan . . . They're testing her. Ricread has a protocol in place to speed up her maturity. He'll breed her before she is even a teenager . . ." Closing my eyes, I drew in a lungful of air, forcing the horror down for now, so I could continue to speak. "We need to get her out of here."

"And we will," he said, with hard determination in his tone, then freed his arm from the cloak, flicking the screen of his device on. "Can you read this out loud, please? In English?" He pointed at the Kealan writings on the screen. "I'll record it right now and send it to your brother."

I skimmed over the words quickly, to get the meaning of the message. Tairan was requesting Tony pick us up in a week, the exact length of time my brother had said he needed to arrange for the aircraft.

"I'll have to find a way to get Elizabeth."

"Here." He pressed a smooth cylindrical object into my hand. "Hide it. Don't let anyone see it."

"What is this?" I examined the heavy, dark-grey cylinder with a metallic sphere on one end.

"A stun gun. I stole it the day Elizabeth was born. Hold it like this." He made me wrap my fingers around the cylinder. "Then press the end with the ball to the person and squeeze the handle right here, to release the charge. It works through several layers of clothing, too, and will keep them out for a few hours."

"Thank you." Now I just had to figure out how to take down two guards, without one of them overpowering me while I neutralized the other. And Zavis . . . The thought of having to hurt her did not sit well with me, but I couldn't risk letting her in on our plans.

"Be careful, please," Tairan begged. "Don't let them get close enough to tackle you. Physically, they're stronger than you."

"I will knock them out," I said firmly, cupping his face. "Promise."

Turning his head, he kissed my hand then tugged his hood over his head again—even in the shade, the traces of the reflective light from outside of the alcove must be still bothering him. "Can you read the message now? I'll record and send it right away." He put the screen in front of me as soon as I hid the gun in my pocket.

"Tairan, it won't be easy—us living anywhere else on Earth," I warned. "Even if Tony manages to find a space underground, deep enough to hide you from sunlight, it will never be as good a shield as this facility. And it may not be near the poles, with extended darkness."

He shrugged one wide shoulder.

"I'm not concerned about myself, Isabella. I know for sure now that Elizabeth can tolerate the sunlight. She would need to wear sunglasses, long sleeves, and some strong sunscreen, but she will be able to stay outside during the day. That's what matters."

"How do you know?"

"Zavis ran some extensive tests and found a way to share the results with me."

"She did? Zavis helped me get out of my room today, too. Did she know you'd be here?"

"They have just allowed me to go for walks again. As much as Ricread hates to let me do anything that brings me pleasure, he needs me fit and healthy in time for the next scheduled insemination. Zavis knows my schedule."

Another prick of guilt hit me at the necessity of having to use the stun gun against the woman whom I had begun to regard as a friend. Yet, Zavis had been following Ricread's orders all this time, and I couldn't risk losing our one chance to escape if fear and compliance prevented her from helping us after I confided in her. Besides, it would be safer for her not to know our plans in case she was questioned at any point.

With a deep inhale, I took a hold of Tairan's forearm, bringing the screen closer, then translated the message out loud for him to record it.

"Just give me a moment, please." He punched at the screen then hit a few keys on his arm device. "It's done."

He lifted his face to mine. Streaks of magenta pink shimmered through the violet rims of his irises.

"What should I pack?" I asked.

"Just our daughter. I'll bring some supplies. Make sure you're both dressed warmly. We'll have to hike past the warning barrier to meet the aircraft. The main Kealan craft is scheduled to be at the South Pole then. It's taking some supplies there in preparation for the next move. The small maintenance vehicles here don't have enough range or speed to chase the Arctic exploration aircraft of humans."

He took my arm, punching a few keys on my armlet.

"The communication between our devices is still blocked. We'll need to agree on the time now and make sure neither of us is late."

He entered the exact time of our escape into my device and set a count-down, visible to me only.

"Tairan, Ricread also has plans to break your agreement with him," I warned. "He wants Erix."

"I knew it would come down to it sooner or later." He didn't seem overly surprised, just calmly determined. "Once you and Elizabeth are safe, I'll be looking for a way to get on the next ship going to Keala."

"Is that even possible? To get on one without Ricread re-capturing you?"

"I'll find a way," he said firmly. "I will get my son back."

I nodded, wishing it for him so badly, even as the dread of all the possible dangers threatening him rose inside me.

"I'll be waiting here on Earth," I said softly, fighting the tears prickling my eyes. "I'll be waiting for both of you."

"I won't leave until I am absolutely sure you and Elizabeth are safe," he assured me.

Not trusting my voice, I nodded again.

Spearing his fingers through my hair, he took my head between his hands. "Isabella," he groaned softly, drawing me in for another kiss—long and tender—I didn't want it to end.

After missing him and fearing for his life all this time, I needed him closer now.

I wanted more.

Tracing the line running along the front of his cloak, I opened it, then eagerly slid my hands inside.

"I was so scared for you, Tairan. I missed you so much," I whispered, hot against his mouth. "Every freaking minute of every day."

With a groan, he deepened the kiss, walking me backwards until my back hit the far wall of the alcove behind the ledge.

I opened his suit swiftly and moaned with pleasure the moment my hands connected with his skin beneath. Touching Tairan was like coming home, every ridge of his hard body loved and familiar.

His arm around my waist, hand under my cloak, he shoved the dress off my shoulder, freeing my breasts.

"I'll need to go soon," I whimpered, as a hot charge of arousal shot through to my belly from his fingers playing with my nipple.

"Don't leave." His voice was thick and raw, heavy with desire. "Just a few more minutes of being with you . . ."

Hands under my backside, he lifted me onto a rocky protrusion in the wall and parted my legs.

I fisted my hands in his braids when he hiked up my skirt and knelt in front of me. Everything inside me trembled with need, making me realize how much my body had needed his touch.

"Oh God. Tairan . . ." I gasped, the air escaping my lungs the moment he put his lips and tongue on me—hot and hungry, just like the way he kissed my mouth.

Gripping his head between my legs, I dug my heels into his shoulder blades, lost in the hot storm of ecstasy that Tairan had plunged me into. Having starved for him all this time, my arousal now was fast and furious, my need for him fierce.

"Wait for me," he rasped, hurriedly rising to his feet, and I whimpered in protest, needing him more than ever. "Come here." Opening the bottom of his suit, he grabbed my hips, yanking me closer. Then I felt his marvellous dick at my opening.

"Come on, honey," I urged, hooking my leg around his waist to bring him closer.

Hands pressed into the rock wall above my head, he brought his hips forward, sliding into me, ridge after a delicious ridge.

"How I've missed this." Wrapping my arms tight around his neck, I breathed in the familiar scent of his skin, holding him close as he moved inside me.

The fire he had started in me burned brighter, flaring with intense desire through my entire body, until it exploded in violent pleasure. Holding me tight, Tairan thrust harder, chasing his own release and making mine stretch longer.

Clinging to him, I felt his climax shudder through him as I rode the final waves of my orgasm, wishing I never had to let him go.

AFTER FINALLY TEARING myself from my husband, I rushed through the gardens then down the grey corridors back to my rooms.

I was deliberately taking a longer route to get back, walking through those parts of the station that I knew were more likely to be free of any passers-by at this time of the day.

Rushing by the turnoff to the pool area, I remembered swimming with Tairan when we were still in Antarctica, protected by the agreement I had made with Ricread. Something akin to nostalgia for those times, when we could roam the station relatively free, overtook me for a moment.

Despite all the pain and suffering that Ricread had put Tairan and me through, I had no resentment towards this place. On the contrary, the facility itself had been a safe haven for Tairan, its walls and ceiling a reliable shield against the burning sun.

With all the wonderful amenities on site, the station was designed not to feel confining. However, the people inside it turned this place into a prison for my family and me, following the orders of one man. Ricread was the one responsible for our running into the unknown.

My heart tightened with worry over the uncertainty of our future, but I did not doubt our decision to leave. Even the life of fugitives that lay ahead of us out there was more acceptable than what awaited us within these walls.

As long as Ricread remained in charge, we could not stay.

Chapter 27

"COULD YOU WATCH HER for me for a second, please?" I asked Zavis, placing Elizabeth on the bed after having just fed her.

Sliding my hand under the blanket, I wrapped my fingers around the smooth handle of the stun gun I had hidden there, willing my heart not to race wildly.

"Sure." Zavis plopped on the bed next to the baby. "Aww," she cooed, stroking Elizabeth's leg. "That's one tired little girl right there. She just can't keep those big, pretty eyes open."

Quickly stuffing the gun in the wide sleeve of my dress, I headed around the bed, as if on my way to the bathroom. Despite my best efforts to calm down, my heart raced even faster, blood swishing loudly in my ears. I forced myself to slow down, keeping my pace as casual as possible.

"Oops." Passing by one of the guards, I pretended to trip and quickly bent over, as if to check my sandal, then pressed the metal ball of the gun to the guard's shin and squeezed the handle—hard—praying that it would work.

With a strangled "Humph," the Kealan collapsed to the ground at once, as if I'd cut his hamstrings.

"What happened?" I exclaimed, in fake surprise, jumping aside and in the direction of the second guard.

He leaped to his buddy's aid, a bewildered expression on his face. And I quickly pressed the ball to his arm, sending him falling heavily on top of the first guard.

Not wasting a second, I spun around to face Zavis, who stood by the bed, her pink-rimmed eyes wide open. To my relief, the shock must have stopped her from raising the alarm—her arms were hanging limply, the screen of her device off.

"You don't have to do this . . ." She took a step to me, lifting both hands up, palms facing me, in a disarming gesture.

"Oh, you know I do." I shook my head, advancing on her. "There is no other choice."

"Isabella, wait . . ."

But I had already lunged forward, pressing the ball of the stun gun to her palm before she had a chance to jerk it back.

Her body shook in a violent shudder, fingers flexed around the ball, ripping the gun out of my hand on her way to the floor.

"I'm so, so sorry, Zavis," I whimpered, covering my mouth with my hand, as mix of intense guilt and compassion rocked through me at the sight of her slim body curled on the floor.

Elizabeth squirmed in her sleep, snapping my attention back to her. A glance at my arm device let me know I had barely a few minutes left before I had to meet Tairan.

Carefully stepping around the guards piled on the floor, I took my cloak out of the closet along with the boots I used to wear whenever I was allowed to walk outside, and a long, wide strip of material I had made out of one of my dresses.

Then I pried the stun gun out of Zavis's fingers and quickly put it in the pocket of my dress.

Returning to the bed, I gently wrapped Elizabeth in her blanket and some of my warmer clothing, then used the strip of material to tie her snugly to my front.

"Sorry, baby," I whispered, patting the small bundle attached to my chest. "I don't know what kind of life I'm about to take you to, but I promise to do my best for as long as I live to make sure you're safe and happy."

I wrapped the cloak around both of us and rushed out of the room.

THE MOMENT I ENTERED the glass room on the way out of the facility, a man in a cloak separated from the shadows by the entrance and pulled me into the corner with him.

"Tairan?"

"Did all go well?" he asked.

I nodded, breathless with worry, stress, and anticipation.

"Give me your arm," he whispered, lifting his hand with a slim object that spewed a thin, white flame.

Without asking questions, I freed my arm from the cloak and stretched it his way. Quickly, he brushed the flame along my arm device, separating it in two halves. I noted that his forearm was bare—his own device had been removed already.

"One more thing." He tossed my disabled device into the corner then took my face between his hands. "Sorry, my *ila* flower," he whispered gently, brushing my lips with his. "This will hurt a little." Turning my head to the side, he yanked the translator out of my ear, sending a sharp lightning of agony through my head and spine and wrenching a cry of pain from my chest.

Feeling the warm trickle of blood down the side of my neck, I bit my lip to stop a groan but only managed to muffle it.

"Shhh. It's done." He cradled me to his chest for a moment of comfort then nudged me to the door. "We have to hurry. They'll be looking for us soon enough."

He slid a pair of goggles over my eyes. "These will help you see better in the dark and wind." Then he took me to the door.

As soon as we stepped outside of the heated area around the perimeter of the facility, the biting cold of the Arctic winter rushed us.

The cloak whipped around me in the wind, but the Kealan-made material clung close enough to my body, keeping me and the baby warm. Drawn low, the hood kept my head and face relatively warm, too, though gusts of wind found their way under the hood now and then, frost nibbling on the exposed skin of my chin and cheeks.

Head down, I huddled into the cloak, nearly blinded by the wind and the darkness.

"I've walked this route already," Tairan yelled through the wind to me. "Twice." He took my elbow, tugging me along. "Just follow me."

Stumbling through the snowdrifts, I felt utterly disoriented by the swirls of white in the night surrounding us, glad I wasn't the one in charge of navigation.

After trudging behind Tairan—his wide back shielding me from the winds somewhat—the sense of my surroundings finally came to me. I glanced back over my shoulder to see the gigantic structure of the facility we were leaving behind.

The enormous building was sparingly lit along the walking path circling it. Numerous tall domes rose into the dark skies, the biggest one being that of the aircraft landing hangar, I assumed.

A small pang of sadness tugged at my heart again. Amazingly, watching the station from the distance felt like leaving a home. No matter how dangerous the occupants of that facility turned out to be, the building itself somehow managed to find a place in my heart.

"Not long now!" Tairan shouted over the wind. "Look!" I followed his gesture with my gaze, peering into the darkness in search of what he was pointing at.

Far on the horizon, I finally managed to spot a few flickering lights. Tony had kept his promise. If I squinted hard enough, I could almost make out the silhouette of the newest model of Arctic exploration aircraft, with its short wings and four horizontal propellers on top, designed to help it land in the harshest conditions.

With another glance back over my shoulder, I spotted some movement at the facility. It appeared as if one of its lights had separated from the building and now was moving our way.

"Tairan." Not trusting he'd hear me over the howling wind, I touched his arm then pointed at the approaching light.

He stopped in his tracks so suddenly it nearly knocked me off balance.

"Keep going." Gently but insistently, he nudged me towards Tony and the airplane. "Tell them to take off as soon as you get there."

"Not without you!" I shouted in Kealan through the wind, shaking my head.

"I'll catch up." His voice was firm. "Or I'll find my way out later. Do not wait for me."

"No." I kept shaking my head, even as he kept pushing me on my way urgently.

"Isabella!" Grabbing me by the shoulders, he gave me a small but firm shake. "You *have to* keep Elizabeth safe."

I still shook my head in denial, but no longer said anything, taking a few steps towards the aircraft when he let go of me.

"Go," he urged. "I'll hold them." The white laser flickered in his hand, signalling to me Tairan was ready to fight. The thought brought tears to my eyes. "Go, please," he begged.

For a few steps, I walked backwards, unable to tear my gaze away from his lone figure standing in the snow and wind—between the approaching danger and me.

Keep Elizabeth safe.

I wrapped my arms around the precious bundle at my chest and headed into the wind.

Chapter 28

TAIRAN

Making sure Isabella was on her way, he turned his full attention to the approaching vehicle.

This was an individual hovering travel device, designed to carry out minor maintenance tasks on the outside of the facility. While it was meant for one person, it could carry two in an emergency. Tairan felt confident that he could slow them down long enough for Isabella to reach safety.

As the vehicle approached, however, he spotted more light dots moving his way from the station. The alarm must have been raised, mobilizing the security team on the hunt for Isabella and him. For Elizabeth.

Desperate to put as much distance as possible between his women and the forces hunting them, Tairan ran towards the vehicles as fast as the uneven ground and wind would allow.

The first reached him soon enough, not slowing down as it approached. The person behind the wheel was obviously aiming to ram it into Tairan.

Jumping aside to avoid the collision in the last moment, Tairan lost his balance and rolled through the snow.

"Saryal!" The familiar hated voice ripped through the freezing air.

Ricread.

Tairan leaped to his feet, getting ready as the vehicle spun around in the air and headed his way again, accelerating.

This time, Tairan sprung high as it approached, aiming for the man steering it. Slowed by the cloak, his arms didn't reach far enough—Ricread's neck slipped from his grip. But the impact of his body against the side of the hover-vehicle jolted it hard enough to tip it to the side, tossing its driver out into the snow.

Tairan landed on his back, a hard ridge of ice and packed snow slammed between his shoulder blades, knocking the air out of his lungs and leaving him winded for a moment.

When he rose to his feet again, he came face to face with Ricread, who pointed a gun straight at him. This was not a stun gun, either. Almost as long as his arm, this was a combat weapon, meant to kill.

"You wouldn't dare." Tairan glared at his enemy. "You need your main *research resource.*"

"Not for long." Caught by the wind, Ricread's words reached him, even though the man didn't shout. "How hard do you think it would be to convince everyone that my agreement with a dead man is null and void?"

"You cannot touch Erix," Tairan gritted through his teeth, his jaw locked so tight it hurt, but he barely noticed the pain.

"He is mine!" Ricread yelled, losing his composure. "Your son, your wife, and your daughter—they are all mine! I'll do what I see fit with each and every one of them. And that'll be the last thing you hear before you die—"

With a growl Tairan launched forward. Rage and terror mixed into an explosive burst of speed, propelling his attack against the gun pointed at him. Ricread fired. A flash of fiery agony hit Tairan's side, but it failed to stop him.

With the power of a man possessed, he tackled Ricread to the ground, knocking the gun out of his hand. The weapon bounced off an icy ridge, rolling away.

Reaching up, Ricread ripped the goggles off his face, the light of the tipped hover-vehicle blinded Tairan for a moment, long enough to allow his enemy to free himself from his grip.

"You're not getting away this time," Tairan hissed, fully surrendering to the rage that detonated inside him.

Tugging hard at the end of Ricread's cloak, he dropped him back to the ground. Rolling through the snow, tangled together, he searched for the other man's throat. His hand landed on something freezing cold and hard, instead.

The gun.

Getting a hold of the weapon, Tairan heaved himself over his enemy.

Ripping off his hood, Tairan grabbed a handful of the professor's braids, yanking them up. The wide bald patch above Ricread's ear came into view. The latest technology had healed the skin smoothly, though no hair grew on this part of the scull. Tairan remembered well the gruesome, bloody wound he had inflicted there, years ago.

"I should have killed you then." He shook his head with a bitter sense of regret. "I should have ended you much earlier. So much pain would have been spared to so many."

But Ricread had always hid behind a security team, even back then. Tairan had been overpowered in his office when he had come to negotiate Erix's freedom, beaten within an inch of his life, and put in a coma during his first weeks as the subject of The Science Group.

"So much progress would have never happened," Ricread bit out. His goggles had slid off during the struggle. A flash of fear crossed his features at the sight of the gun pointed straight into his face.

"You will leave my family alone," Tairan demanded, with a firm tug on Ricread's braids to ensure his full attention. "Once and for all. Do you hear me?"

From the corner of his eye, Tairan noted the security vehicles already surrounding them in a circle. Ricread must have seen them too, as the fear melted away from his expression, the usual cold arrogance settled firmly back over his face.

"I am no longer making deals, Saryal," he scoffed, haughtily.

"Neither am I."

Tairan pressed the trigger.

Chapter 29

I'D ONLY MADE IT A hundred metres or so away from Tairan before my legs refused to obey my brain, and I stopped, frozen in place. Unable to take another step away from him, I watched the vehicles move in from the facility, circling my husband who rolled on top of Ricread and leaned back, pointing the gun at his head.

I saw the bright flash of the gunshot, though the sound never came, lost in the wind and cold.

Pressing my hands to my sides, I felt the hard cylinder of the stun gun in my pocket and yanked it out.

The cloaked figures of the security personnel jumped off their vehicles. The guards pointed their weapons at Tairan as he rose to his feet, and suddenly, I was able to bring my body into motion once again, running through the night to him instead of to the aircraft that waited to take me to safety.

Pressing one arm to his side, Tairan lifted the other up, slowly pointing the gun along the line from one guard to another.

The last flying vehicle arrived from the facility, and a tall, cloaked figure stepped into the circle, prompting Tairan to jerk his gun to the newcomer. The man raised his arm, and the guards lowered their weapons, as if by magic.

"Let us go," Tairan demanded, loud enough for me to hear as I approached.

The wind must have quieted somewhat because I recognized Valran's voice as he replied.

"I prefer not to do that, Commander. I am willing to re-negotiate the terms of your staying at the station."

"I am past the point of negotiating with anyone representing The Science Group."

"Would you hear what I have to say if I told you I speak on behalf of all of Keala in this negotiation?"

"*I* want to hear it!" I yelled in Kealan, panting from my run as I entered the circle. "Make it quick and keep your distance."

"Isabella!" Tairan swayed my way.

Only now did I spot that his side was soaked with pale blood. Deceptively innocent in its strawberry-cream colour, it trickled down his cloak and dripped onto the snow.

Rushing to him, I yelled over my shoulder at Valran, "You get him medical attention, right now! And this is *not* part of the negotiations."

One arm supporting Elizabeth under my cloak, I hugged Tairan with the one gripping the stun gun, helping him stay upright.

"You didn't leave." He pressed his forehead to mine.

I never took the wedding band off my finger, but it wasn't the ring that tied us together. We never got to say our vows, but in my heart and in my mind Tairan was my true husband—my friend, my lover, my protector, and the father of my child.

"We are a family, honey. And families stick together." I gave him a quick kiss on the lips. "Besides, you just took care of the biggest monster here."

"That alone will have consequences," he warned grimly.

Valran came closer. "We will need to take him back in, Isabella, to stop the bleeding. I know you're not wearing your translator. How well can you understand me?"

"Perfectly well," I replied sharply in Kealan. "You will need to give me some very firm promises here—before I let you take him inside that place again—and give them quickly."

"I will not withhold medical attention or use it as leverage in negotiation." Valran's voice was firm. "We will help the commander regardless of whether or not you decide to stay."

"Get it in writing," Tairan said with a thin, crooked grin.

"What he said." I tipped my head his way.

Valran nodded and opened the screen of his device. Instead of typing in, he spoke into it, the words appearing then in black on the white screen. Adding the swirl of his signature, he turned the screen our way.

"Can you read Kealan, too?" he asked with a note of genuine curiosity.

"Yes, I can." I read the written promise he had just made, making sure it matched what he had said. "I learned your language. Knowledge is power, isn't it?"

Valran paused for a moment as if absorbing my words then turned to one of the guards, "Take Commander Saryal in, quickly. Bring him—"

"To our rooms," I interrupted. "No more clinic."

He nodded again, helping Tairan to get on the vehicle behind the guard.

"You can come with me, Isabella." Valran gestured at the vehicle he had arrived in.

"Alright, but can someone dash over to that aircraft over there, please, and invite my brother to come in, too? It's way too cold to make him wait out here."

BY THE TIME WE GOT back to our rooms, Elizabeth woke up and I fed her while several from the research team took care of Tairan's wound—a long gash with ragged edges—on his side.

"How is she?" Zavis hovered over me.

I lifted my gaze to her, meeting her beautiful pink-rimmed eyes. "I'm sorry I had to use the stun gun on you."

She blinked, rubbing her upper arms with her hands. "Well, that was not a pleasant experience. Thankfully, it didn't last that long, the charge in the gun must have been low."

"I'm sorry," I said again.

"I understand why you did it." Her gaze flickered to Elizabeth in my arms and she asked again, "How is she?"

"Good." I saw my baby's eyelids slowly drop as she fell asleep again. Her eyelashes, pure white as if frosted with snow, rested on her pale, chubby cheeks. "I don't remember my sister's twins being this calm. It must be the Kealan in her."

"Um, I don't know." Zavis turned to Tairan, who was reclining on the other side of the bed. "Is it normal for Kealan babies to be this quiet?"

"Not really," he replied, with a brief laugh. "I remember quite a few nights when Erix kept me up to the point of near insanity."

"Lucky us then." I smiled.

His wound had been treated. A generous layer of pink healing gel glistened against his pale skin, covering the scar on his side from lower rib to hipbone.

"How are you?" I got up, and Zavis readily grabbed sleeping Elizabeth out of my arms.

The Kealans who treated Tairan moved away, taking the equipment robots out of the room.

Tairan got up.

"Shouldn't you rest?" I tried to stop him.

"No." His voice was firm. His expression turned hard and serious. "I'm well enough to keep going."

The door hadn't solidified after the medical team left, and Valran entered the bedroom, accompanied by several others from the research team, but no Sikril, I noted. Valran still had his cloak on, although his goggles were gone.

"We need to go," Tairan wrapped his arm around my shoulders.

"Where is Tony?" I asked.

"In the lounge by the swimming pool, along with his crew," a female from the research team, Laylee, replied. "Yaee is feeding them some Kealan food." She paused for a moment, a confused expression on her face. "He said 'You're really hot for an alien' to Yaee. What exactly does that mean? Her body temperature is not elevated."

"Oh, boy," I groaned and turned to Valran. "We need to leave soon, before my brother finds some way of getting into trouble."

Valran inclined his head, drawing in a long inhale. "I offered to discuss the new conditions of your staying here," he reminded. "I sincerely hope you'll reconsider your leaving us."

"No." Tairan's hand squeezed my shoulder.

"How far are you willing to go in your concessions?" I asked, tentatively.

"Isabella," Tairan warned me. "They always skew deals in their favour."

"*We* have never made a deal," Valran pointed out. "All your agreements have been with Ricread."

"You have been his right hand for years, a part of everything he had ever done."

"Not exactly." Valran gestured to the living room. "Would you like to sit down? I want to explain, but it may take some time."

"You promised to let us go," I reminded.

"And *you* promised to hear me out," he retorted. "We can part amicably once both sides of that agreement are fulfilled."

Gripping Tairan's hand in mine, I tugged him to the living room. The others followed. We sat on the couch, Tairan's thigh pressed to mine, with Valran taking the seat opposite of us. The rest of the

Kealans who came with Valran took their seats on the swing chairs or stood nearby.

"Ricread was a member of a small but powerful elitist fraction of the Kealan government," Valran started. "The so called 'purists' only agreed to breed our race with humans on the condition that the human DNA would eventually be reduced in the offspring, brought down to the same ratio it is in Kealans now. This process takes time. Ricread was determined to come as close as possible to that goal with his work before his death, speeding up the experiment, even at the expense of ethics and decency."

"How are you any different?" Tairan challenged, gruffly.

"You *know* I am." Valran kept his head high under Tairan's reproachful glare. "You once entrusted me to look after someone very dear to you." His gaze moved to me. "Your wife."

"You did?" I asked Tairan. "When?"

"Your husband saved your life by ensuring a necessary procedure was performed on you during your labour with Elizabeth," Valran explained. "I was there when he immobilized Ricread and ordered a human doctor save you and the baby."

"The C-section?" I pressed my hand to my belly over the barely-there scar hidden under my dress. "Ricread was against it?"

"The commander ordered the procedure then gave himself up."

I squeezed Tairan's hand in both of mine. "You knew he'd take it all out on you. What kind of torture did he put you through?"

"I needed some time to work out the details of getting you and the baby out of here," Tairan replied simply.

"Oh, my love . . ." I leaned into him, burying my face in his shoulder for a moment to collect myself and fill up with his strength. "This needs to stop." I straightened and turned to Valran. "No one will ever touch him again. Do you hear me?"

Tairan slid his arm around my waist, drawing me closer to him as if afraid I'd lunge into a physical attack.

Valran jerked his head, his cool composure wavering for a moment. "Despite how it may seem, Ricread and I have not shared the same principles for a long time now, Isabella. Personally, I believe in a different approach to our research. Instead of re-creating our race, I want to let it develop in a more natural way. Evolution instead of simply duplication. That was where the cloning failed for us. A race needs to evolve instead of simply copying itself over and over. Kealans are an intelligent, proud, noble race. But we have strayed away from what should have been our main goal."

"*That* I agree with." Tairan exhaled heavily.

"I want to preserve our culture," Valran proceeded. "Our language, traditions, and history. I want our cities to burst with life again. However, I'm not particularly concerned about the specific make-up of the DNA of the people who will populate them." He glanced my way. "I agree, a race that has lost its values, its morals, and its kindness is not worth preserving. Kealans had it all, until Ricread managed to convince them that in order to survive they had to give that up. After years of research, I believe there is another way, but we need your help."

"What exactly are you talking about?" I asked carefully.

"We have been doing testing on both males and females of Earth. However, under Ricread's orders, the priority was to find a suitable female match for our one and only male subject. Meanwhile, a large amount of data has accumulated on the Earth's male population. And I've started to identify possible female matches on Keala for them."

"You want to breed Kealan women with human men?" I frowned, worrying about *how* he planned to implement that.

"Not the way it was done with you," Valran rushed to reassure me. "Human sperm can survive outside of the male body. It can be frozen and transported with no damage to the genetic material. I would like to open a program for human men donating their sperm to artificially inseminate Kealan females, who may still have some viable eggs left in their ovaries. With the help of our most current technology, I'm estimating the pregnancy success rate would be well in double digits, and we can further improve it, using the data collected during your pregnancy and labour."

"Why hasn't it been considered before?" Tairan asked, his arm around my waist flexed, and I stroked his hand soothingly.

"The idea was outlined in Ricread's plans. However, he never went ahead with its implementation. The chance of a successful pregnancy was initially estimated even lower than yours. Only now, having analyzed most of the data collected during your pregnancy and Elizabeth's birth, we are confident the chances of success are significantly higher than was first thought.

"Another reason, I suspect, was Ricread's inability to gain absolute control over the free-born Kealan females and their offspring the way he was able to do with a human female from a conquered race. All his political influence went into entrapping and retaining the commander. Additionally, the great physical distance of this lab facility from Keala helped him to disregard many of the laws we have on our planet that protect personal freedom."

"So, you do have those, huh?" I couldn't help the snappy remark.

Valran heaved a sigh, letting my sarcasm slide. "I used to be a long-time admirer and supporter of Ricread's work. When I got accepted into his team, I was thrilled to be a part of what he was doing. His genius seemed unparalleled, and his achievement in the field unmatched by anyone else. After a while, however, I began to question the methods he used to achieve his incredible results. Ever since we came to Earth, I've been diligently recording all violations of the law on his part."

"That must be a long list by now," Tairan said with a bitter laugh.

"It is," Valran admitted. "You see, I do not agree that the results justify the means. You are right, Isabella," he turned to me, "going against one's beliefs chips away at who you are, until there is nothing left worth to keep."

"Why have you been allowing all of this to happen then?" I asked, hurt and anger stirring in me again. "Even as recently as a week ago? You must have known he'd started tests on Elizabeth."

"That was done without anyone's knowledge. Ricread did it entirely on his own. But we have been able to stall the implementation of the aging protocol on her—nothing has been done in that regard."

"Well, that's a relief." I exhaled, although not entirely pacified.

"What have you been doing with that list of violations, Valran?" Tairan asked. "Anything? What is your plan, if you have one?"

"I've been sending reports to the Committee of Five at The Science Group, to whom Ricread was accountable. As you know, he has been gaining power in all levels of science and government on Keala, making it practically impossible to so much as disagree with him on anything. After the birth of Elizabeth, however, public opinion played in our favour."

He shifted in his seat, leaning forward. "Elizabeth is a real celebrity on our planet now. Although none on Keala have ever met her, she is loved and treasured by all. She embodies our hope. I've collected firm evidence that by continuing the experiment as intended, Ricread was going to harm her. I detailed the physical and emotional damage that would occur due to what he had planned for her. My last report stirred the strongest concern among the members of the committee. Especially, because if made public, it has the potential to cause a riot in the general population, undermining all work of The Science Group to date."

"That would be a disaster for them all." Tairan's expression was cynical.

"I just got official instructions to halt the whole experiment until a full review by the Group," Valran continued. "I already submitted a revised schedule to them last week, outlining the plans regarding artificial insemination of Kealan females with human sperm. I have full confidence that this plan will be enthusiastically received by the general public. Many Kealans are yearning for children and family, but none have been given this chance until now."

"How does my family fit into your new plan?" Tairan asked, his eyebrows knitted together again, hard mistrust etched on his face. "Why do you need us to stay?"

"I'll be completely honest with you." Valran leaned back, unflinchingly holding Tairan's stare. "Elizabeth is the culmination of the work of many people here, myself included. We all feel invested into her future. Aside from the concerns for her safety, I simply don't want you to take her away. I would love for you to stay here, where living conditions are perfect for her and where we all can watch her grow. The only thing I would ask from you in return would be your permission to monitor her development, by non-intrusive means."

"Like what?" I stirred in Tairan's arms.

"I would love to observe and record every developmental milestone she reaches, like walking, talking, and other mobility and cognitive functions. She would also be fitted with an arm device when she is old enough—around ten. Aside from the continuous data collection by these means, there would be no other tests and no interfering with her natural growth process."

"What will happen after she is done growing?" Both Tairan and I asked almost simultaneously.

"Once she reaches adulthood, I would like to be able to discuss any further involvement in our research with her and you, but nothing will take place without her approval."

"How about Erix?" Tairan asked.

"I will certainly extend the same offer to him too, when he reaches his natural age of maturity."

"Erix needs to see his father," I said firmly. "As soon as possible."

Valran's seemed to think about it for a moment. "I can arrange for a video transmission. The connection may take some time to establish, though."

"How long?" Tairan's body stiffened beside me.

Valran glanced at one of the other men in the room.

"About an hour or two," the man said. "Considering the current conditions of the atmosphere."

"Well then, make it happen." I turned to Tairan next. "Do you think Erix would like to move here and live with us? If not, we can think about moving to Keala."

The opportunity to go to Keala was not currently on the table, but I felt that if we decided that planet was the best place to raise our family, we could negotiate our terms of making a life there.

One thing felt certain, Valran was definitely not Ricread. Talking to him, I believed he was concerned about all of us as individuals, not just the subjects of his research. This alone made it easier to breathe.

"Would you move to Keala for me?" Tairan asked, brushing my hair back.

"Anywhere," I replied without a shadow of a doubt in my heart. "I'd move worlds and galaxies for you." I smiled. "Literally."

He gazed at me for a moment, his hand cupping my face. "We can talk about that." He turned to Valran. "There is another problem, though. I just shot a man. There will be murder charges against me."

Valran straightened in his seat. "I've put the insident in my report. It is going to be viewed as an unfortunate accident. No murder charges."

"Can you guarantee that?" I was afraid to believe it had already been dealt with.

"You *know* it was no accident." Tairan fixed his stare on Valran. "There were a number of witnesses, including Sikril."

"Sikril has just accepted a position as the security head with a private company on Keala. He is moving out with the next ship. With

Professor Ricread's untimely death, I am the head of this facility now. Sikril and I have never had a wholesome working relationship, and he made the decision to pursue other opportunities."

"Did he make it all by himself?" I wondered.

"Well, the idea came from me, but he agreed." A smile ghosted Valran's lips. "Almost without a fight."

"Almost?" I wished I could share his lighter mood, but the worry refused to leave me. "Don't you think he'll use the knowledge of what happened here today against you? And us?"

"I know for a fact he has considered that." Valran nodded. "He let me know in no uncertain terms that he will take Commander Saryal and me personally to court for murder and assisting murder respectively.

"I managed to convince him, however, that he would not succeed. If the case went to court, it wouldn't be hard to prove self-defence on the commander's part. Ricread clearly attacked first, and the weapon he was shot with was his. Also, the circumstances leading up to the incident would be enough to acquit the commander of murder charges, according to Kealan laws. The years of physical and emotional abuse that this man has been put through would justify his decision to stand up for himself and his family.

"Sikril has been made aware that if the matter went to court, I would make public every detail of Ricread's violations I have scrupulously documented over the years, including Sikril's personal involvement in them all.

"As a result of our conversation, Sikril chose to accept his transfer and retain his honour. As the matter stands, Ricread's remains will be transported to Keala where he will be given a hero's funeral. In exchange, you won't have to face any murder charges. I hope this deal is acceptable to you."

A small vindictive part of me wished Ricread's criminal behaviour was exposed and his reputation was tarnished. However, I also realized that this was a small price to pay for keeping Tairan out of jail and away from a death sentence. No matter what, he was now free, and his tormentor dead. This was an outcome I hadn't dared to dream about before.

"What do you think?" I turned to Tairan. "I mean, provided we get it all in writing, of course," I added with a smile.

"I'll get a friend's lawyer from Keala go through it, point by point, to make sure all loopholes are closed." He threw a glance Valran's way. The suspicion was definitely there, I understood it was hard for Tairan to trust someone from The Science Group again. Although I didn't spot any direct hatred for Valran in Tairan's expression. That was a start.

"Living on Keala may be better for the children," I thought out loud. "Especially if there are plans for other babies to be born there. Kids need the company of other children growing up." I looked at Valran for his reaction.

He shifted under my gaze, drawing in some air to reply, obviously still intent on persuading us to remain on Earth. "We have plans to open up our stations for human crews of scientists, donor volunteers, and their families. I want to invite them to work in a partnership. Your children will have friends here. There will be school classes organized by age." He rubbed the back of his neck. "We just need to find a better understanding with the coalition of Earth's Governments. Until now, Ricread has done nothing in terms of building a relationship with your officials. Whatever he needed, he simply threatened them to get his way."

"You do have your work cut out for you in building that relationship," I agreed. "Your first impression was horrible, coming here. Now, I would suggest you ask for Barbara Adan, one of the three North American representatives to the coalition. I know for a fact she considers Kealans an intelligent race who can be *reasoned* with. I'd say that's a start."

AFTER HAMMERING OUT the main points of our new agreement with Valran, Tairan immediately forwarded the whole thing to his group of lawyers in Atal on Keala.

Following a short discussion between the two of us, we decided to stay on Earth for now. It was liberating to know that we were no longer prisoners and had a choice to move anywhere anytime. At the moment, though, the station seemed the safest place for Elizabeth. I had peace of mind, knowing that everything she needed to stay well and healthy was right here for her.

When this stage of negotiations was done, Tairan left for the communication station of the facility for the first video conversation with his son in over four years. I'd offered to come with him, but ultimately, we both decided that it would be best for him to talk to Erix one-on-one first.

Instead, I had dinner with my brother, who was in awe of Elizabeth when he saw her.

"She's like a porcelain doll," he exclaimed, touching her silky white hair, which now reached her shoulder blades. I had to use a hair elastic to gather it on top of her head. The hairdo looked like a funny little water fountain, but it kept the hair out of her eyes and her mouth. "I'd never think someone could be this weird and beautiful at the same time."

"Did you hear that, baby?" I smiled. "Your uncle thinks you're weird. Should we tell him everything we think about him?" I nudged him in the ribs with my elbow.

"I also said she is beautiful." He sulked, making me laugh.

"Do you think you could come home for a visit maybe?" Tony asked when we sat in the living room after the dinner. "Mom would love to meet Elizabeth. Mary, too. They both have been asking me constantly about your alien guy. You can bring him as well, of course."

"I'd love to, Tony. But I'm not sure how safe that would be for both of them. Tairan can't tolerate sunlight. The trip may be uncomfortable for him. And Elizabeth has to get a little older for travelling."

He squinted at me, lifting an eyebrow.

"You realize I came to take you away from here? You were ready to spend the rest of your life outside of this place."

"That was an act of desperation, Tony." I said, feeling relief that the escape didn't happen.

"Do you think you'll be safe here now?

"I believe so, Tony. Evil people happen in every nation, but I have faith in Kealans as a whole."

"Well, you know who to call if the aliens start misbehaving again." He puffed his chest, wiggling his eyebrows.

"Oh, Tony." I hugged his neck, laughing. "You are the best big brother!"

I heard a noise from the entrance and turned that way.

"Tairan!" I exclaimed at the sight of my husband walking in, his expression a little stunned. "How did it go?"

"Good." He nodded. "Erix has grown so much. And it's not just his height, the way he speaks, like a grown-up already—" he cut himself short, spotting Tony behind me. "I am honoured to meet my wife's brother." Tairan stepped to him, his hand outstretched in greeting.

"Um, hi!" Tony jumped off the couch, energetically shaking the offered hand. "Me too. Honoured, I mean . . ."

I smiled, taking in this moment—my husband and my brother shaking hands. Considering my brother's earlier resentment towards 'the aliens', this seemed like a good sign for the relationship between humans and Kealans in general.

"You know, just because it isn't easy for us to travel right now, it doesn't mean that all of you can't come here for a visit. What do you think?" I asked Tony.

"Do you really want all of us visiting you here?" He laughed.

"Why not? What's the worst that can happen? As long as you promise not to hit on the staff, of course." I pointed my finger at him.

His expression softened, eyes glossing over. "Who knew the alien girls would be that cute out of their cloaks," he said, as if thinking out loud. "Those tight uniforms—"

"Tony!"

"Got it, got it." He lifted his hands up, in a pacifying gesture. "No hitting on the staff, no matter how hot they look."

I just shook my head with a sigh.

AFTER TONY LEFT, I started feeling the effects of the day. My limbs were heavy with exhaustion and my head felt fuzzy.

"We should go to bed." I walked over to Tairan, who stood at the living room window, staring out into the dimly lit snowy landscape. "How is your wound?"

"It's fine." He wrapped his arm around me, drawing me into his healthy side. "I had easy access to the painkillers this time." He kissed my hair then stared back through the window again "I want Erix to come live with us as soon as possible."

"Of course, darling. When can he be here?"

"He needs to finish his semester in school then my friends will help him get on the next ship coming to Earth."

"Good." I drew in a cleansing breath. It felt so right to have Tairan reunite with his son, after all this time. "I'm really looking forward to meeting him. Can I come with you next time you have a video call with him?"

"Of course you can. I told him about you, he wants to meet you too."

We stood in silence for a minute, locked in an embrace and our thoughts.

"It's hard to believe we're back where we started," Tairan said as he moved his gaze around the room.

"This is not where we started, honey," I disagreed. "We've come a long way. And it's been quite a journey. We've earned every moment of peace we have ahead of us, because we fought hard for it."

He gazed at me with one of his rare smiles that I loved so much. "It's been an honour to fight side by side with you."

"I'll live, love, and die by your side, Tairan. Always."

He brushed my nose with his, gently. "I love you, Isabella," he whispered against my lips. "Kiss me, my Earth woman."

And I did. I kissed him like a true Earth woman—deep, long, and hot—the most wonderful kiss on the planet and all of the Universe.

EPILOGUE

AFTER WEEKS OF SCRUPULOUSLY working out every detail of the agreement between The Science Group and us, Tairan finally felt confident enough to sign it.

Even before it was finalized, though, our life on the station had already changed from what it was when Ricread was alive.

Neither of us had any daily schedule forced on us. We gained full control of our time as well as of our bodies and had the freedom to move anywhere within the facility and beyond.

Both Tairan and I got new arm devices, but none of the functionality was restricted anymore, including our ability to communicate with each other and with anyone outside of the station.

I got in touch with my family again, and they were able to watch Elizabeth grow via our regular video calls. We were also planning their visit to the station soon.

Tairan had weekly talks with Erix up until the end of his school semester. He would have had them daily if it was technically possible. Unfortunately, because of the enormous distance between our planets, the video calls were not always possible. They ended up being interrupted and needed to be regulated.

A month after we signed the agreement, Tairan got an offer to return to the City Defense Force as head of training, a position he could hold remotely. He came to discuss it with me. I saw the light in his eyes the moment he told me about the opportunity to go back to the job he loved, and my heart swelled with pride and happiness for him.

Since accepting the offer, Tairan spent a big portion of his day working in the office that was added to our rooms for that purpose. He also dedicated a couple of hours a day to working out combat tactics with security staff in the training hall.

One morning a month before Elizabeth's first birthday, when we were back at the Northern station after another six months spent in Antarctica, Tairan got up way before our usual time. Today was special—a ship was arriving from Keala, and Erix was on it.

Our rooms had been further expanded in anticipation of his arrival. New entrances in the walls had been activated, adding a separate dining room, a bedroom for Erix, and a nursery for Elizabeth, who had been sleeping in a crib by our bed until then.

"You can go back to sleep, my *ila* flower." Tairan kissed me on the cheek. "It's still too early to get up."

"Nah-uh." I climbed from under the covers. "No way I'm going to miss the arrival of Elizabeth's big brother." I hoped I could call Erix 'son' one day, but I didn't want to impose it on him, feeling he might need some time to accept me as his father's wife and his stepmother.

Elizabeth stirred in her crib too, as if she couldn't wait to go meet her brother, either.

After a quick shower and breakfast, we made our way to the landing hangar, just in time to watch the giant space ship glide in through the opened dome of the ceiling.

The material over the entrance to the craft liquefied then shifted down, forming stairs to the ground. Several cloaked Kealans exited one by one.

The figure in the middle was much shorter than the rest, and I realized this must be Erix. When the dome closed, he took off his goggles and shoved the hood back, revealing a thick mop of snowy white braids, just like his father's.

Tairan rushed to him.

"Father." Erix stepped into his open arms.

My eyes watered as I watched them hug for the first time in years, overwhelmed by emotion for the two of them. Pressing Elizabeth to my chest, I sighed into the mass of her little braids as she cooed and tugged at my hair.

"Come meet Isabella." Tairan led Erix to us.

We had spoken via video calls a number of times, which helped me not to feel like a complete stranger to the boy now.

"Hi, Erix." Making an effort to compose myself, I brushed away an errant tear and smiled brightly.

"Mother." He bowed politely.

"Oh . . . You don't have to call me that," I mumbled, a little lost but definitely touched. "Unless you want to, of course. Then I'd be delighted . . ." I trailed off.

"I have no one else to call by this name," he replied, looking a little unsure, his navy-blue-rimmed eyes moving from me to Tairan then back again. "You are the only mother I know."

"Oh, God . . ." I exhaled, losing it after all, my voice cracked. "Come here." Shifting Elizabeth to my hip, I crushed Erix into a hug—a little awkward, but so very wonderful. "You are my boy now. My baby, too."

Coming closer, Tairan wrapped his arms around all of us. Squished in the middle, Elizabeth wiggled impatiently then got hold of one of Erix's braids and tugged hard enough to make him cry out.

"She is small but fierce, this one." I exhaled a laugh.

"Your sister, Elizabeth," Tairan introduced her.

Erix stared at the baby in bewilderment. "I can't believe she is real." He shook his head. "She is so small."

"Oh, she's growing," I assured him.

Erix freed his braid from her grip, and she immediately got hold of his finger, dragging it into her mouth.

"Watch out," Tairan warned. "She has a few teeth now. And they're very sharp."

Erix only laughed, watching Elizabeth try to chew on his finger with her gums where the molars hadn't come through yet.

"Can I hold her?" he asked.

"Sure." I handed her over to him as Elizabeth cooed and giggled in delight, waving her arms wildly. "She definitely likes you."

My heart squeezed a little tighter. This was the first time ever that Erix was meeting a child younger than himself. And Elizabeth hadn't seen any children before her brother at all.

All that was about to change, though. The space ship that brought Erix to us was taking the first shipment of donated human sperm to Keala. A specifically assembled group of scientists and medical professionals was ready to implement the next phase of the experiment—artificial insemination of several Kealan female volunteers. It was now reasonable to expect that there would be babies born on Keala soon, giving the planet a real future.

The first group of human scientists and volunteers to the Kealan station on Earth had also been selected and approved. Within weeks, they would be arriving here with their families, many of which included children of all ages.

Elizabeth and Erix would have the chance to make friends and to go to the school that was being organized at the facility.

"Father, mother, look, she can walk!" Erix exclaimed in wonder, bringing me out of my thoughts.

He had set Elizabeth down, and she was chasing after him now, moving her chubby legs quickly, even if still a little unsteady.

Laughing, Erix ran aside then caught Elizabeth in his arms when she wobbled to him. He swung her in the air, eliciting another bout of loud giggles from her.

"Well." Tairan lifted an eyebrow with a smile, pressing me to his side in a hug. "They get along."

"They sure do." I laughed, nuzzling his shoulder, and wrapped my arms around him.

Peace settled over me, watching my children play.

We'd earned this moment. We deserved our peace.

Not ready to say goodbye to Tairan and Isabella?

DOWNLOAD BONUS EPILOGUE /Slice of Life story by subscribing to my newsletter, for news, updates, giveaways, and ARC's of new releases, here:

https://dl.bookfunnel.com/101lp5qb0z

If you already are a subscriber, keep an eye on my emails for this story, which is exclusive to my newsletter.

Wicked Warlock

Cursed Coven – Excerpt

A SUDDEN LOUD NOISE from inside the suite made me shrink back. The floor under my feet seemed to lurch up before all went quiet again.

Unsure what to do next, I went to lean my ear against the door, only to jump back again—the surface proved to be too hot to touch.

Fire!

Alarm shot through my brain, and I yanked my walkie-talkie from on top of the stack of clean towels then tossed it back on the cart when nothing but static came out of the device. My cell phone was downstairs in my locker, along with the rest of my stuff.

It wouldn't take long for this old building to go up in flames. The best idea was to get out as soon as possible. I turned toward the stairs with the intention of pulling the fire alarm on my way down.

A deep groan reached me through the door of the suite. The sound was followed by more noise and cursing. Someone was definitely inside that room . . .

"You need to get out!" I hammered on the door with the toe of my shoe, not willing to risk burning my knuckles.

My worry was rapidly turning to panic, as no one replied and nobody exited the room. What if they were trapped? Or hurt, unable to move?

Quickly sliding my key through the slot, I wrapped my apron around my hand before pressing the handle down then opened the door while hiding behind it.

No fire burst out, though. There was no smell of smoke in the air. I carefully peeked around the door.

Semi-darkness greeted me. All the lights were off, and the curtains had been drawn closed on the large bay window. The interior of the spacious living room was illuminated by whatever daylight came through a perfectly round hole that seemed to have been cut out through the glass and the curtains on the window. Green-and-yellow lights curled and sparkled along the edge of the cut-out.

"What is that?" I mumbled, stepping into the suite.

There was no sight of fire or smell of smoke inside, either.

"Fuck me!" A deep voice sounded right behind me, making me jump. "Who the hell are you?"

"April," I mumbled, cautiously watching a dark, menacing figure by the wall rise to his feet. "I thought there was a fire . . ."

Dressed in a thin, black coat that reached his knees, he drew the hood low over his face, then yanked the silk scarf up over his mouth and nose, before I had a chance to see his face.

"No fire. And why April?" The silk scarf now muffled his deep, rumbly voice.

"*I'm* April," I clarified. "It's my name. I work here."

"Right." His eyes glistened from under the hood as he stared at me. With a grunt, he straightened then leaned side to side, stretching his back.

Even if there was no fire, I remembered there had still been some noise and ground shakes. Also, there was that weird hole in the window.

"Are you okay?" I asked. "Do you need a doctor? Should I call the hotel management? The police, maybe?" I darted my gaze around the room again, searching for anything else that would help me determine the kind of authorities I should be calling.

There was something intimidating in the man's size and the all-black outfit that concealed his face and body, making me anxious to get someone else to deal with him and whatever had happened here.

"I was about to make a call," he muttered, grabbing a cell phone off the side table by the couch, "but I got interrupted."

The hostility in his tone made me wonder if he was annoyed with *me* for disturbing him, and I took a cautious step back to the door. Of course, he could be referring to some earlier interruption—maybe the one that had heated the door to his room, and possibly made that weird looking round hole in the window? What on earth could that have been, anyway?

The phone in the man's hand crackled with the same yellowish-green light as had just calmed down around the hole in the window. The licks and sparks of it ran around his hand and spread up his arm. With a curse under his breath, he tossed the cell phone onto the couch.

"It looks like I will need your help, April." He glanced up at me. "I need you to make a call for me."

I threw a suspicious glance at the device on the couch cushions.

"Um, I'm afraid your phone's broken, sir." The green sparks stopped as soon as the stranger tossed it down, but I really didn't feel like touching it myself.

He must have caught my hesitation, his chest rose with a sigh as he explained, "It's not the phone, it's me."

"You? How?"

The whole atmosphere in the room felt unsettling. Something had happened, but I didn't care to find out. The sooner I could leave, the better.

"Please, April," his voice unexpectedly softened with the plea, which was inexplicably disarming. "I won't be able to use anything electronic for a while, but I really need to call someone for help."

"What's wrong with you and the electronics?" I asked warily but took a few hesitant steps toward the couch. "Could I use the room phone, maybe?"

"If you wish." He shrugged. "But you won't be harmed by using mine. I promise." The confidence in his tone was encouraging, and I tentatively picked up his cell phone, holding it between my thumb and forefinger.

No sparks or crackles happened.

"Okay." I exhaled, glancing his way. "Whom do I call?"

He told me the code to unlock the device then the number to dial.

"Oliver!" A female voice sounded on the other end of the line after the first ring. "You have some nerve! After all this time—"

I thrust the phone toward the stranger, for him to answer. A green string of sparks suddenly licked the screen as it came near his body. Startled, I yanked my hand back, dropping the phone to the carpeted floor. The crackling static broke the voice of the woman on the other end.

The man in black quickly retreated to the wall, putting some distance between him and the phone, which seemed to calm the sparks.

"Oliver? Are you there?" Although faint now, the voice clearly sounded annoyed and impatient.

With a pleading glance my way, he gestured at the phone, prompting me to continue the conversation on his behalf.

Crouching in front of the device, I cautiously hit the speaker button, so at least he could hear her. From the distance where he stood, she probably wouldn't catch his replies if he spoke.

"Um . . . my name is April—" I said.

"April?" The woman on the phone sounded indignant, as if my name alone was offensive. "Who are you?"

"I—I'm calling on behalf of Oliver . . ." I stared at the stranger pointedly, waiting for him to confirm that it indeed was his name, then continued after he had nodded, "He is unable to use the phone himself."

She paused for a moment.

"He can't?" Her voice softened. "Does it have anything to do with Thea and the ball last night?"

'Does it?' I mouthed to the man in black, since I had no clue what she was talking about.

He rubbed his forehead.

"I need her help," was all he said.

His back to the wall, he slid to the floor. Sitting on the ground, his legs bent, he placed his arms on his knees. Only now did I notice that his right hand had a black leather glove on. It seemed padded with something—the hand appeared larger than the other one, the leather stretched over an uneven surface.

"He needs your help," I repeated mechanically. He spoke way too softly for the phone speaker to pick up his words.

"Does he now?" Her voice slithered through the room, with a seductive note woven through it. "And what makes him think I'd consider helping him after the way he left me, with not even a phone call all these years?"

"Um . . ." I stared at him, waiting for an answer. Although, I wouldn't have wanted to be in his position. The woman seemed angry, the calmness of her voice only amplified that.

"What does she want for helping me?" Oliver sounded tired.

"What would you want from him for your help?" I repeated into the microphone.

She laughed. "I could definitely come up with a number of things . . ."

"Not happening!" Suddenly, he leaped to his feet. "Do you have anything to do with this, Louise?" He shouted the question, loud enough for the woman on the phone to hear this time.

"Me?" Her voice remained calm and even, although with a sharp note added to it. "You know I don't meddle in the affairs of mortals. I stay away from the business of your coven, too. Yet here you are, begging me for help, the moment you get yourself in trouble."

"It wasn't my fault." He paced the room along the wall. "I hardly know Thea. Her fight was with my father not me, but he's dead, so she took it out on me."

"You're not alone, I've heard many of your coven are affected." Louise sounded mildly curious.

"I thought you didn't meddle in our business."

"I don't, but it doesn't hurt to stay informed," she retorted.

They both seemed to have forgotten about me being there. Finally, Oliver stopped pacing and faced me where I still crouched over his phone on the floor.

"Will you help, Louise?" he asked.

She took some time to answer. I could almost feel the tension emanating from him as he waited.

"Are you willing to reconsider coming back to me?" Her voice was sweet and irresistibly enthralling. For a moment, I honestly believed I would have gone to her myself had she but called me like that. "My magically delicious Oliver," she cooed.

His shoulders dropped with an audible exhale from him.

"No, Louise." He fisted his hands at his sides. "I don't particularly enjoy your chains and whips."

"Don't I know that," came with a long sigh. "So, you expect me to help you, while giving me nothing in return?" A steely note of sarcasm rang through the seductive velvet of her voice now. "Why would I help? For old times' sake?"

"Yes," he replied, with hard confidence. "No matter how you choose to view it, you do owe me for the fifteen months of my life wasted in your basement."

"Oh, I can't believe you're still holding a grudge over that," she replied, light and airy, followed by a laugh, melodious like silver bells. "Fine. Come over. I'd love to see your face, or whatever is left of it. You'll need to leave by dinner time, though. Unless you're willing to feed me, in which case I'd need to cancel my date for tonight."

"I'm coming right now." In quick determined strides, Oliver headed for the exit. "Keep your date, Louise," he threw over his shoulder. "I'll leave well before dinner."

Reaching the door, he stopped abruptly, as if remembering something, then slammed his right hand into the wood.

"April," he turned around slowly. "I will need your help with getting there. I won't be able to drive for a while, just like I can't use the phone right now."

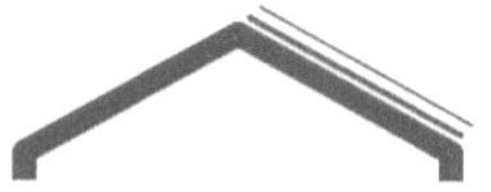

More By Marina Simcoe

Demons Series
Demon Mine
The Forgotten
Grand Master
The Cursed – 2020
The Last Unforgiven – 2020

Standalone Paranormal Romance
The Real Thing
To Love A Monster

The Midnight Coven Author Group
Wicked Warlock

Science-Fiction Romance
Enduring (Valos of Sonhadra)
Experiment

About the Author

MARINA SIMCOE LIKES to write love stories with characters, who may or may not be entirely human, because she firmly believes that our contemporary world could always use a little bit of the extraordinary.

She has lots of fun exploring how her out-of-this-world characters with their own beliefs, values, and aspirations fit into our everyday life.

She lives in Canada with her out-of-this-world husband, their three little offsprings, and a cat, who is into all kinds of experiments himself.

For more illustrations of all of her books please visit Marina Simcoe Author page on Facebook or www.marinasimcoe.com.

Please Stay in Touch

Newsletter signup: http://eepurl.com/c__RGn
Readers' Group
Marina's Reading Cave https://www.facebook.com/groups/
621598474945014/
www.instagram.com/marinasimcoeauthor
www.marinasimcoe.com
www.facebook.com/MarinaSimcoeAuthor/
www.amazon.com/author/marinasimcoe
www.bookbub.com/profile/marina-simcoe
www.goodreads.com/MarinaSimcoe